The Mark of the Horse Lord

ROSEMARY

The Mark of the Horse Lord

SUTCLIFF

FRONT STREET
Asheville, North Carolina

Other books by Rosemary Sutcliff
Dawn Wind
The Eagle of the Ninth
Knight's Fee
The Lantern Bearers
Outcast
The Shield Ring
The Silver Branch
Warrior Scarlet
Rudyard Kipling (Walck Monograph)

First Front Street paperback edtion, 2006

First published in the U.S. 1965 by Henry Z. Walck, Incorporated

LIBRARY OF CONGRESS CATALOGING-IN-PUBLICATION DATA
Sutcliff, Rosemary.
The mark of the horse lord / Rosemary Sutcliff.—1st Front Street pbk. ed.
p. cm.
Summary: Bearing an uncanny resemblance to the now blind displaced
King of the Scots, former gladiator and slave Phaedrus impersonates
the Horse Lord to regain from the Picts the control of the Scottish kingdom.
ISBN 1-932425-62-4 (pbk. : alk. paper)
[1. Kings, queens, rulers, etc.—Fiction. 2. Slavery—Fiction.
3. Gladiators—Fiction. 4. Scotland—History—To 1057—Fiction.] I. Title.
PZ7.S966Mar 2005
[Fic]—dc22   2005025568

FRONT STREET
An Imprint of Boyds Mills Press, Inc.
A Highlights Company
815 Church Street
Honesdale, Pennsylvania 18431

Contents

VERRERA
Oban
CAVE OF
THE
HUNTER
CRUACHAN
CALEDONIA
LOCH ABHA
Dun
Monaidh
LOCH FHIONA
LOCH
LOMOND
FIRTH OF THE WAR BOATS
Theodosia
CLUTA
ANTONINE WALL
SIGNAL
POST
EARRA-GHYL
RIVER CLUTA
N
ARRAN
W
E
S
VALENTIA
FRONTIER OF EARRA-GHYL
Scale of miles
0
25

AREA OF
LARGER MAP
ANTONINE
WALL
HADRIAN'S
WALL
Corstopitum
(Corbridge)
Eboracum
(York)
Londinium
(London)

BRITAIN in the
SECOND CENTURY

palacios

Historical Note

MOST PEOPLE KNOW THAT AT ONE TIME SCOTLAND WAS inhabited by Picts and Scots, but they are probably a little hazy as to the difference between them. Broadly (very broadly) speaking, they started out the same; both part of the great Western drift of peoples who rose somewhere in the great emptiness of Asia and spread across Europe in succeeding waves through the last two thousand years or so before Christ. The Picts were a confederacy of tribes whose "Master Tribe," the Caledones, settled in the land that later became Scotland. The Scots were the tribes who went on farther to make their homes in Ireland and, long after, returned—some of them—to settle in the Western Islands and coastal districts of Scotland. At the time of this story, the Caledones had begun to be great among the tribes, but the Pictish confederacy did not yet exist; while "Scot" or rather "Scotti" was the Roman name for a people who called themselves Gael, or Dalriad. So in *The Mark of the Horse Lord* I have written of Caledones and Dalriadain, and not of Picts and Scots, but it comes to much the same thing in the end.

In the years since they parted company, the Gael had become a Sun People, worshiping a male God, while the Caledones had held to the earlier worship of the Great Mother, and like most people with a woman-worship, they traced their family and inherited even the kingship through the mother's side. (Even in medieval Scotland it was quite common for a king's eldest son to find his claim to his father's throne after him indignantly denied by his sisters' husbands, who claimed that they were the true heirs by right of being married to the Royal Women.)

The traditional founder of the Dalriadain is the Irish Prince Cairbre Riada, who, driven out from his own land of Munster by famine, led his kinsmen and followers first North into Ulster and then overseas to the Western Islands and Highlands, in the year A.D. 258, which is quite a bit later than the date of this story. But there are traces and traditions of Irish settlement on the West Coast in A.D. 177, in 200 B.C., and even 300 B.C.; so that the answer would seem to be that no one knows quite when they came, but that they probably arrived in waves over several hundred years, and the most famous Irish leader would come in time, in the usual way of folklore, to have the credit for all the rest.

You will not find the Cave of the Hunter anywhere; but on the coast, close by Oban, there are caves that show clear traces of Stone Age occupation, and the coastline has changed so much through the ages, that the cave with the Horned One daubed on its back wall might have been among them once, and been claimed by the sea.

Nor, at present, will you find the ruins of a Roman Naval Station at Dumbarton Rock; though a strong tradition says that there was once one there, and that it was called Theodosia.

But if you go looking for it a few miles South of the head of Loch Awe, not far from the modern Crinan Canal, you will find Dunadd, which was once Dun Monaidh, with the traces of its five courts cropping through the turf, and in the highest court but one, the great Rock of the Footprint, where Phaedrus the Gladiator (whom you will not find anywhere outside this book) was crowned Horse Lord and King of the Dalriadain.

The Mark of the Horse Lord

1 | *The Threshold*

IN THE LONG CAVERN OF THE CHANGING ROOM, THE LIGHT OF the fat-oil lamps cast jumping shadows on the walls; skeleton shadows of the spear-stacked arms racks, giant shadows of the men who crowded the benches or moved about still busy with their weapons and gear; here and there the stallion shadow of a plume-crested helmet. The stink of the wild-beast dens close by seeped in to mingle with the sharper smell of men waiting for the trumpets and sweating a little as they waited. Hard to believe that overhead where the crowds had been gathering since cockcrow, the June sun was shining and a fresh wind blowing in from the moors to set the brightly colored pennants flying.

But the man in the farthest corner, who sat hunched forward, arms crossed on knees, seemed lost to all that went on around him, deep sunk in his own thoughts. One or two of his fellows glanced at him in passing, but left him alone. They were used to Red Phaedrus's moods before a fight; he would come out of it and laugh and turn tiger when the trumpets sounded.

Phaedrus was indeed very far away, back beyond the four years that he had been a sword-fighter here in the Gladiators' School at Corstopitum, and the two years before that, back in the small pleasant house in Londinium on the night his father died ... Ulixes the Arcadian, importer of fine Greek wines. He had never owned Phaedrus for his son, only for a slave, the son of Essylt who kept his house for him. But he had been fond of them both, when he could spare a thought from his business; he had seen that the boy got some schooling; he had been going to free them, one day. But in the end he had died too suddenly, slumped over his office table with a half drafted letter to his agent in Corinth under his hand, and the autumn wind whirling the leaves of the poplar tree against the window.

Everything had been sold up, the household slaves included. Everything but Phaedrus's mother. "I am too old to go to a new master," she had said on the last day before the sale, and she had sent him on an errand into the town. And when he came back from the errand, he had found her in the arbor at the foot of the narrow garden, where the master had liked to have his breakfast on fine summer mornings. She had used the slim native hunting dagger that had served Ulixes as a papyrus knife; but there was not much blood because she had stabbed herself under the breast, not cut her wrists as a Roman woman would have done. Phaedrus, not yet come to his fourteenth birthday, had changed from a boy into a man that day.

He had been sold off next morning, along with the part-Lybian chariot-horses, for he had the makings of a charioteer—and after changing hands a couple of times, and learning something of sword-play from his last master who wanted someone to practice on, had been sold into the Arena to help pay a gambling debt. ("It's you or the team, and it won't be easy to get another pair of matched bays," his master had pointed out.)

At first he had been wild with loathing of his new life, but in four years it had become part of him, so that whether he hated or loved it no longer mattered. It ran in his veins like the fiery barley spirit that the tribesmen brewed: the roar of the crowd that set one's pulses jumping, the warmth of sunlight and the sweetness of cheap wine and the fierce pleasure in one's own strength and skill, heightened by the knowledge that tomorrow, next week, in an hour's time, it might all end on the squared point of a comrade's sword.

Four years. Not many lasted so long at the deadly trade. If he could last another year or so, they might give him his Wooden Foil with the silver guard, and he would be free. But his mind never got beyond the first triumphant moment of gaining his freedom, any more than it got beyond the sting of the death blow, because he had been born a slave and knew no more of what it would be like to be free than he knew of what it would be like to die.

"Wooden Foil?" Somebody's voice exploded beside him. "You've been dreaming, lad!" And the words, striking in so exactly upon his own thoughts, splintered them apart and brought him back to the present moment and the scene around him.

"I have not, then," said Lucius the Bull, leaning back and stretching until the muscles cracked behind his thick shoulders. "Someone is to get their Wooden Foil, earned or no. Trouble and expense no object in *these* Games, so long as the Province remembers them afterwards and says, 'Good old Sylvanus! *Jolly* old Governor Sylvanus!—Gave us the best Games we ever had.'—I heard the Captain talking to Ulpius about it—neither of them best pleased by the sound of it; Ulpius was cursing by all the Gods he knows."

"Well, you couldn't expect any Arena Master to be *pleased*," someone said. "Maybe he reckons he's going to lose enough of his little game cocks without losing that one more." And there was a burst of reckless laughter from those near enough to overhear and join in.

Phaedrus stooped and rubbed his palm on the sanded floor, an old trick when one's sword hand grew sticky. In the moment of silence that followed the laughter, he heard the rising murmur of the crowd, and from the beast den a wolf howled, savage and mournful as a lost soul; *they* knew that it was almost time. Without meaning to, he glanced across the crowded place to where Vortimax stood under a flaring lamp, preening the crest plumes of his helmet before he put it on. The big-boned Gaul turned his head in the same instant, and their eyes met. They both looked away. ...

In the ordinary way, the Master of a frontier circus could not afford to use up his gladiators too fast, but Sylvanus Varus, the new Governor, who was giving these Games to celebrate his appointment, had paid for four pairs of Sword-and-Buckler men to fight to the death. Four pairs—including Phaedrus and Vortimax. He still could not quite believe it. They had come up the School together from the first days in the training yard. They knew each other's sword-play as well as they knew their own; they had shared the same food-bowl and washed each other's hurts in the same water; and in all the School, the big fair-haired Gaul was the only man whom Phaedrus had ever counted as a friend.

A forceful step sounded in the corridor, and Automedon, the Captain of the gladiators, appeared in the dark entry. He stood an instant looking down at them, and the livid scar of his own gladiator days burned in a crimson brand across his cheek as it always did in the moments before the trumpets sounded.

"Time to helm-up, lads."

Phaedrus got to his feet with the rest, catching up his plumed helmet from the bench beside him, and stepped forward from his dark corner. The light from the nearest lamp showed him naked like the other sword-fighters, save for the belted leather loin-guard and the sleeve of supple bronze hoop-mail on his sword arm; a young man with hair the color of hot copper, lithe and hollow-flanked as a yearling wolf, the tanned pallor of his face slashed across by red brows and a reckless, faintly smiling mouth.

He put on the heavy helmet and buckled the chin strap. Now he was seeing the world through the long eye-slits in the molded mask, and thought, testing the buckle, "My last sight of the world will be like this, looking out at it sharp-edged and bright from the darkness inside my helmet." And then pushed the thought away. It wasn't lucky to have that kind of thought, going into the Arena. That was the way one's nerve began to go.

Automedon stood in the entrance, watching from the vantage point of the two steps that led up to it, while they took down spears and heavy bronze-rimmed oblong shields from the arms racks and straightened themselves into roughly ordered ranks; then looked them over with a nod. "Good enough. Now you know the order of events for the day: the wild-beast show first, the boxers and then the General Fight; the Net-and-Trident men, and to wind up with"—his glance went to Phaedrus and Vortimax and the rest of the rear rank, and his voice was grimly sardonic—"you lucky lads in the place of honor. For the rest of you—I don't want any more careless casualties like we had last month! Casualties of that kind don't mean courage—nought but slovenly sword-play, and the Circus doesn't pay for your keep and training for you to get yourselves hacked to bits before it has had its money's worth out of you! Any man who comes out of the Arena today with a hole in his hide deep enough to keep him out of the Consualia Games will have to account for it to *me*, and if I am not satisfied with the accounting"—he smiled at them with narrowed gaze and lip lifted over the strong yellow dog-teeth—"both he and the man who gave it to him will wish they had never been born! Understood?"

They grinned back, one or two tossing up their weapons in mock salute. "Understood, Automedon! Understood, Noble Captain!"

"That's well." His face lost something of its grimness in a gleam of humor. "This new Governor is fresh out from Rome, and maybe he doesn't expect much from a frontier circus, so show him that even if he has seen bigger fights in the Colosseum, man for man the Corstopitum lads can give Rome a bloody nose any day of the week!"

They shouted for him then in good earnest, tossing up swords and javelins as though to Caesar himself, and while their shouts still rang hollow under the roof beams, Phaedrus heard the silver crowing of the trumpets, and the grinding clang as the Arena doors were flung wide.

Automedon turned on his heel with a rapped-out command, and the Arena guard stood back on each side of the broad stone stairway that led up to the open air. Two by two, the gladiators stepped off and swung forward.

Phaedrus shortened his stride at the foot of the stairway, clipped steps, head up, sword drawn and shield at the ready. The lamplit gloom fell away behind, and the light of day came down to them with the swelling voice of the crowd. They were out from the echoing shadows of the arched stairway into the sudden space and wind and sunshine of the Arena, the yielding sand underfoot, the greeting of the multitude bursting upon them in a solid wave of sound, hoarse under the clash of the cymbals and the high strident crowing of the trumpets. They swung left to circle the Arena, falling into the long swaggering pace of the parade march, past the Altar of Vengeance at which they had sacrificed at first light, as always before the Games; past the mouth of the beast dens, past the dark alleyway giving onto the rooms where the Syrian doctor and his salves were waiting to deal with such of the wounded as seemed worth trying to save, past the shovels and sandboxes and the Mercuries with their little flapping gilded wings and long hooks. Phaedrus looked up, seeing the tiered benches of the amphitheater packed to their topmost skyline: Roman and Briton, townsfolk and tribesmen, easy figures in purple-bordered tunics in the Magistrates' Gallery, and everywhere—for Corstopitum was a depot town for the frontier—the russet red cloth and glinting bronze of the Legions. Faces stared down at them, hands clutched the barriers in the excitement of what was to come. The usual flowers and sweetmeats began to shower down upon favorite gladiators. Phaedrus caught a white briar rose in the hollow of his shield, and flashed his trained play actor's gesture of thanks up at the fat woman in many jewels who had thrown it.

Full circle round the wide rim of the Arena, they were close beneath the Governor's box now. Automedon snapped out a command, and they clashed to a halt and wheeled to face the big bull-necked man who leaned there with the glowing wine-red folds of his cloak flung back from the embossed and gilded breastplate beneath: Caesar's new representative, the giver of the Games. Their weapons flashed up in the windy sunlight, and they raised the full-throated shout, as though Caesar himself had leaned there.

"Hail Caesar! Those about to die salute you!"

Then they were breaking away to take station round the barricades. Phaedrus swung his shield into its resting position behind his shoulder and, straddling his legs, stood with hands on hips, deliberately wearing his courage at a rakish angle. That was what the crowd liked to see; the crowd that had come to watch him or Vortimax die.

The attendant Mercuries were hauling back the bars that closed the dark mouth of the dens, and the proud ten-point stag came flying in, half mad already with fear of the wolf-smell in his nostrils, and a few moments later the wolves were loosed after him. Six wolves in a dark low-running pack. He killed two with his terrible antlers and left them ripped and broken on the bloody sand, before the rest pulled him down to a red rending death amid a great yelling from the onlookers. The bodies were dragged away; a third wolf who lay snapping and snarling with a broken back was finished off by one of the Mercuries. The remaining three were decoyed back to their cages for use another day, and fresh sand was spread over the stains in the Arena. After that came the boxing match, and the big sham fight which pleased the crowd better, especially when blood began to flow—for despite Automedon's orders, there was seldom a sword-fight that did not end in a few deaths and maimings. Now it was the turn of the Net-and-Trident men, and all across the Arena they and the swordsmen matched against them were zig-zagging like mayflies in a wicked dance of death.

Suddenly Phaedrus realized that the open expanse before him was empty of tense and running figures, the Mercuries with their hooks were dragging another dead man away, and for the last time the filthy sand was being raked over and the worst of the stains covered.

And he thought in a perfectly detached way, "Our turn now."

The trumpets were crowing again, and, as one man, the chosen eight strode out from their station close under the Governor's box to the center of the Arena where Automedon now stood waiting for them.

They were being placed in pairs, ten paces apart and with no advantage of light or wind to either. It was all happening very quickly now; from the Governor's box came the white flutter of a falling scarf, and the trumpets were sounding the "Set on."

Phaedrus took the customary two steps forward and one to the left, which was like the opening move in a game of draughts,

and brought sword and shield to the ready. With that movement he ceased to be aware of the other pairs, ceased even to
be aware of the suddenly hushed onlookers. Life sharpened its
focus, narrowed to a circle of trampled sand, and the light-fleck
of Vortimax's eyes behind the slits of his visor. ("Watch the eyes,"
Automedon had said on the very first day in the training school.
"Always be aware of the sword hand, but watch the eyes.") They
were circling warily, crouching behind their bucklers, ready to
spring. Phaedrus's head felt cold and clear and his body very
light, as it always did the moment the fight began, whether in
earnest or in practice. Practice. He had fought out so many practice bouts with Vortimax. The surface of his mind knew that this
was different, that this was kill or be killed, but something in
him refused to believe it. This *could* be no more than a trial of
skill between himself and Vortimax; and afterwards they would
slam the swords back into the arms rack, and laugh and go off
to the wine booth together. ... He made a sudden feint, and the
Gaul came in with a crouching leap. Their blades rang together
in thrust and counter thrust, a fierce flurry that struck out
sparks from the gray iron into the windy sunlight. The sand rose
in little clouds and eddies round their feet; they were circling
and weaving as they fought, each trying to get the sun behind
him and the dazzle of it in the other's eyes. Phaedrus felt the
hornet-sting of the other's blade nick his ribs, and sprang back
out of touch. Vortimax was pressing after him and, giving back
another step before the darting blade, he knew that the Gaul's
purpose was to drive him against the barricade, where he would
have no space to maneuver. He could sense the wooden barrier
behind him, some way off still, but waiting—waiting—and side-
sprang clear, at the same time playing a thrust over the shield
that narrowly missed the other's shoulder. "A feint at the head, a

cut at the leg, and come in over the shield with a lunge." Autome-don's voice sounded in his inner ear as he had heard it so often at practice. The crowd was crying *"Habet!"* as a fighter went down; and almost at once the shout was repeated, one wave crashing on the tail of another, and the Mercuries were dragging two bodies away. Only two pairs left now. Phaedrus knew it, on the outer edge of his consciousness, but it had no meaning for him; it was beyond the narrow circle of trampled sand and the sparks of living danger behind the eye-slits of Vortimax's visor. They had returned for a while to more cautious play, and the blades rang together lightly, almost exploringly; but they had no need to explore, they knew each other's play too well. It was that, partly, that made the whole fight seem faintly unreal, a fight in a dream. And the sense of unreality took the edge from Phaedrus's sword-play; he knew it, and tried to break through, and could not.

Ah! Vortimax's guard was a shade more open that time! Phaedrus's blade leaped, and it was the other's turn to spring back out of touch, with a red gash opening like a mouth in the brown skin over the collarbone. He had the Gaul now, and began to press him back—back—Vortimax's turn to feel the waiting barrier. But still the odd sense of fighting in a dream was upon Phaedrus, and the inability to bring his sword-play out of the practice yard and set it to the real work of killing. ...

He saw the flicker behind Vortimax's eye-slits in the split instant before the deadly low stroke came. He sprang sideways, pivoting on the ball of his foot, and felt a white-hot sting like that of a whiplash across the side of his left knee. The stroke which, had it landed square, would have cut the tendon and left him hamstrung and helpless on the sand. It was a brilliant, wicked stroke, an almost outlawed stroke for it crippled instead of killing, and could bring your enemy down broken and at your mercy;

but if it failed, it left your own guard wide open. Like the sudden opening of a cavern in his head, reality burst upon Phaedrus, and in that ice-bright splinter of time he understood at last that this was a fight to the death, that he was fighting, not his comrade Vortimax, whom he had fought scores and hundreds of times before, but death—red rending death such as the stag's had been, and the hooks of the Mercuries in the dark alleyway. And the man before him was the enemy, and he sprang to finish him. But in the same instant the Gaul, nearly knee-down in the sand, twisted aside and up in an almost miraculous recovery, and again sprang back out of touch.

Phaedrus set his teeth and went after him, warned by the warm flow down his leg that he had not much time. He did not hear the crowd cry *"Habet!"* for the third time, nor the mounting roar as all along the benches they shouted for himself or Vortimax. He had another enemy to fight now; the rising weakness of blood loss creeping through him. Soon he felt his sword-play growing less sure. No onlooker could guess it as yet, but he knew, and so did Vortimax. Once, the Gaul's blade was within a nail's breadth of his throat before he turned it aside. His heart was lurching in the sick hollow of his body, his teeth were clenched and his breath whistled through flared nostrils. The crowd had fallen suddenly silent, but he heard their silence no more than he had heard their yellings. He was fighting on the defense now, he had begun to give ground—a little—a little—and then a little more—and he knew with sick despair that he was very nearly done. Suddenly his blade wavered glaringly out of line, and Vortimax sprang in under his guard. How he avoided that thrust he never knew, but as he leaped sideways without thought, like a wounded wolf, Vortimax's foot slipped on Phaedrus's own blood in the sand, and in the instant that he was off balance with lowered shield,

Phaedrus gathered the last of his strength and struck home.

Vortimax gave a small surprised grunt, and pitched forward, twisting as he fell, so that he landed face upward, still part covered by his buckler.

Phaedrus stumbled to one knee over him, and caught himself back from crashing headlong. He heard the voice of the crowd now, but distantly, as one heard it from the underground changing-rooms, and stood with raised sword, drawing his breath in great sobbing gasps, while he waited to hear the *"Habet"* and see the thumbs turned down. But the signal did not come; instead, a long roar of applause, and then he understood. Vortimax's chin strap had snapped in his fall, and the plumed bronze helmet had fallen off, leaving his face bare. He was quite dead.

Phaedrus thought without emotion, looking down at him, "That was almost me."

He just remembered to turn and salute the Governor's box, which swam in his sight as the Arena floor was swimming under his feet, then Automedon was beside him, growling in his ear, "Hold on! Hold up, lad! If you go down now I swear I'll get the Mercuries with the hot irons to you!" And the Captain's hand was clenched on his arm, turning him back toward the arched entrance of the changing-rooms. The Mercuries were already dragging Vortimax's body away. "Come on now, a drink is what you need!" and he thought with a sick shock of laughter, "I'm being decoyed away, just like the wolves from their kill—decoyed away for another day." He managed something of his usual swagger as he passed out of the westering sunlight, leaving a heavy blood trail behind him, into the gloom of the stairhead and the smoky glimmer of the lamps still burning below. His foot missed the top step, and he stumbled forward, and somebody caught him from a headlong fall, saying cheerfully, "Drunk again? This is no time to go breaking your neck!"

He was sitting on a bench, with head hanging, while the long, crowded changing-room swirled around him. They had taken off his helmet, and the Syrian doctor was lashing his knee in linen strips, so tightly that he could not bend it. There was a sudden splurge of voices with his own name and the words "Wooden Foil" tangled somewhere in the midst of them. They were thumping him on the shoulders to rouse him, pouring the promised drink down his throat. The barley spirit ran like fire through his veins, and the world steadied somewhat.

"Now—up with you!" Automedon said. "Up!"

And he was being thrust back toward the entrance stairway and the evening sunlight wavering beyond the great double doors; and all at once the truth dawned on him!

Somehow—the barley spirit helped—he pulled himself together and put on the best swagger he could with a rigid knee, and managed the few paces to the Governor's box with a kind of stiff-legged fighting-cock strut. Sylvanus's coarse, clever face seemed to float in clouds of bright nothingness, and the rest of the world was the merest blur so that he never saw the sandy, withered-looking man with silver and coral drops in his ears, who leaned forward abruptly from a nearby bench to stare at him out of suddenly widened eyes.

He saw nothing but the Governor's big fleshy nose and small shrewd eyes, and the foil with its blade of smooth ashwood as white almost as the silver guard. He took it from the Governor's hands into his own, feeling how light it was after the heavy gladius that he was used to, how lacking in the familiar balance when he brought it to the salute.

The crowd were shouting for him: "Phaedrus! Red Phaedrus!"

The fat woman who had tossed him the briar rose threw an enameled bracelet at his feet, and two or three others followed her. But Phaedrus was scarcely aware of the gifts. He knew only that he was a free man; that he had come to one of the two thresholds that had waited for him and, for all the triumph and the shouting, he must step over it alone, into the unknown world that lay beyond.

2 | *Corstopitum by Night*

HE STOOD OUTSIDE THE GATEWAY OF THE GLADIATORS' SCHOOL, under the sculptured helmet and weapons of the pediment, and pulled his cloak round him against the chill mizzle-rain that was blowing in from the moors. It was a new cloak, very fine, of saffron-colored wool with a border of black and crimson and blue, and had been given him by a certain admiring merchant who had seen him kill Vortimax and win his Wooden Foil. A tall man, dried and withered and toughened like a bit of old weather-worn horsehide, but with heavy drops of silver and coral swinging in his ears. He had brought his gift in person, on the morning after the Games, and stared into Phaedrus's face as he gave it, so intently that the gladiator laughed and said: "You'll know me another time, even if I should not be wearing this sunburst of a cloak!" And the man had lowered the fine-wrinkled lids over his eyes, but gone on staring under them, and said, "Aye, I'd know you another time," with something in his tone behind the words that had made Phaedrus suddenly wary. But he had kept the cloak; it was a rich cloak, and he had not lived four years in the Gladiators' School without learning never to turn down a gift.

He looked up the street toward the transit camp, and down the street toward the baths and the lower town, wondering which way to go, now that all ways were open to him, and feeling suddenly a stranger in the town that he knew as well as he did the cracks in the wall plaster beside his sleeping bench. Well, no good standing here all day, he must find another sleeping bench. He hitched up the long bundle containing his few possessions, including the Wooden Foil, and set off down the street, limping because the half-healed gash on his knee (they had kept him until it was half healed; a clear two weeks) was still stiff.

He found lodgings at the third attempt, a filthy room in a house down by the river, kept by an ex-army mule driver with one eye, and leaving his bundle there, went out again to the baths. He had the full treatment, with a breathtaking cold plunge after the scalding steam of the hot room, and then lay like a lord while a slave rubbed him with scented oil and scraped him down with a bronze strigil; finally he had the tawny fuzz of his young beard shaved. It cost a good deal, but there was the fat woman's bracelet and a few other bits and pieces in the small leather bag hung round his neck; and in the circus one got out of the way of saving for tomorrow in case there was no tomorrow to save for. Also it helped to pass the time.

But the depot trumpet was only just sounding for the noon watch-setting when he came out again into the colonnade. Two or three men strolling there looked at him and said something to each other, recognizing him. The rain had stopped and a pale gleam of sunlight was shining on wet tiles and cobbles and drawing faint wisps of steam from sodden thatch. He went down the colonnade steps, the red hair still clinging damply to his forehead, and the beautiful cloak flung back now from his shoulders giving him a kind of tall, disreputable splendor like a corn-marigold, and strolled off along the street as though he was going somewhere, because he knew that they were still watching him.

For the next few hours he wandered about Corstopitum. He bought a brown barley loaf and strong ewe-milk cheese at a stall, and ate them on the river steps in another scurry of rain, and then wandered on again. He was free! A free man for the first time in his life! His official manumission signed by the Circus Master and a magistrate in the small bag round his neck, his name struck off the muster roll of the Gladiators' School with the words, "Honorably discharged" instead of the more usual "Dead" against it. No man was his master, there was nowhere that he must report back to after his day's leave. Yet more than once that day he found himself back at the double doors with the sculptured weapons over, or wandering in the direction of the turf-banked amphitheater beyond the South Gate.

The last time it happened, he pulled up cursing and, looking about him, saw that it was dusk and a little way down the street someone had hung out the first lantern of the evening. The first day was drawing to a close, and suddenly he thought, "This is only one day, only the first day, and there'll be another tomorrow, and another and another ..." and panic such as he had never known in the Arena where one only had to be afraid of physical things whimpered up in him so that for a moment he leaned against a wall, feeling cold in the pit of his stomach. Then he laughed jeeringly and, pushing off from the wall, turned back the way he had come, toward the narrower streets where the less respectable wine shops were to be found. "Fool! You want a drink, that's what's the matter with you—a lot of drinks. You can get as full as a wine skin tonight, and sleep it off like an emperor! Won't have to be out on the practice ground with a head like Hephaestos's forge and seeing two of everything at first light tomorrow."

The first wine shop he came to, he passed by. It was a favorite haunt of the gladiators on town leave, and he didn't want to run into old comrades. It was odd how he shrank from that idea now— a kind of embarrassment, a feeling that they would not know quite how to meet each other's eyes. Only one of them he would not have minded meeting again, and he had killed him two weeks ago.

Jostling and jostled by the people who still came and went along the streets, he pushed on until the Rose of Paestum cast its yellow stain of lamplight and its splurge of voices across his way. He went in, swinging his cloak behind him with the play actor's swagger of his old trade, and, thrusting across the crowded room to the trestle table at the far side, demanded a cup of wine. He grinned at the girl with greasy ringlets hanging round her neck, who served him, and flung down the price of the wine lordly-wise on the table, with a small bronze coin extra.

She half moved to pick it up, then pushed it back. "This is over."

"Best keep it for yourself, then."

"Best keep it for *yourself*," she said. "I reckon you've earned it hard enough, lad."

"Sa sa, have it your own way. This instead—" Phaedrus leaned across the table, flung an arm round her shoulders, and kissed her loudly. She smelled of warm, unwashed girl under the cheap scent, and kissing her comforted a little the coldness of the void that had opened before him in the street.

He picked up his cup, and the extra coin. She was his own kind, part of his own world, and to leave the coin after all would have been a sort of betrayal of his own kind. Lounging over to a bench against the wall, he sat down.

He gulped down most of the wine at a draught, though it hadn't much flavor somehow, and sat for a long time with the almost empty cup in his hand, staring unseeingly over the heads of the crowd toward the opposite wall and the faded fresco of a dancing girl with a rose in her hand which gave the wine shop its name.

What was he going to do with the days ahead? It had been stupid, that moment of panic in the twilit street, the appalling vision of emptiness that was simply today repeated over and over again for all eternity; stupid for the beautifully simple reason that to go on living you had to eat, and to go on eating you had to work—the fat woman's bracelet wouldn't last forever. What about the Eagles? Oh, not the regular Legion, the Auxiliaries of the Frontier Service? It might be worth trying, but he didn't see old one-armed Marius who commanded up at the depot taking on an ex-gladiator. Well then, if he could get a job as a chari-oteer? Any kind of job to do with horses? But men who owned horses didn't want free grooms and drivers when they could get a slave for twelve aurae. No, sword-play was the only trade for him; he could probably get himself taken on by a fencing master somewhere in one of the Southern cities, and end up teaching the more showy and safest fencing strokes to young sprigs of the town. The prospect sickened him.

There was a movement in the crowd, and a shadow fell across his hand holding the wine cup, and he looked up quickly to see that a young man had risen from a nearby table and checked beside him. Phaedrus knew him by sight, Quintus Tetricus, the Army Contractor's son, and recognized one or two others among the faces at the table all turned his way.

"See who sits drinking here alone!" Quintus said, clearly speaking for the rest. "Ah now, that's no way for a man to be cele-brating his Wooden Foil!"

"I fought for it alone, and I may as well drink the Victory Cup alone—the wine tastes just as sweet," Phaedrus said harshly, "and snore alone under the table afterwards."

"Come and drink with us, and we'll all snore under the table afterwards," Quintus said, and the men about the table laughed.

"I do well enough where I am." In the mood they were in, if a sad showman's bear had shambled in through the door they would have called it to drink with them, and Phaedrus was in no mood to dance to their whim.

"Even with an empty cup? Na na, my Red Phaedrus! Come and drink off another with us; we've got a flask of red Falernian—eagle's blood!"

Other voices were added to his, the rest were shifting closer on the benches, making room for one more.

And suddenly, because nothing mattered much anyway, it was too much trouble to go on refusing. He shrugged and got up, and, not quite sure how it happened, found himself sitting with Quintus and his friends, the cup brimming with unwatered Falernian in his hand. Flushed faces grinned at him round the wine-dabbled table. A complete stranger with hair bleached lint white as some of the young braves among the tribesmen wore it—it was the fashion just then to be very British—leaned forward and clapped him on the shoulder, shouting, "Here he is then; let's drink to him! Aiee, my lucky lad, that was a pretty fight!"

Cups were raised on all sides. "Red Phaedrus! Joy and long life to you!"

Phaedrus laughed, and drank the toast with them, gulping the cup dry. It would be good to get drunk. "A pretty fight. You saw it?"

"Wouldn't have missed it for all the gold in Eburacum Mint!"

"I thought the Gaul had you with that low stroke," another said.

"I thought so too." Phaedrus drained his cup and threw the lees over his shoulder where they lay dark as the grains of old blood on the dirty floor. "What's a friend after all? I'll drink again if anyone asks me."

Presently, he had no idea how many wine cups later, he realized that the place was emptying, and the serving girl and a couple of slaves were gathering up empty cups and mopping spilled wine, while at the far side of the room benches were being stacked one atop the other. "Shutting up, by the look of things." A plump dark youth who had been quieter than the rest of them all evening looked about him somewhat owlishly. "S'tonishing how quick an evening runs its course in—good comp'ny."

"Ah now, who says it's run its course? I'm shtill—*still* thirsty." Quintus flung himself back against the wall behind him, and beckoned imperiously to the girl. "Hai! Pretty! More wine."

The girl looked up. "We're shutting up now."

"Not while I'm here, we're not."

She glanced toward the wine shop owner, who came waddling across the room toward them, his paunch thrust out beneath a dirty tunic stained with old wine splashes. "We don't keep open all night in the Rose of Paestum. This is a decent house, sirs, and we need our sleep same as other folks."

Quintus lurched to his feet, flushing crimson, his hand fumbling for his knife, but Phaedrus, with a few grains of sense still in him, put a hand on his shoulder and slammed him down again. "Softly! The Rose of Paestum isn't the only wine shop in Corstopitum."

And a big red-faced young man with a loose mouth grinned in agreement. "Tired of that girl on the wall, she's coming off in flakes anyhow. Le's go 'nd find some real dancing girls."

Somehow, matters were sorted out, and the remains of the score paid with a good deal of bickering, and they were spilling out into the street, hotly arguing as to where they should go next. They had been no more than loudly cheerful and from time to time a little quarrelsome in the hot room, but the fresh air went to their heads and legs like another kind of wine. "I'm drunk," Phaedrus thought. "I haven't been drunk as this since Saturnalia!"

Well, he had meant to get as drunk as an emperor tonight,

and the feeling was good. He was not lonely or cold any more, and tomorrow could look after itself; he felt seventeen hands high and curiously remote from his own feet. He could fight a legion singlehanded, and whistle the seven stars of Orion out of the sky. It was not such a gray world, after all.

They had forgotten about the quest for dancing girls, and for a while they wavered their way about the streets, singing, with their arms round each other's necks. Respectable people scurried into doorways at their approach, which seemed to all of them a jest for the Gods, so that they howled with laughter and began to kick at doors in passing and yell insults at any protesting face that appeared at an upper window. They had no clear idea of where they were heading, but presently they found themselves in the center of the town, with the square mass of the Forum buildings and the Basilica rising before them cliff-wise out of the late lantern light into the darkness. Among the small lean-to shops, closely shuttered now, that lined the outer colonnade, the gleam of a lantern here and there told where a late wine booth was still open, and the sight of the little groups gathered about them made Phaedrus and his boon companions thirsty again.

"C'mon," Quintus said, "let's have another drink."

"Had enough." The dark plump boy still had more sense left in him than any of the others. "Maybe we'd best be jogging home."

"Roma Dea! The night's still in swaddling bands, there's two full watches of it left yet." And another of the band lifted up his voice in mournful song:

"Oh do not drink so deep, my son,
My dear and only child!
And do not lie down in the street
And look so strange and wild."

The others joined in the chorus:

"Yellow wine of Chios
And dark wine of Gaul,
But the blood-red Falernian,
The ruby-red Falernian,
The fire-red Falernian,
Is the Emperor of them all."

Then in a blurred gabble, "I've-a-fine-and-noble-reason-for-lying-here-a-season-but-what-it-is-I-cannot-quite-re-call."

And baying each other on to further efforts, they headed for the nearest of the still-open wine booths, close beside the main gate with its triumphal inscription and attendant stone lions.

The booth, which was no more than a trestle table under the roof of the colonnade, with a couple of coarse wine and water jars behind it, a few horn cups and a red pottery lamp in the midst of all, was kept by an ex-Legionary who had had trouble with drunks before. He eyed them with grim disfavor as they drew near, and began ostentatiously to stack the horn mugs together. "And what might you be wanting?"

Quintus propped himself against the trestle table. "What's one generally come to a wine booth for, eh?— Tell me that. Wha's one gener-rally ..."

"Well, you've come too late," said the booth's owner. "Can't you see I'm shutting for the night?"

Quintus shook his head, and said with elaborate care, "That was what they said at the Rose of Paestum. The very words they—and it wasn't *true!* They jus din'—*didn't* like our faces. You don' like our faces either, do you?"

"I've seen ones I've liked better."

"Our money's good 'nough though." Quintus flung down a scatter of coins and thrust a suddenly darkening face into that of the ex-Legionary. "An' tha's all that matters t'you, isn't it? Now we'll have some wine. Me an' my frien's, we'll *all* have some wine."

"Not here, you won't." The man pushed the money back at him. "Now pick up this lot, and get off to bed, the pack of you."

The rest of the party had begun crowding closer, and there was an ugly murmur. Phaedrus, with his beautiful, prancing mood suddenly checked, aware once more, through the bright haze of the Falernian, of the gray flat future that he had thought successfully drowned, had a strong desire to fight somebody. It did not much matter who. He elbowed his way to the forefront of the group beside Quintus. "And supposing there's no wish in us for bed? Suppose we feel like a cup of wine all round, and nothing else in the world?"

The mood of the whole band was turning ugly; he felt the ugliness growing and gathering strength behind him, and saw the recognition of it in the ex-Legionary's suddenly alerted gaze. Legionary of the Eagles that he, Phaedrus, was not good enough to join! For the moment it seemed to him that he had actually gone up to the depot, and been turned away.

"Then you'll have to try another booth, gladiator. *I'm shutting up for the night!*" The man raised his voice abruptly to a parade-ground bellow, as he clattered horn cups into a basket that a boy behind him had dragged out from under the trestles. Out of the tail of his eye, Phaedrus was aware of several other men moving up; the wine-booth owners were mostly old Legionaries, and held together when there was trouble.

"Right! Then we'll help you!" Quintus shouted, and kicked over the biggest wine jar; and in the same instant, even as the booth keeper lunged into battle like a bull with a gadfly on his tail, Phaedrus seized one end of the trestle board and heaved it up, sending everything on it to the pavement with a deeply satisfying crash. On the instant a free fight was milling round the wreckage, and the raw red Sabine wine running like blood between the cobbles. The lamp had gone over with the rest, and little rivulets of burning oil mingled with the wine. Then someone shouted, "Look out! It's the Watch!" and the thing that had begun as little more than a savage jest tipped over into nightmare.

Somebody—in the confusion Phaedrus did not know who it was—drew a knife. He caught the flash of it in the flickering light of the burning oil about their feet; somebody shouted "Don't be a fool! For the Gods' sake—" and a Legionary of the Watch went down with a sharp bitten-off cry.

One of the little runnels of fire had caught the dry timber of a shop-front nearby, a wavering tongue of flame licked up as though tasting it, and then the fire was roaring up the shutter, and in the red flare of it Phaedrus saw the crested helmet and mailed shoulders of the officer of the Watch patrol lowered to charge, and more men thrusting grimly behind him. The little band of revelers was scattering, melting away at panic speed. Phaedrus sprang back into the shadows and turned to run. But sometime in the fighting he had caught a kick on the half-healed wound, and now suddenly his knee gave under him.

He heard a shout and the pounding of feet and, even as he struggled up from his headlong fall, two of the Watch had flung themselves upon him. "Here's one of them, anyhow!" a voice shouted, and merciless hands dragged him to his feet and back into the light of the blazing shop-front, where others of the patrol were already getting to work with water from the Forum fountain. He caught a brief glimpse of the officer's crest, tall and arched like a stallion's against the sinking fire; and a coldly disgusted voice from under it said, "One of them! And they have half gralloched Gerontius."

All sounds of the chase were pounding away into the distance. Phaedrus twisted in his captors' hands and began to fight. Four years of the Gladiators' School, where private quarrels were settled without weapons and far from the eye of authority, had taught him other ways of battle than those of the sword, and he used them all, every clean and dirty trick of them. But the part-reopened wound hampered him, and when he tried to knee one of his captors in the groin it again played him false.

"Ah! You would, would you, you stinking polecat!" someone snarled, and he was wrenched sideways, and something that felt like a thunderbolt took him under the left ear. Jagged flame shot from the point of impact through the top of his head, and he plunged down into a buzzing blackness between spinning sun-wheels of colored light.

3 | *Midir of the Dalriadain*

PHAEDRUS SAT ON A PILE OF FILTHY BED-STRAW IN THE CORNER of the cell, scratching at the blood-stained rag that was tied round his knee and watching the last daylight fade out beyond the high narrow window-hole.

It had been noon when they hauled him out of the main prison hall and flung him in here. At the time he had been too sick to care, almost too sick to notice. There was something odd about that sickness; it had leaped upon him as soon as the morning bannock and water was down his throat, so suddenly and horribly that he had wondered if he was poisoned—until he stopped being able to wonder at all. His head still ached, but dully, a leaden soreness instead of the black pounding of a few hours ago; and his belly crawled clammily within him; but he no longer sweated and shivered. And he had begun to wonder with a growing urgency why he had been shifted into this small cell shut away from the rest of the prisoners. Because of that sudden sickness? Had they feared that it might be something that would breed and spread and break loose of the prison into Corstopitum? Or had the wounded Legionary died? He had not been dead when Phaedrus was thrust into the city jail six days ago, that much they had told him, but he could have died since. Was this solitary cell perhaps the place where prisoners on a death charge were held for trial? It was one thing to make a good end with one's sword in hand and the packed theater benches baying, quite another to die like this. Not a pleasant thought, and it brought with it an unpleasant sense of the damp stone walls closing in.

He pushed the walls back with care, and steadied his breath. The fact that he had not struck the blow would stand him in no kind of stead; he realized that. In the eyes of Roman justice, they had all struck, had all, equally, drawn the knife. And the others had all got clear. Well, he would do for a scapegoat—ex-gladiator, paid off with the Wooden Foil, gets drunk to celebrate and knifes one of the Watch in a street brawl; it made a nice, neat story for the records, all the ends properly tied in; no need to look any farther.

There was a heavy step outside, and the jailer appeared beyond the iron grid of the cagelike door, stooped to thrust the evening food bowl under the lowest bar, and tramped on without a word; a few moments later Phaedrus heard the sudden uproar from the main hall that always greeted the food pail. He looked at the bowl which the man had left on the floor, but the look of the black rye bread and watery bean stew made his stomach heave, and he left it where it was and went on sitting. It was dusk in the cell now, though there was still light in the sky outside the small high window; and beyond the cagework door there began to be a faint tawny glow, an echo of the torch that burned all night at the head of the steps.

Presently the jailer returned, but instead of merely reaching in for the bowl and passing on, halted and produced from his belt something that jangled. His hands were out of sight beyond the edge of the door, but Phaedrus heard the metallic hiss and click of the lock, the long bar which held the door was freed and dragged back, and the door itself swung open.

"Out with you," the man said, standing back.

Phaedrus's muscles had already tensed to the chance of freedom, with the quick reaction of the Arena-trained, but he made no movement. No point in trying to rush the door when it was already open—and the Gods knew what lay beyond. ...

"Out, I said! Come on now, outside."

Phaedrus stood up in no hurry. "Am I to go before the Magistrate? Well it's about time—six cursed days he's kept me waiting."

"At this hour of night? Besides, he's not back yet. Do you think he's going to shorten his hunting trip for the likes of you?"

"Hardly," Phaedrus said, and then, "Is the man dead?"

"Him as you knifed? Not that I've heard of."

That was something, anyway, but still Phaedrus stood wary, back against the wall, misliking the man's furtive manner. "Then where are you taking me? Why am I to leave my cell at this hour?"

The jailer shrugged broad shoulders. "How should I know? My orders don't go beyond the guardroom steps. Are you coming or do I have to call my mate?"

"I am coming," Phaedrus said, and pushed off from the wall. As he ducked through the cell doorway, the man sidestepped, quick as a cat for all his size, and he felt the prick of a knife point under his ribs. "Quietly, now."

Phaedrus checked an instant at the touch of the cold iron. He had half hoped for the moment that someone was working his rescue; but the knife would seem to put an end to that idea. It had been a stupid one, anyway; the School stood by its own, bound by odd pack loyalties however much it fought among itself, but once you were out, living or dead, you were *out,* and the pack hunted without you.

"Down here—out of the light."

Well, whatever was happening, whatever all this meant, he hadn't much to lose. Phaedrus was used to taking chances. Now, quite deliberately, he let go, and abandoned himself to events like a swimmer pushing off into the current; and as the prick of the knife came again, warningly, under the ribs, he gave a low breath of a laugh and moved off down the stone-flagged corridor away from the torchlight. The main hall was behind them, with its wild-beast stink; once more they crossed a patch of torchlight, shining across a narrow courtyard from the open guardroom door; then they turned another corner, mounted some steps, and cool air stirred in their faces, clearing Phaedrus's head somewhat from the fumes of the strange sickness.

Another figure, tall, but shapeless in the dusk, moved from beside an open postern doorway; there was a quick, muttered exchange between him and the jailer: "All well?" and "All well." And then to Phaedrus, "Put on this cloak—so, the hood forward over your face. It is a fine night for a walk, my friend."

Then he was out in a back alleyway, walking as though all this was a perfectly usual thing to happen, beside the muffled figure of his new guide.

"Walk as though we were bound for the nearest wine shop— nowhere more important," said a dry voice under the other's hood; a voice that seemed faintly familiar, speaking in the British tongue.

Phaedrus glanced aside at him. "And since that seems unlikely, where *are* we bound for, on this fine night's walk?"

"Not into any trap, if that is what you are thinking."

"I can be sure of that?" Phaedrus said on a faint note of mockery.

"Na, you cannot be sure until the thing is proved. You have only my word for it, but there are places where the word of Sinnoch the Merchant is counted binding."

Phaedrus wondered whether this was one of them, then shrugged beneath the greasy-smelling folds of the cloak, and, his weakness beginning to wear off, fell more easily into step beside the other man.

Among the drifting evening crowds, they went by narrow ways and back streets, emerged at last into the Street of the Trumpeter, and turned down it. It was almost dark now, with a faint mist creeping in from the moors to make a yellow smear about the lanterns that hung here and there at street corners or over shop doorways. A stain of light fell across the roadway from an open door, and with it the blur of voices and the throaty blackbird notes of a pipe, and Phaedrus realized, with a nightmare sense of having traveled in a circle, that the doorway and the voices and the lamplight were those of the Rose of Paestum.

But the man beside him touched his arm, and instead of passing in beneath the hanging ivy bush, they turned off short into the mouth of a small dark passage way beside the wine shop; and the circle was broken.

A few paces into the darkness, Phaedrus sensed rather than saw the door that barred their way. It opened to the merchant's hand as though it had been left on the latch for them, but once inside the man said, "Wait!" and standing in the dark Phaedrus heard the sounds of key in lock, and then the light grating of a bar being slipped into place. If this was a trap after all, he had walked into it, and the trap was sprung. It was odd still to hear the voices and the blackbird piping, and know that on the far side of the lathe-and-plaster wall was the lamplight and the cheerful evening gathering of the wine shop, while he was here in the dark with whatever was coming toward him out of the Unknown.

Sinnoch the Merchant led the way to another door, which also opened to his touch, and this time did not pause to secure it behind them. They were in a narrow wailed space, half courtyard, half garden, where a lantern hanging from a rickety vine-trellis lit up the nearest of a few dejected rose bushes growing in old wine jars. There was a stable close by, to judge from the smell of hay and horse dung, and at the far side of the place a thin line of light showed through the chink of a door in what looked like a barn or a range of storerooms.

The man crossed to it, breaking into a soft haunting whistle as though to give warning of his coming to someone inside, and, lifting the wooden doorpin, went in. Phaedrus followed close behind.

The light of a fine red earthenware lamp hanging by a chain from the rafters showed him a storeroom of sorts, with dim-seen bales and boxes stacked along the walls together with coiled hide ropes, a couple of riding-pads and all manner of horse gear; showed him also a couple of benches strewn with rugs and pillows of striped native cloth, and a table with a bronze wine jug and cups on it. Clearly this was a private room of the Rose of Paestum, such as a merchant who did not wish for the company of the big posting inn by the South Gate might take for himself and his wares.

But though his first glance took in all these things, his whole attention went in the next instant to the man seated at the table, and remained there. A man in his full prime, certainly well under forty, and of giant strength, to judge by the almost grotesque thickness of neck and shoulder and the hand clenched, as though it did not know how to hold anything lightly, about the bronze wine cup he had just set down. His mouth was dry and ragged at the edge, as though he had a habit of chewing his lower lip; black brows almost met across the bridge of his nose, and on cheek and forehead showed the fine blue spiral lines of tattooing that had earned the far Northerners the name of the Painted People.

Whatever Sinnoch might be, *this* was certainly no merchant, Phaedrus thought.

He heard the doorpin falling, and Sinnoch passed him, pushing back the hood of his cloak and letting it drop from his shoulders, and the lamplight jinked on a silver and coral earring. It was the man who had given him the saffron cloak.

More and more, there were things here that he did not understand.

"I have brought him," Sinnoch said.

The man at the table answered him with a nod, and spoke directly to Phaedrus in an outlandish form of the Celtic tongue. "Take off that cloak."

Still deliberately going with the current, Phaedrus flung back the hood without a word, and let the heavy folds drop to the floor, and stood confronting the stranger, his head up, and on his lips the faint insolent smile that his comrades of the Arena knew.

There was a long moment of complete silence, in which Phaedrus could hear the distant hubbub from the wine shop mingled with the drubbing of his own heart. Then the stranger said, "It is in my mind that you will have spent an evil day."

Phaedrus took one long pace to the table and stood looking down into the eyes that were tawny as a wolf's. "That was your doing?"

"It was needful to make sure you would be lodged alone. It was needful also that there should be something—some mark of sickness on you to be remembered afterwards."

"Afterwards?"

"After they find the body."

Phaedrus felt a small icy shock in the root of his belly, and his hand flew to the place where his dagger should have been, then dropped away. It was in that instant that he became aware for the first time of a curtained inner doorway half lost in the farther shadows.

"Ach no, not *your* body." Sinnoch, who had sat himself down on the bench a little to one side, said in his dry, amused voice. "There are always bodies to be had in every city—a beggar in a back street—anybody not too closely seen will serve the purpose—and once it has been tipped into a hole in the prison yard. ..."

Phaedrus said slowly, "And all that is arranged?"

"All that is arranged. It might have been a harder matter if him they call the Chief Magistrate had not been off on the hunting trail; but it is wonderful what a few little lumps of yellow gold will do among men; most wonderful. Merchant that I am, I know the buying power of gold. They will put him in his hole quickly, lest the thing spread in the summer heat, and when the hunter returns from his hunting, there will be nothing left to see of Phaedrus the Gladiator but a little turned earth in the prison yard." The dry tone deepened into melancholy. "It is very sad. He was young and strong and good to look upon; but he took a sudden sickness in the jail, and was gone like a lamp pinched out between thumb and finger." Sinnoch made the gesture sharply and precisely, then dusted his leathery fingertips together as though to rid them of the snitch of the charred wick.

Phaedrus caught the gesture out of the tail of his eye; he had never taken his gaze from the man at the table while he listened to Sinnoch the Merchant.

"You must have wanted me sorely, to go to so much trouble," he said, and his mouth felt dry.

"We—had a certain need of you."

"What need?"

All this while the other man had sat unmoving, the bronze wine cup gripped in his hand. Now he pushed it away, so sharply that a few drops of wine leaped over the rim and splashed like blood upon the table top, and lunging to his feet came tramping round the table to where Phaedrus stood. Seated, he had seemed a big man, but the gladiator found with a sense of shock that he was looking steeply down at him, for his body was set on strong bowlegs so short that he was almost a dwarf.

"Turn to the light."

Phaedrus obeyed. He could scarcely see the other's face now, only the darkly blotted shape of him with the lamplight on the top of his head and shoulders; but he was aware of the bright, tawny stare that raked him from head to foot; and aware also, though he could not have said how, when the purpose of the stare changed, and it was no longer his outer seeming but his mettle that was being judged.

Until now, he had gone unresisting where the current carried him, but something in that ruthless probing scrutiny raised his hackles, and he locked his gaze with the other man's and strove to beat it down as though it were an opponent's weapon.

It was the merchant, lounging among the striped rugs on the bench, who broke the silence at last. "I was right, Gault the Strong?"

The other nodded, turning back to the table. "You were right, Sinnoch my brother. He may serve the need."

Phaedrus shot out a long arm to the shoulder of Gault the Strong, and swung him round again. "And now that seemingly you are satisfied, in Typhon's name you shall tell *me* this need, and we will see if *I* am satisfied also!"

Suddenly the dark man smiled, and with a lightning movement, chopped Phaedrus's gripping hand away so that he felt for an instant as though his wrist was broken. "When you lay hands on me, do it in fellowship and not in anger! Now pull that stool to the table and sit down, for you have a long listening before you."

Phaedrus stood for a moment, his fists clenched, then

shrugged, and pulled up the stool. When they were facing each other across the table, Gault said, "Can you be understanding all that I say, or shall Sinnoch here turn the words from my tongue to yours?"

Indeed the tongue he spoke was full of odd inflections and cadences that would have made it almost a foreign tongue to most of Phaedrus's kind. But his mother had been part of the spoils of some far northern battle before ever she came to a Roman slave market, and had spoken in much the same way when they were alone together. "I understand well enough," he said.

"Sa. First then, drink, my friend." Gault the Strong splashed more wine into his own cup and pushed it across the table.

Phaedrus left it standing there. "I've an empty belly and I'd as soon listen to what you tell me with a clear head."

"Maybe there is wisdom in that. Later then, we will eat and drink together." Gault had dipped a finger in the spilled wine, and as though not conscious of what he was doing, had begun to draw patterns on the table top as he talked. It was a trick that Phaedrus was to come to know well as time went by.

"In my grandfather's time, we, the Dalriadain, the People of the Gael, came from Erin over the Western Sea, and conquered the land and the people of the hills and the sea lochs below Cruachan, the people who were called the Epidii in those days; and we made our hunting-runs where theirs had been, so that all that land became Earra-Ghyl, the Coast of the Gael." He looked up, his finger pausing an instant in its making of curved and crosswise lines. "Since long and long before that, we have been a Horse People, a People of Lugh the Sun Lord, holding to kings who passed the kingship down from father to son. But the Epidii, though they too were a Horse People, were even as the Caledones are still, a people of Cailleach, the Great Mother, and to them the Queen was all, and the King for little save to give the Queen children. Therefore our King mastered and mated with their Queen, as the Sun Lord masters and mates with the Mother who is both Earth and Moon; and we and the Epidii became, in some sort, one."

"This, one may learn from any harper who sings of the old days and the death of kings. Why will you be telling it to me now?"

"For a good reason, that you shall know in time. ... Seven winters ago, Levin of the Long Sword died when the boar of his hunting turned at bay; and the kingdom should have gone to Midir his young son. Maybe that would have been the way of it, if the boy's mother had been yet living; but she was dead, and Liadhan the King's half sister was the Royal Woman of the Tribe—a woman like a she-wolf in a famine winter. The Earthling blood was in her, and the Old Ways, for her mother was a princess among the Caledones. She chose out one of the Royal Bodyguard to be her mate— her first marriage-lord was lately dead—and seized the rule. So for seven years we have followed the Old Ways again."

"Just like that. Did you not fight?"

"Some of us fought." Gault fingered a long white scar that writhed up his forearm, and left it streaked with the crimson of the spilled wine that stained his fingers. "Most of us died. She had the northern clans, where the Old Blood runs strong, behind her; she had the power of the priest-kind, who hoped for greater power under the Mother than they had known in the Sun Lord's day; she had made sure of young Midir. The thing was done between a winter's dusk and a winter's dawning, and we of the Southern clans were weak with fighting, for we had joined shields with the Caledones in the past summer, to break the Red Crests' Northern Wall. We had no rightful king to raise for a battle cry against her. The longer-sighted among those that were left of us urged peace; and in the end we made what peace we could—such as may be made with the wolf-kind—and waited for a later time."

He paused, and dipped his finger yet again in the spilled wine, and added a carefully judged flourish to his pattern. A small muscle twitched in his cheek. "At Midwinter, it will be the seven years that we have waited."

"Seven years?" Phaedrus said, puzzled.

And from the rug-piled bench, Sinnoch the Merchant put in dryly, "You have been too long among the Roman-kind, for all the color of your hair. You forget the ways of your own people."

"Every seventh year the King dies," Gault said, as though there had been no interruption. "Liadhan has chosen already the man who is to fight the Death Fight with Logiore and take his place until in another seven winters it is time for his own death, and another King."

For an instant, Phaedrus's Arena training almost made him say, "What if it is the Old King who wins the Death Fight?" He had lived all his life among the Roman-kind, but something in him was beginning, all the same, to remember the ways of his own people, a memory of the nerve-ends rather than the mind. And he knew that the Old King would not win the Death Fight. Maybe there was a drug used; maybe it was simply that he knew winning that fight was not in the pattern of his fate.

He began to catch the first and most distant flicker of an idea as to where all this might be leading. "And the Old King does not care for the end made ready for him?"

Sudden and unexpected laughter twitched at the corners of Gault's bitten lips. "Ach no. The Old King has the Old Blood in him. For him it is the pattern of things. It is the Young King who balks. At Beltane, the Queen sent her token to Conory of the Kindred. It was unwelcome."

"And so?"

The dark man leaned forward, one elbow smearing out his pattern to a red blur on the table top; and all at once his eyes were burning like those of a man with fever. "And so the time has come that the Dalriadain set aside Liadhan the Queen, having borne her rule long enough. Already the horns are blowing in the hills, and the black goat dies. Even among the northern clans many have come over to us in their hearts, weary of this dark woman's rule that calls for the death of men. We of the Kindred, the Royal Clan, are of one mind in this matter; Conory stands with us, and certain of the Companions, the Bodyguard, will follow him. There is yet one more that we need—Midir!"

Phaedrus stared at him under frowning brows. "And since Midir is dead?"

Gault made a quick gesture of one hand, as though to say, "Let that pass for the moment." "We need our rightful King to raise and follow against the Woman, as we needed him seven winters ago. He would have been worth two—three thousand fighting men to us then, boy that he was. As a man, he would be worth more." The tawny eyes were fixed upon Phaedrus's face. "A man much about your age; much such a one to look at, too."

"I am not certain what you mean," Phaedrus heard his own voice after a sharp pause, without even being aware that he had spoken. "But it is in my mind that you would have me play this lost prince for you."

"We need Midir."

Phaedrus flung back his head and laughed. "Fiends and Furies! You're more of a fool than you look, if you think I could be doing *that*."

The tawny eyes never swerved. "You can if you will."

"If I will? I have the choice then?"

"It is a thing that can only be done of the free choice."

"Are you asking me to believe that if I refuse you will let me go free, loaded with all this that you have told me? Tell that to the green plover."

"Na, we will not be troubling the green plover. Refuse, and bide captive in our hands until all is over, then go free and shout your story where you will. I will swear that, if you like, on all our hopes of victory."

Phaedrus said, "But if he is dead, she will know—all the Tribe will know it for a trick." It seemed to him as he spoke that the rug that hung across that inner doorway stirred, but when his gaze whipped in that direction, the heavy folds were hanging straight and still. It must have been only the trick of the lamplight.

"The tale runs that the boy was drowned bathing in the loch, and his body never washed ashore. Only the Queen, and those who did her will, can know it for a trick, and for good reasons they will not be seeking to prove it."

"A pity, for her, that she did not have the body washed ashore, for all men to see."

"That would have been beyond even her powers," Gault said. "He was not dead."

The words seemed to hang echoing among the bales and boxes, until Phaedrus said at last, "Not dead?"

"Even Liadhan would not quite dare the slaying of the King. She—made sure of him."

"Then what if he comes back to claim his own?"

"He will not come back to claim his own."

"How can you know? If he is lost. ..."

"He is not lost." Gault's finger had returned to its half-unconscious pattern-tracing in the spilled wine. "He works for a leather merchant in Eburacum. We sought him from the first, and found him three years and more ago."

Phaedrus was beginning to feel that he was caught up in some fantastic dream. "Then if you have your own prince to your hand, why me? *Why me?* There is something here that smells strange to me, and I do not think that I like the smell!"

"There is a price offered."

"This time I am not for sale."

"For gold, maybe no. There are other kinds of price."

"A kingdom? How much of a king should I be when all is done?"

"As much of a king as you would be showing yourself strong for. That I promise you, I who am not without power in the Tribe. The price I had in mind was no more than the balance of a sword in your hand, a few risks to be run, maybe a lost flavor to be caught back into life."

"You choose the price you offer well," Phaedrus said after a moment.

"And your answer?"

"Give me a sword, and I'll use it well for you. I'll not meddle with a kingship that isn't mine; ill luck comes that kind of way."

Silence lay flat and heavy in the room, a silence that seemed tangible as the air one breathed. And in the silence, Sinnoch the Merchant looked on as though at some scene that interested him but was no concern of his; and the two pairs of eyes, slate-gray and tawny, held each other across the table.

Then Gault turned on the bench, and shouted into the gloom behind him, "Midir!"

And even as Phaedrus's gaze whipped toward that inner doorway, the hanging rug was dragged aside, and a man stood on the threshold. A young man in the rough tunic of a craftsman, who checked on the farthermost edge of the lamplight, his head alertly raised like a hound's when it scents the wind. Phaedrus caught the glint of red hair, and something in the shadowed face and the line of throat and shoulders and long flank that made the hair lift a little on the back of his neck. He might have been looking at his own fetch.

"Did someone call my name?" The voice was different, at all events, lighter and harder, glinting with a bright febrile fierceness that flashed into Phaedrus's mind the image of a panther he had once seen in the Londinium Circus.

"I called," Gault said. "I have failed, Midir. Now let you try if you can do better."

The young man walked forward. Phaedrus, with a quick suspicion of the truth, thought that he followed the sound of the other man's voice, and as he came full into the lamplight, saw that there were only scarred hollows under the straightened brows where his eyes should have been. Saw also the great puckered scar on his forehead where something, some pattern that had been tattooed there, had been dagger-gashed across and across and across in a sickening savagery of destruction, a long time ago.

He had enough of his mother in him to know that among the tribes no maimed or blind or crooked man could hold the kingship, lest his rule bring disaster on the People. So that was how the Royal Woman had made sure of Midir, the rightful King whom she had not quite dared to kill! His gorge rose in his throat.

"Will you speak, Phaedrus the Gladiator, that I may hear where you stand."

"I stand here, a spear's length from you, Midir of the Dalriadain."

"You give me a name that I have not borne these seven years. I am Midir the leather worker." The other had turned full face to him at the first sound of his voice, and came toward him unerringly, seeming to know the position of table and benches by the sound of his own footsteps, or by that mysterious "shadow" that blind men speak of. "And so you are like-looking to me. Like enough to take my place?"

"It is in my mind at least that any man who has seen neither of us in seven years might well take one for the other."

"That should make you proud. It is not every slave gladiator could pass for a prince of the Dalriadain."

Phaedrus felt the angry blood rushing to the roots of his hair, but before he could retort, the other added with a crack of laughter, "Or, of course, every prince of the Dalriadain who could pass for a leather worker."

"I do not see why not, if he had the training of his craft," Phaedrus said in a tone of cool effrontery; but his sudden anger had begun to flicker out.

"I wonder. Is it the same with the prince's craft, should you be thinking?" The laughter lingered in Midir's voice.

"Na. The prince's craft is another matter. No man needs to be born a leather worker and the son of a leather worker, but can you think of any training that would change a slave gladiator, in truth and not mere seeming, into a prince of the Dalriadain?"

"The seeming might be enough—if he were not afraid."

"Afraid?"

"A man who set out to play such a part would have good cause to be afraid. ... But if you are like enough to pass for me, and not easily made afraid, then maybe the Gods have sent you to us."

Phaedrus asked with a detached interest—he could still think himself detached, because he still believed that he was going to refuse—"And you? Could you stand aside while another man took your place?"

Midir's head was up, the lines of laughter in his face suddenly thin and hard as sword cuts. "Listen, my friend, Gault has used me as a weapon against you tonight—ach yes, he has, you know it as surely as I do—and if old Fox Sinnoch had not found you, they would have used me as a weapon against Liadhan, for want of a better. They would have made me their accusation against her before all the Tribe. 'See, Warriors of Earra-Ghyl, Lords of the Horse Herd, here is Midir who should have been your King, but the She-Wolf clawed out the daylight for him and made him an insult to the Gods! Strike now against the Woman who has done this accursed thing!' It is better than no weapon at all. But to shout 'Brothers! Here is Midir your King! Liadhan would have slain him, but he escaped and now he is come back to be the battle standard of the war host!' That is a sharper weapon, and the sharpness of the weapon is all I care for, now."

His hands had come up while he spoke, feeling for Phaedrus's shoulders, and clamped down on them with a fiercely urgent grip.

And Phaedrus thought again of the chained panther, and was not sure why; only as surely as though he had shared these seven years, he knew that this red-haired other self had never come to any kind of terms with his fate, never for an instant accepted, never for an instant ceased to rage against the darkness, unbroken, unsubmitting, unreconciled. Knew also that he was without pity either for himself or for anything under the sky. For that instant, as though one life flowed through them both through the other's hands on his shoulders and his own that he had brought up to cover them, he knew the Prince Midir as he had never known anyone since the day that he was born.

The two onlookers had ceased to matter; the world contracted and sharpened focus as it had used to do in the Arena, until it contained only himself and the man before him.

"You bid me to take your place, Midir?"

Midir was faintly smiling, and he spoke lightly, but the words came widely spaced like small bright drops of blood. "Take my place, Phaedrus, and with it, take my vengeance, and keep it safe—warm with your own warmth, like a little polished throw-stone in the hollow of your shield until the time comes to throw. But cry my name when that time comes, so that both the Sun Lord and the Woman may know that it is my vengeance, not yours."

4 | *The House of the Fighting Cocks*

COCKCROW HAD JUST SOUNDED FROM THE FORT, AND THE long narrow sprawl of native hovels, wine shops and bath houses, granaries, married quarters, horse corrals and temples to a score of alien Gods that made up the town of Onnum on the Wall was stirring into wakefulness. Not that any of the Wall towns ever slept, save twitching and with one ear cocked and one eye open.

In the loft of a ramshackle house close to the fortress gate, where Florianus the old Syrian archer bred his fighting cocks, the birds roused and rattled their feathers, stretched their necks and crowed defiance to the Roman trumpets.

Most mornings, the crowing of the cocks roused Phaedrus and Midir in their quarters beyond the rough partition walls. Then whoever's turn it was to forage would go down the rickety loft ladder and out to the well at the street corner, draw himself a pail of water for a hurried splashing wash, and on the way back collect the platter of oaten bannock and jug of buttermilk or sour watered wine which the old crone who owned the house would have left out for them overnight. The one whose turn it was to have his food brought up to him like an emperor went without washing that day. They never broke cover together, for though it was still half dark the lantern burned until dawn above the doorway of the Bacchus's Head close by, and they took care not to impress it needlessly on the minds of chance beholders that there were two men lodging in the House of the Fighting Cocks—two men who looked so exactly alike, unless you came near enough to realize that one was blind.

But today they had been astir before the cocks, and were sitting on the edge of the makeshift plank bed, jug and platter almost finished with between them. The lamp on its niche high on the wall was getting short of oil; the flame leaped and fluttered, and its unstable light sometimes found and sometimes almost lost the two young men, showing them stripped to their plaid breeks as they had slept, for it was close in the little room, and already the day creeping up behind the narrow window gave promise of heat later.

Perhaps it was because of the thundery heat, Phaedrus told himself, that he was not hungry. But he knew it was not. Fiends and Furies! One would think to be glad enough at the prospect of getting out of this place!

He looked round at Midir, sitting with a half-eaten lump of the mouth-drying oatcake in his hand, and realized with a kind of exasperation that the heat had killed Midir's hunger as well. The flaring lamp made harsh shadows where his eyes should have been, and cast the puckered scar on his forehead into cruel relief. It was almost a month now since the night just after they came here, when they had lain side by side while Gault, with his curious skill for such things, had remade the lost pattern with a cock's hackle dipped in woad, and then copied the main lines of it onto Phaedrus's forehead; those potent, interlocking lines and spirals and double curves of Sun Cross and Stallion Symbol that formed between them a device not unlike a four-petaled flower. And after that, the old woman he had brought with him had taken over, with her tattooing needles and pots of woad and crimson dye. The memory of that small prickling torment made the nerve-ends crawl between his brows even now, and Phaedrus put up his hand unconsciously and felt the faintly raised lines on the skin. The Royal Flower, the old woman had called it, the Mark of the Horse Lord.

"Does it still feel strange?" Midir said, with that disconcerting awareness he sometimes had of what one was doing.

"Not so strange as it did a month ago."

"A few months older, and I'd have had more than the Mark of the Horse Lord for the beldam to prick into your hide with her sharp little needles."

Phaedrus thought of Gault, who had gone North again now; Gault the Strong, with the warrior pattern tattooed on breast and shoulders, thighs and cheeks and temples.

"All the warrior patterns that they prick onto the boys' skins at the Feast of New Spears," Midir was saying.

"At the next Feast it would have been my turn to go into the darkness of the Place of Life, and come out from it a man, to take my place among the Men's Side, with the warrior patterns princely thick upon me."

Beyond the thin partition a cock crowed in fiercely shining challenge, and was answered faintly across the roof tops from some other cock loft on the far side of the town.

"Why not Sinnoch?" Phaedrus asked suddenly.

"Sinnoch is only half of the Tribe. His father was a Roman merchant—they get everywhere, the merchant-kind—who came to his mother on the night she hung up her girdle for the Goddess. There was a bad harvest that year, so I've heard. The priestess said the Great Mother was angry and must be appeased; and when they drew lots among the maidens, to sleep at the river crossing for the first stranger who passed that way, the lot fell upon her. And so Sinnoch was born and she died bearing him. ... I think he never greatly wanted to be a warrior; I suppose his father's wanderings were in him, too, so he trades horses to the Roman-kind, with an unmarked skin, and Gault says there is not a noble of Tribe he could not buy up if he wanted to. It is strange—he did not want to be a warrior, and the Dalriadain have always accepted him in other ways; but it hasn't made him love the folk who whisper in the dark to the Great Mother."

"I think it would not make me, either," Phaedrus said.

He got up and crossed to the window. The lamp was finally dying in little gasps of flame, and the roofs opposite were already touched with morning, though night still lingered in the narrow chasm of the street below. He stood gazing down into it while he tied his hair back out of the way with a leather thong as he had been used to do before putting on his helmet. He knew that street—what one could see of it from the window—as well as he knew the room behind him, with its gap-toothed floorboards and the scattering of bright feathers that drifted through with the smell of droppings from the cock loft, and the places where the daub had fallen from the walls and the laths showed through like the bare ribs of something dead.

"Close on time for you to be away," Midir said behind him.

"Sa sa. No time for a wrestling bout this morning."

Every morning, since they had been cooped up here, they had wrestled together, at first simply to keep themselves from going soft, because they had no other way of getting exercise; but later, because they enjoyed pitting strength and skill against each other. Well, all that was done with now. ... "I must not be keeping my new master waiting," he added, and thought, "It seems a lifetime that I have been mewed up in this place, learning my trade, and in a little while it will still be here, but I shall be gone. I shall be away up the street to join Sinnoch and take the pack beasts North—to win myself a kingdom that isn't mine, or more likely end as wolf-bait. And Midir?" Somehow the past month had seemed so shut away from the run of life, so turned in on itself, that he had never wondered before. He swung round from the window. "And you? What road for you now, Midir?"

Deep in the shadows the other shrugged. "The road back to Eburacum and my *old* master and the dressed hides. This was only to be a free time to visit my aunt in Segedunum. He's a good old man; he said I had earned the holiday."

"One advantage of being a free man. A slave never earns a holiday." (Midir had never been sold as a slave, Phaedrus knew. Who would buy a blind slave unless he could sing? He had simply been turned adrift like an unwanted dog among the beggars of Eburacum, and his one piece of good fortune had been when the harness maker who was now his master had seen him rough-mending a broken pack-strap for a traveler outside the posting inn, and noticed the skill in his hands.)

"I've an idea he did not mean so long a holiday as this one," Midir said wryly.

"But he will take you back?"

"Ach yes. I'm a good craftsman. You don't need to be able to see to work the skins or cut a belly-strap—only to be a king. I am wondering if this seems a noble jest to any God that chances to look this way. I wonder if the Gods laugh at the things that happen to men, as we laugh at someone slipping on a kale stalk—or if they simply don't care. ... My father went out to meet his boar. There had been much fighting, and the Red Crests had burned off all the pasture that they could reach, and then a wet autumn and the cattle died. It was famine time, you see. And look what came of it. That will have made the Gods laugh, too."

"Don't be talking like that," Phaedrus said quickly. He did not understand what Midir was talking about, but he knew that it was dangerous. "It is only a fool who sets out, like a man poking at a stallion with a little stick, to make the Gods angry!"

Midir shrugged. "Ach well, it is I that said the thing, not you." He leaned forward and felt for the jug, and with a quick gesture flung the lees of the watered wine on the already stained and filthy floor. "See, I am making an offering—what is it you call it in your Roman tongue? I pour a libation to the Sun Lord, a peace offering." Then leaning back against the wall, hands behind head, "Come now, I'll be hearing you your lessons one more time while you make ready for the road."

Phaedrus had begun to move about their cramped quarters, gathering his few belongings and bundling them into an old cloak. A small part of his mind was wondering what had happened to his Wooden Foil and the fat woman's bracelet—probably the lodging-house people had taken them and whatever else was in the bundle, when they heard he was dead. The rest of him was waiting, his mind poised to leap this way or that, for whatever question Midir would toss at him first.

Midir said, "What happened after Liadhan had you stunned and flung into the river?"

Phaedrus frowned. ("Do not seem too sure," Sinnoch had said when his training began, "not so sure as to make men think 'This is a lesson learned by heart.' ") "How would I be knowing in the dark and I hit on the head with a stone? The last thing I remember is Liadhan's men; the one of them with a stone in his hand. For the rest—" he shrugged. "I suppose the man did not strike hard enough—maybe he did not mean to. Or else it was that my time had not come. And I must have lodged among the rocks under the overhang of the shore, with my face above water. And seemingly they did not wait to be sure the work was finished, for when I woke, there was no one there. I was half drowned and very sick, and there was no strength in me to make the bank again, and I—I must have struggled and rolled clear of the rocks; the run of the river took me and carried me away, and washed me up at last, away down at the Crinan ford, where the chariot road runs

South. A trader going that way with horses to sell to the Wall garrisons found me. ..."

"What was he like?"

"A small man—I do not remember clearly. I was in no state to be taking account of faces; and it was a long time ago."

"That is fair enough. Go on."

"He would not believe me when I told him who I was; he was a stranger and did not know the Royal Mark. He took me South with the horses and sold me when he sold them; and the man who bought me sold me again, and—shall I go on?"

"No need. So far the story is a credit to Sinnoch. For the rest— you should know your own story well enough without my hearing it again. Na, we'll try something else." He made no move from his lounging position, but the next question came silken-swift as a dagger thrust. "You see a man with a small sickle-shaped scar slicing through one eyebrow. Who is he?"

"Dergdian, Son of Curoi, one of the Guard in my Grandsire's day."

"Which eyebrow does the scar cut through?"

"The left."

"How is it that you remember so clearly? It is a longer time since you saw Dergdian than it is since you saw the horse trader."

"It was I that gave him the scar, throwing a stone at what I thought was a fox in the tall bracken; and he gave me the choice of taking my beating from my father, or from himself and no more said." Phaedrus sounded rueful, hitching at his shoulders as he spoke, as though indeed remembering the weight of Dergdian's arm. It was like that with him sometimes, now. He turned to the narrow window and stood looking out. "Conory helped me wash the blood off, and begged some wound-salve from old Grania to ease the smart."

"Conory?" said Midir's voice behind him.

"Conory was—is my cousin, born in the same summer to Lorwen, my father's younger sister. I know him by his having one eye set higher than the other, and a brown fleck in the apple of it." There were other things he knew about Conory, a great many other things, including some that Midir had never told him. But he did not recite them now. They had had to be learned, but though the Arena years had hardened him to most things, he still disliked trampling more often than need be in another man's private territory. "It was to Conory that the Queen sent her token at Beltane," he said, and then, watching a pigeon on the opposite roof, "It seems the Queen likes her kings young."

"The Sacred King must be always young, and strong, lest the harvest fail and the mares grow barren. It is maybe a fine thing for the Queen, but the needs of the harvest come first."

"You've not told me much of Liadhan the Queen. Very little beside all that you have told me of other men and women."

"What should I tell you of her? She has long fair hair and a long fair face, and all her movements are slow and strong and rich—like corn that is heavy in the ear. They say that Maeve of Connacht was such a one, who fought against us in the High and Far Off days, in the land our people came from. But there's small need to tell you the look of her, you'll not be mistaking her for another woman. I saw her in the Royal Woman's place at the feasts and sacrifices, but her life never touched against mine, until"—he broke off, and Phaedrus, looking round, saw his face for the moment no more than a mask—like the calmly molded features of the helmet-mask over the sweating, snarling features of the gladiator beneath. Even his voice seemed masked with that same artificial calm, when he spoke again. "The boy Midir hated and feared her always—that is all that the Prince Midir, returned to his rejoicing Tribe, need remember of Liadhan. Not even that she had him blinded to make him unfit for the kingship, and stood by to see it done. That story is done with and best forgotten, now that there is a new story to take its place."

"Nevertheless, the part of me that remains Phaedrus the Gladiator will not quite forget that story until the account is settled with Liadhan."

"Na! Forget it!" Midir dropped the mask, and springing up, came striding across to him. "You've a wild enough team to drive without *that* mare yoked among them."

"It was you who bade me to avenge you, that first night behind the Rose of Paestum."

"I spoke in a black moment," Midir said.

And there was a small sharp silence. Then Phaedrus said, "You must have hated me."

"You can scarce expect I would be loving you."

A cart came rumbling up the street, the wagoner cursing his team; there was the crack of a long rawhide whip, and the slow hoofbeats of the file of oxen died into the distance. Then Phaedrus said:

"Give me a right to the kingship, Midir."

"I have told you ..."

"I want more than words."

Midir stood thoughtful for a moment, then he pulled the dagger from his belt where he wore it night and day ("A man needs to know where to lay hand on his knife in the dark," he had said once), feeling with a finger along the blade to the tip, and made a small precise movement quicker than the eye could follow. A thread of crimson sprang to life on the fine brown skin inside his wrist, and a few beads of blood welled up. He reversed the knife with a flick and held it out by the blade. "Now you."

Phaedrus took it, and stood for a moment balancing it in his hand. He was not even sure that he liked this uncomfortable man, certainly he felt none of the easy comradeship with him that he had felt with Vortimax; but none of that mattered. During this long enclosed month they had grown together at the edges in a way that had nothing to do with liking but belonged somewhere far down at the root of things.

He made his own small quick movement, watched the blood spring out on his own wrist.

Midir flicked up his head at the sound of the movement. "Done?"

"It is done."

"Bring yours to mine, then."

Phaedrus did so, feeling the mouth of the tiny wound on the mouth of the other as they pressed their wrists together. Three drops of mingled blood escaped between them and made three brighter spots among the spilled lees of the wine on the floor where Midir had poured his libation to the Gods.

"So now we are of one life blood, you and I," Midir said, "and you have the blood of the Horse Lord mingled with your own, if ever the Gods call you to account for taking the kingship." There was a note almost of laughter in his voice. Then as he took back the knife and sheathed it and brought up his hands to feel Phaedrus's shoulders, he was in deadly earnest. "Listen! *You* cannot be taking the kingship from me. Liadhan did that, once and for all. But it is not hers, even by reaver's right, for she has turned back to the Old Ways and so there is no Horse Lord to lead the Dalriadain and answer for them to Lugh of the Shining Spear. The kingship lies free and waiting. ... Take it if you can— and a good war trail to you, Phaedrus my brother-in-blood."

Phaedrus set his own hands for an instant on the other's, as he had done that first night of all. "It may be that we shall meet again one day," he said. "The Sun and the Moon on your path, Midir."

He turned and caught up his bundle, and went clattering down the rickety stair and out into the street, all but colliding with a man carrying hot loaves. The man swore at him, and Phaedrus swore back, with flowers and flourishes of insult learned in the Arena which left the other open-mouthed and envious, then turned to look up at a small window high under the gap-toothed slates, from behind which came the sound of whistling, a short five-note phrase jaunty as a water wagtail, that he and Midir had used for a signal at their comings and goings all this month. He whistled back and, hitching up his bundle, set off for the inn on the outskirts of the town, where Sinnoch and the horses were lodged, falling as he went into the old play actor's swagger.

He had entered into this business partly for the sake of the things that Gault had offered as a price, partly because of that sudden feeling of oneness with Midir; and then he had not been sure what strange waters he was getting into, nor where he was heading. But now, striding up the already crowded street where light and color were seeping back into the world, and the pigeons wheeled above the roof tops, suddenly he felt light on his feet and lucky. Every gladiator knew that feeling; the day when the Gods' faces were toward you, your lucky day, when it was your adversary's guard and not yours that flew wide. He dodged a cart laden with wine skins, and swaggered on. Once or twice a head turned to watch the tall man with the red hair under a Phrygian cap pulled down to his eyebrows, who wore the rough clothes of a pack-train driver and walked with braced instep of a dancer or a swordsman.

It was almost full daylight when he came to the stable court of the Golden Fleece.

5 | *Frontier Post*

TOWARD EVENING, SIXTEEN DAYS LATER, WITH ALL THE BROAD slow heather hills of Valentia between them and the Onnum Gate, the little pack train swung northward from the broadening Cluta, which they had been following since dawn, and turned into the track that rose gently from the river marshes. And it was then that Phaedrus saw a faint haze of smoke hanging beyond the ridge, and said to the merchant riding beside him, "What lies ahead? It does not look like heath fire, though Typhon knows the furze is dry enough."

"It isn't a heath fire," Sinnoch said. "That is the smoke of the Northern Wall cooking its supper."

It was late into August by now, and the dust cloud rose from the track under the ponies' hooves and settled slowly again after their passing, a gray bloom of dust that powdered beasts and men from head to foot, parched the throat, and stung the eyes, and seemed to fur over even the sound of the bell that the train leader wore about his neck to warn off the Evil Eye. And Phaedrus, constantly on the move to and fro along the plodding line, envied Vron, who had been Sinnoch's fore rider for a score of years, ambling ahead on his small ragged pony, his feet almost brushing the ground on either side, his old sheepskin hat hanging loose and easy on the back of his head.

It was a very small pack train, only four burden-beasts and the three riding ponies; for Sinnoch was a horse trader before all else. Once a year he made the trip South with a score or more rough-broken three-year-olds, herded by drovers on little shaggy ponies much as sheep dogs herd their flock. He would give the lads a few days to make Corstopitum a still wilder place than it was the rest of the year, and then send them North again, and himself follow later with no one but old Vron and maybe one other, his ponies' yellow bale-cloths laden with a few luxuries chosen with care and long experience of knowing his market: a few fine bronze weapons, ornaments of amber and jet, a cup of violet-colored glass, a length of emerald silk, a couple of jars of Etruscan wine slung one on either side of a pack-saddle.

Phaedrus had asked him one day why he did not keep the drove-boys with him to act as guard for his small rich cargo, and Sinnoch had said, "Ah now, that would be to cry aloud to the very hills that the goods in my bales were worth taking; and what could a handful of drove lads do against a reaving party? Na na, it is better not to be putting ideas into honest folks' heads."

A short while later they had crested the ridge and were looking down at the Cluta marshes again, where the river flung one of its great loops northward. A broad tongue of low sodden land reaching far back into the hills flaming like gorse along its backward fringes, blurred with saltings and mouse-pale dunes toward the coast. And away across the flatness of it, where the lane began to rise again, was the square-set mass of a big turf and timber fort with the usual huddle of native bothies in the stockaded cantonment; and on either side, the turf banks and ditches of the Wall itself. The Wall that ended, westward, in some kind of block-house or signal station far out on the marshes, and eastward, climbed away and away onto higher ground, strung with other forts— Phaedrus could make out two, from the low ridge where they had checked to breathe the ponies—until it lost itself in distance and heat-haze and the great dust-dark Caledonian Forest that lay like a thunder cloud on all the inland country. And beyond the Wall, range behind range, trembling and transparent on the sultry air, the mountains of the North, seeming less substantial than the smoke of the cooking fires that hung above the fort. ...

Eight years ago, the smoke hanging above the forts of the Northern Wall had been war smoke, the dark snitch of burning timbers, rolling over dead men in the ditch. That was the last time that Dalriadain and Caledones had joined spears, the second time that the Wall of Lollius Urbicus had gone up in flames. But each time it had been patched up and garrisoned again, and now the smoke was the quiet evening smoke of cooking fires, and the place looked secure and set in its ways between the marshes and the wooded hills.

"A pleasant change, to see smoke rising from a hearth again," Phaedrus said, his mind going back over the cold hearths, the remains of deserted villages, the steadings and cattle folds whose stones were laced together with brambles and bindweed about their doorways, that they had passed more than once on their way North. Oh, there had been living settlements, too, but even they had had a chill about them: too many old women with hollow faces, too few men, and too few children.

"Aiee! Lollius Urbicus made a fine clean sweep of Valentia while he was about it," Sinnoch said. He spoke the General's name as though it smelled; a tone which Phaedrus had heard before among the men of the North. "More than forty summers ago but the scars still show. *And* still ache when the wind is in the East, as old scars have a way of doing."

Phaedrus glanced round with quickly raised brows. "Meaning another rising, one day?"

But the merchant, sitting loose on the saddle rug, the great oxhide whip resting across his pony's withers, had nothing in his eyes but distance and heat-haze. "Maybe one day when and if the lowland tribes grow strong enough. That won't be in your time or mine; Lollius Urbicus knew what he was doing when he made his demands on the province—drafts for the Auxiliaries has a fine respectable sound to it—and marched all the young men away to serve the Eagles at the other end of the Empire."

"One might be calling that a kind of murder," Phaedrus said thoughtfully, "only the murder of a whole people instead of one man."

Sinnoch's voice was dryly and bitterly amused. "Ah na, it is just the Red Crests making the *Pax Romana*." He whistled to the pack team, cracking the long whip above their backs to set them again in motion.

"And then he built his fine new Wall," Phaedrus pondered, as they plodded on and the choking dust cloud rose again, "to say to all men 'The *Pax Romana* runs to *here*. This far the sun shines, and beyond it is the dark, that had best keep out.' "

"Not quite. There were forts along that line a hundred years ago, so I've heard, and there are still outpost forts and the old warship base at Are-Cluta, a full day's trail beyond it. And as for keeping anything in or out. ..."

"What purpose does it serve, then?"

Sinnoch shrugged. "It serves as a check-line, by which the Red Crests can keep track—after a fashion—of who comes and who goes, and how many, and how often."

"After a fashion?"

"There are ways through without troubling the Red Crests. There are the coastwise marshes at either end, if one knows the tides and troubles to learn the habits of the patrols. But the game's not worth the lamp oil unless there is something of especial value to be smuggled through."

"Such as?"

"Arab mares, for instance. The Romans will wink quite happily at the odd stallion, fairly bought in the horse market, going through to improve the stock—the more so that they buy our three-year-olds for cavalry remounts. But mares are another matter."

Phaedrus nodded. A stallion could sire many foals in a year, but a mare bore only one. That was why no war host ever put its mares in the fighting line unless it was desperate for horses, why no province would allow good mares out over its borders if they could possibly be stopped. "Then if it is only to improve the stock, why not leave the mares alone and bring North only the stallions that the Red Crests wink at?"

Sinnoch looked round at him. "A charioteer you have been, among other things, but it is in my mind that you know little of horse breeding. Have you never heard that a horse gets his strength from his sire, but his courage from his dam? And valiant though our little hill-run mares may be, there's nothing like an Arab mare for setting fire in her foals. Besides, it would be a poor cold world in which a man was only doing what the Red Crests allowed."

Phaedrus said softly, "Have you taken mares through, yourself?"

"I may have done, from time to time, when I was young and rash. If it served no other purpose, it taught me the hidden ways of my own hills as few save the Little Dark People know them. But *this* trip we are not looking for trouble; also I've a mind to visit an old friend who keeps the wine shop in the cantonment yonder. So tonight we shall sleep safe and respectable under the fortress walls, and pass through with Rome's blessing in the morning."

And so late that evening, having unloaded the pack bales and left Sinnoch in the back room of the wine shop exchanging the news of the Frontier with his old friend, who proved to be an immensely fat old woman in a dirty pink tunic, Phaedrus and Vron took the ponies down to water them at the stream below the fort that, born somewhere among the furze and birch scrub inland, came down in a chain of looped shallows and widening pools on its way to join the Cluta.

A patrol of the Frontier Scouts had just come in and were watering their mounts, and Phaedrus, well aware of the caste difference between pack pony and cavalry mount—though indeed these particular cavalry mounts were just as rough-coated as his own charges and not much larger—followed Vron down to the pool below that at which the troop ponies were drinking. It was cool under the alders that trailed their branches toward the water, though the midges still danced in the sunlight and a breath of air stole up from the marshes, salt-laden after the heat of the day. You could see the long soft breath of it coming, silvering the marsh grasses all one way. Phaedrus and the old fore rider dismounted, knotted up the halters, and let the ponies make their own way down the bank; and the cold peat-brown water riffled round the seven eager muzzles as the weary little beasts dropped their heads to drink.

Vron squatted onto his heels, his back against an alder trunk, tipped his sheepskin hat over his eyes and became instantly and peacefully one with the landscape. But Phaedrus, making sure that the halters were secure so that the ponies could roll without danger of getting entangled, before going back to the corral, kept one eye on the men upstream.

He had seen bands of the Frontier Scouts once or twice since coming North of Hadrian's great Wall, but they were a strange breed to him, not like the Legionaries or the Auxiliaries of the Wall garrisons who came down to Corstopitum on leave. Of course he had heard stories. ... They were lean, rangy men who he knew could cover the hills on foot almost as quickly as on horseback if need be; many of them British born. A wild lot, the stories said, but said it in a tone of unwilling respect; and watching them as they stood by, relaxed but watchful while the ponies drank, one leaning against a hazel trunk and whistling through his teeth, one frowning over some adjustment to his bow—a light horn bow such as the Cretan Auxiliaries used, good for work on horseback; two more arguing softly and fiercely, an argument that looked as though it had gone on all day and might well go on all night, but each with an eye on his mount to make sure that he drank what he needed and no more, Phaedrus could believe something of their reputation and understand something of the respect. No Legion would have been seen dead in their company, breeched like barbarians, wolfskin cloaked, some with the wolf's head drawn forward over their own in place of cap or helmet. Something about them seemed familiar, making an odd pang of longing in Phaedrus that surprised and puzzled him until he realized that it was the one-ness of the pack, the strong bond that he had known in the Gladiators' School.

But the little red-roan pack mare was water-greedy, and in seeing that she did not guzzle half the pond and give herself colic, he lost track of the Frontier Scouts until a twig cracked, and he looked round to see that the Captain of the band had come strolling down the stream side with an eye cocked on the ponies.

He nodded toward the mare. "She looks as though she had a bit of breeding to her."

"She's not—" Phaedrus began, instantly on the defensive.

And the other laughed. He was a thin, very dark man, maybe in his late twenties, with a hooked nose too big for his narrow face and a pleasant pair of eyes set deep and level on either side of it. "Ah no, I'm not accusing her of Arab blood! I was thinking merely that she seemed a bit too good for pack duty. She might make a hunting pony. I wonder if Sinnoch would sell her."

Phaedrus, beginning to coax the mare back from the water ("Enough, greedy one! Back, now! Back I say!"), looked round at the soldier. "You know my master?"

"I have been in these parts three years now—seen him through three times into Valentia with his re-mounts, and three times back into the hills again with his wine and amber. Everyone on this sector of the Wall knows Sinnoch, and relies on him for news of the outer world. But as to the mare. ..."

"You had better ask him."

"Maybe I will." The man had put up a hand that was thin and dark like himself and begun fondling the mare's wet muzzle as she turned unwillingly from the water, coaxing her to him. "There's my girl. See, we are friends already, you and I." But his gaze was still on Phaedrus's face, considering; and suddenly he said, "You're a new man of Sinnoch's, aren't you?"

"Yes."

"And like the mare, you have not the look of the pack train."

"I have been other things—more than one—in my time."

"Among them, perhaps—a gladiator?"

Phaedrus's head jerked up. "I gained my Wooden Foil something over two months ago."

"So—o. This seems an unlikely way of life for a gladiator to turn to."

"It's meat and drink. My kind still needs to eat, even when the Arena gates are closed to us. Is it written all over me, then?"

"It is my business to know the looks of fighting men. You are a fighting man, but you have the look that does not come from Legionary training."

Phaedrus grinned. "Is it only the training then, that makes the War Hound or the Arena Wolf?"

"Generally something more, I grant you. Assuredly the gladiator, once trained to the sand, makes a very bad soldier."

"I was right then. I did think to go up to the Fort—that was at Corstopitum; but I reckoned it would be a waste of time."

The other nodded, his hand still on the little mare's neck, while she nuzzled with delicately working lips against his breast. Then he added abruptly, "The Frontier Wolves, of course, might be another matter. We also make very bad soldiers by Legionary standards."

Phaedrus was silent a moment in blank surprise. "You would not be offering me a Scout's dirk for my Wooden Foil?" he said at last.

"Hardly. But if you were to go to the Commandant at Credigone, I *think* you might not find it a waste of time."

They stood confronting each other while the slow heartbeats passed; the silence full of the soft stamping and sucking of the horses and the woodwind call of an oyster catcher from the marshes. Phaedrus thought with detachment what it would be like to break away from the wild venture he was bound on and ride behind this man or another of his kind, one of a close-knit company again. It was a thought to play with for an instant, like a little sharp dagger that one throws up and catches by the blade. ...

Then he shook his head. "Too late now; I've another trail to ride."

"No turning aside from it?"

Phaedrus had a sudden vision of the kind of thing that would happen to him if he tried to turn aside from this particular trail now; and knew in the same instant that if there had been no bargain made in the back room of the Rose of Paestum, no mark like a blue four-petaled flower tattooed on his forehead under the close Phrygian cap, still he would have done no more than play with the thought for an instant.

"No turning aside. To speak plain, I'd not care to spend the next twenty years patrolling this desolation of Valentia, with a skirmish with cattle raiders now and then by way of salt in the stirabout. Not that I'd be lasting twenty years. I'd be cutting my throat by spring."

"So? Are you so much of a townsman? The hills are lonelier, North of the Wall, than the hills of Valentia."

"But maybe not so desolate. There are too many dead villages and cold hearths between here and the Southern Wall."

"That is an old story now, though it was an ugly one in its day," said the Roman officer. "Punitive work is always ugly."

"More than forty years old, they tell me, but the little villages are still dead and the hearths cold, as Lollius Urbicus left them."

"You're British, aren't you?" the Captain said. "Well, upward of half my scouts are native to the land."

"They have chosen their loyalties, and I choose mine," Phaedrus said, and checked, trying to find words for what he meant. "My mother was from somewhere in these northern parts, and knew the inside of a slave market. My father was—of another conquered people. There are too many conquered peoples in Rome's world."

"At least we have brought some kind of order, even some kind of peace, to a world that was ancient chaos before."

"The *Pax Romana*," Phaedrus said. "My fa—my first master had me taught to read and write, though I have lost the trick of it now. He let me read his books. There was one, a history that a man called Tacitus wrote of the General Agricola's campaigns, a hundred years ago. He fought a great battle, this Agricola, with a war leader called Calgacus, far to the North somewhere; and there was a fine fiery speech that Calgacus was supposed to have made to his warriors before the battle joined—no Roman could have heard a word of it and so it must have been Tacitus's speech really—you see that? He made Calgacus say of the Romans, 'They make a desolation, and call it peace.' So even Roman Tacitus could have his doubts." He was surprised and infuriated even while he was speaking to find how much of his mother race those dead villages had roused in him. Fool, to be crossing swords with this dark man, just when it was most needful that he should not get into trouble or draw attention to himself in any way! But still, he did not stop until the thing was said.

Mercifully it seemed that the Roman officer was unusually slow to take offense. There was no gathering frown of affronted dignity on his face, only the look of a man arguing with another who has different beliefs from his own, and who respects those beliefs even while he will not yield to them one hair's breadth. "I think you must have been almost as unlikely a gladiator as you are a pack driver. I'm sorry I can't persuade you; I believe you would have made a good Frontier Wolf."

There was the jink of a hanging bridle bit as one of the cavalry ponies tossed up his head, and from the fort a trumpet call sounded through the evening air; and Phaedrus realized that the shadows were beginning to thicken among the alder roots. "Aye well, I'll have a word with Sinnoch about the mare," the Captain said, and turned on his heel to stroll back upstream to his own men.

Phaedrus stirred Vron out of his sleep with a friendly foot. "Come on, Grandfather, time to be getting them corralled."

Late that evening, in the lamplit store shed behind the wine shop, when the fat woman had gone waddling off to attend to her customers and Vron had betaken himself to a cock fight, Sinnoch said, "And what were you and the Captain, Titus Hilarion, talking of so earnestly, down at the horse pool?"

"*That* will be Vron," Phaedrus said. "I doubted he could have gone to sleep so suddenly."

"Vron always sleeps like a hound—one ear cocked and one eye open."

"Sa—I have noticed. Well then, he can tell you what we talked of."

A dry smile twitched at the corner of Sinnoch's mouth. "Alas, you spoke in the Latin tongue. Vron has only three words of Latin, and one of them is 'drink.' What did the Captain want?"

"He was interested in buying the roan mare."

Sinnoch nodded. "I thought he might. He was needing a new hunting pony when I came by on the road South, so I kept my eye open in Corstopitum horse markets."

"You thought—then why all this pretence of her being a pack pony?"

"Why bring her all this way like a fine lady eating her head off, when she can earn her keep on the trail? Besides, it was in my mind that he would be well pleased with himself to discover breeding under a pack saddle, and a man pleased with himself pays the better."

"You wily old fox," Phaedrus said in admiration.

Sinnoch made a small depreciatory gesture, as of one modestly turning aside a compliment. "It is merely a matter of knowing one's market. He is a bright enough lad, our Captain—good at his job. He'll be commanding one of the outpost forts in a year or two, if he isn't broken for going too much his own way, or dead in a bog with an arrow of the Little Dark People in him; but like most of his kind, his mind works in straight lines. Maybe that is what has made Rome the ruler of the world, but there's no denying that when it comes to buying or selling a horse, the man who can think in curves has the advantage." He leaned forward abruptly, his face in shadow, one heavy eardrop of coral and silver catching the lamplight as it swung. "What else did he say?"

Phaedrus frowned, and was silent an instant before answering. "That an ex-gladiator might do well enough among the Frontier Scouts."

"And you are thinking it, maybe, a sad pity that you never thought of that before you went the first time to the Rose of Paestum, and ended in the town jail?"

Phaedrus rubbed his knee, where the scar was pulling as it still did when he was tired. "We have a saying in the Circus, that life's too short to waste it in saving for the future or regretting the past. I told the Captain Hilarion I'd be cutting my throat by spring, if I took service in this desolation."

"You may not last so long in Earra-Ghyl."

6 | *Eyes*

NEXT DAY WHEN THE BARGAINING FOR THE RED MARE WAS
over and she had changed owners, they pushed on northwestward into the tribal lands beyond the shadow of Rome. Gault met
them two nights later, a picked handful of warriors with him. And
after that there were days and nights—so many that Phaedrus lost
count of them—among the coastal marshes and steep woodland
glens and great inland-running arms of the sea, with always the
huge mountain mass that Sinnoch said was Cruachan, the Shield-
boss of the World, towering higher and higher into the northern
sky. A constant shifting from place to place, strange faces seen in
the firelight and gone again next morning; word spoken softly
and passed on, in herdsman's bothy or at river ford. Little bands
of men with spears who appeared as it were from nowhere in
the half light of dusk or dawn, and were given their orders and
merged into nowhere again.

They came at last to those great cliff caves that must once have
had their feet in the Western Waters, though now there was a
strip of rocky shore between them, and made their fire in the
heart of the largest of them; and after that for a while there was
no more changing camp.

It was well into autumn by now; the great gales came booming
in from the sunset, leaping the back of Inshore Island that crouched
as though to give what shelter it could to the rocky coast behind
it, and the seals had left their basking rocks for deep water. And
a certain autumn night came, a soft dark night between storms,

bringing with it a moment that seemed to Phaedrus very like the moment before the first trumpets sounded and one heard the clashing open of the Arena gates.

The branching gallery in which he stood was no more than a fault in the living rock, so narrow that a man's shoulders might brush against either side, but running up to unknown heights overhead. The rocks were slippery underfoot, and somewhere in the depth of them was the sound of running water; and the heavy cold air was full of hollow sighings of the sea. There was a faint blur of light at the far end where the lamp still burned in the small inner cave, and close at hand a fiercer gash of torchlight shining through a chink in the heavy sealskin curtain that covered the mouth of the gallery.

Low voices sounded beyond the curtain, as the three of them checked an instant in the all-enveloping dark between the two gleams, and they too had a hollow sound, and set strange whispering echoes running. Then Gault—he knew that it was Gault by the kind of leashed ferocity of the movement—reached out and dragged the heavy skins aside, and torch and firelight flooded in to meet them.

Phaedrus, caught full in the smoky light with all the darkness of the gallery behind him, checked an instant on the lip of the rock-tumble that led down into the huge main cavern. Trained as he was to make an entrance and an impression, he was vividly aware of himself, aware that gladiator and pack rider had both gone, and that in their place stood a prince of the Dalriadain, in breeks of checkered stuff and tunic of fine saffron wool, rawhide brogues on his feet, a bronze sheathed dagger at his belt and everywhere about him, on arms and neck and in the fillet of twisted wires that bound back his hair, the glint of yellow river gold.

The voices in the cave had suddenly stopped. Faces were

turned and eyes fixed hungrily upon him. He sprang down over the loose stones into the cave, Gault and Sinnoch following more soberly in his wake.

As always in the first instant of coming into the great cavern, he cast one swift glance toward the innermost wall where the masses of volcanic rock, which elsewhere upheaved themselves in gigantic zigzag layers, rose in sheer slabs as flat and level as though cut by hand; and on the smooth surfaces still showed the dim and fragmentary traces of animals and birds drawn in red and ocher and black: wild ox and bear, boar and wolf and what looked like a wild duck rising, and in the midst of them, towering into the upper gloom, gaunt and grotesque but magnificent, the figure of a man with the head of a twelve-point stag. No one knew how long he had stood there, only that he was very, very old. And Sinnoch, who knew many things beside how to sell horses, had said once that he was the Lord of Herds and the Hunting Trail, and something strange about his dying for the People whenever the Sacrifice was needed. It was only a flung glance as his feet touched the cave floor, then he turned to the five men who sat or stood beside the driftwood fire on the raised central hearth.

"Well?" Gault said, beside him, and then, "Look him over, my brothers; will he serve?"

It seemed to Phaedrus that there were nothing but eyes in all that great sea-echoing cavern, and behind the eyes the judgment of five men, focused on him. He felt them burning him up, as he stood confronting them, head raised and mouth curving into a smile that he did not know was faintly insolent.

A big, freckled man with the blurred outlines of an athlete run to flesh was the first to speak. "It is hard to tell, with a boy of fourteen summers, what like the man will be; but the King his father—" he checked an instant and corrected himself. "This man is much such a one to look at as the King, Midir's father, was at his age."

Another nodded in agreement, and the third said, "It takes more than the shape of a nose to be making one man able to pass for another, but so far as outward seeming goes, aye, he will serve."

But the fourth member of the group, an oldish man with hot, clever eyes and a sour mouth with no teeth in it, said fretfully, "I wonder, Gault the Strong, that you are troubling yourself to bring him to the Council fire at all, since it seems that you have decided the thing to suit yourself already. Or do I dream in my old age, and only think to see the Mark of the Horse Lord on his forehead?"

"Na, you do not dream, Andragius my Chieftain," Gault said. "The Mark is there. But maybe your memory plays you tricks, and you forget that because you among the rest of the Council chose me, I am the leader in this matter as I have been from the first. There was no time to call a Council; indeed if Sinnoch had not had calm weather for the boat crossing and found me in my own Dun of the Red Bull, but had come on North to Dun Monaidh seeking me, it is in my mind that there might have been no time to carry the thing through at all. The Mark had to be made at the first possible moment, that there might be time for the look of fresh tattooing to wear off from it, and in such a case it must be for the leader to decide what shall and what shall not be done! Will any of you say that I have gone beyond the powers you gave me?"

There was a moment's silence, only the sea echoes and the crackle of the driftwood spitting on the fire. Then Andragius shrugged, and said unpleasantly, "If my brothers are satisfied, then I suppose I have little choice but to be satisfied, too."

Gault dropped the subject as though it was a dead mouse and turned to the fifth member of the Council. "You have not spoken yet, Tuathal the Wise, Cupbearer of the Sun: you who should speak first among us."

The fifth man, who had been sitting on a skin-spread stool, unmoving all this while, his eyes fixed on Phaedrus's face, got to his feet, slowly uncoiling his full magnificent height, and instantly became the core and center of the scene. He was maybe not much younger than Andragius, but of a very different kind. A man with a great curved nose like the hooked beak of a bird of prey; his robe of finely dressed horseskins, supple as cloth, fell around him in folds like a king's mantle; his head was shaved save for a single broad strip from forehead to nape, which sprang up and arched back with the proud sweep of a silver stallion's crest. His eyes too were like those of a bird of prey—a falcon, not a hawk, the dark full glowing eyes that, alone of all eyes of men or beasts, could outstare the sun without being blinded. He said, "Come here to me, you who are now called Midir."

Phaedrus went to him, and found himself caught and held by those eyes.

"You understand, to the full, what we demand of you? Not only the Council here, but the People who will be your People?"

"I know and I understand the demands of the Council. Can any man not born to it understand the demands of a People, save by learning them as they come?"

"No," said Tuathal the Wise. "No. ...Yet even that is a thing worth understanding, and the rest may come with the need. ..." He seemed to be speaking to himself, rather than to Phaedrus, his gaze going past him to the great daubed figure on the wall behind. Then abruptly the bright, piercing gaze returned to Phaedrus's face. "You have learned the part that you must play? The ways and customs—and the memories? You know your way through the five courts of Dun Monaidh? When a kinsman speaks to you, you will know what name to call him by?"

"I was a full month with Midir, and I think I did not waste it."

"No?" Tuathal waited, clearly for some proof.

Phaedrus smiled, knowing that he could give it. "Shall I call you by all your titles, Tuathal the Wise, High Priest of the Burning One, Mouthpiece of Lugh Shining-Spear, Cupbearer, Foal of the Sun? And—the one more, not for speaking aloud." He leaned closer and murmured the fifth name, the taboo name that could only be spoken between the Horse Lord and the Priests of the Sun.

Something flickered far back in Tuathal's eyes, and the proud arched lids widened a little, but he gave no other sign.

Phaedrus turned to the big fleshy man who had been the first of the five to speak. "Oscair Mac Maelchwn, is there still a cub of white-breasted Skolawn's among your hearth hounds?"

Then, as Oscair nodded, he turned to the third man, meeting little, bright, lively eyes like a grass snake's, in a big-boned, ruddy face. "You will be here in the Chief your father's stead, Cuirithir? He was a sick man, growing old before his time, seven years ago, and yet you do not wear the Chief's arm-ring."

And then it was old Andragius's turn, and Phaedrus longed to say to him, "Poor old man! Do you know that they only brought you into the Council because you are too great a Chieftain to be left outside?" Instead he said, "My Lord Andragius, you were never quite believing that I did not trip your grandson on purpose in the boys' Spear Dance, so that he went heels over head and everybody laughed. But truly, it was no more than clumsiness. I have learned to use my weapons better now."

And last of all, to a thickset, dark man, younger than the

rest, with a gay and ugly face, he said, "Gallgoid, are you still the Prince of Charioteers in all Earra-Ghyl? You used to take me up into your chariot, and drive like the west wind with me, and I'd not have changed places with all the Gods and heroes rolled into one!"

"There's none risen to supplant me yet," Gallgoid said, with a flash of white crooked teeth.

"You have put your month to good use," the Sun Priest said after a moment, "but let you tell us one thing more. Why are you doing this?"

Oscair put in gruffly, "He is doing it. Does the reason matter?"

"It is in my mind that there are reasons and reasons—though maybe this one is not far to seek. A kingship must seem good enough reason to such men as I have heard fight to the death to amuse a Red Crest crowd for the price of their next meal."

"Both Gault and Sinnoch will bear me out that that at first I swore I'd not meddle with a kingship that was not mine."

"Sa sa—what made you change your mind?"

There was a long silence, and Phaedrus heard by the changed sea echoes in the cavern that the tide was on the turn. "Midir, as much as any other thing," he said at last. Then with a kind of defiance, "Na, it is simpler than that. Gault offered me a price—oh, not in gold: the whetted edge to life that I had missed somewhat since I gained my freedom from the Gladiators' School. The price seemed to me a fair one, and so I am your man, in the way of any other mercenary who strikes a fair bargain for his sword."

"So, you give us two reasons; and together I find them good." Tuathal turned to the others beside the fire. "For myself, I am with Gault the Strong in this. How say you, my brothers?"

"I also," Gallgoid said vehemently.

"And I."

Only Andragius shrugged, and held his hands to the fire. He would be able to say that he had warned them all along, he would even be able to claim that he had never agreed but been overruled by the rest of the Council, if trouble came later.

Presently they were all sitting about the fire, while the mead horn passed from hand to hand and Phaedrus, as the youngest man there, tended the thick hunks of pig-meat broiling on the red peat heart of the blaze.

They went over plans as they waited for the food to be ready, the plans that were to become action on the night before the Midwinter Fires. But, indeed, all things had been worked out long since ("Already the horns are blowing in the hills, and the black goat dies," Gault had said, months ago in Corstopitum), and there was only some small point here and there to be altered because now, instead of a blinded prince to avenge, they had a long-lost prince to set back in his father's place.

Even the mark that would tell friend from foe had been decided on, and every man of the Sun Party would wear the temple-locks of his hair plaited, the rest hanging loose. Conory, it seemed, was to manage that, setting the fashion and making sure that it spread naturally, as a fashion does, between this and the night of the uprising.

Oscair said suddenly, "You are sure that Conory can handle it? He is more skilled with the sword than the ways of guile."

"He'll handle it. He's no fool."

"I still think," Gallgoid the Charioteer put in, "that we should have been telling Conory the truth of this matter."

"If he suspects. ..."

"Why should he suspect?" Gault demanded harshly. "It is seven years since he last saw Midir, and they were both fourteen.

And in any case, it is less risk than telling him would be. He's as unpredictable as a woman, and once told, it would be too late to untell the thing again."

The Sun Priest, who had seemed to be far withdrawn into some inner distance of his own, looked up from the fire. "Furthermore, in Conory we have our one sure test. They were closer to each other than most brothers, those two; if Conory does not know that this is not Midir, then unless he makes some very great mistake no one will ever know."

Many torches burned at the upper end of the cavern, and in the unaccustomed light that leaped from his feet to the proudly antlered head high among the hearth smoke, the painted figure of the Horned God seemed to stand clear of the rock wall behind him. An apron of skins across the seaward entrance had been drawn tight over its pegs against the wild autumn night, and the storm wind coughed and roared against it like the open palm of a giant on the stretched skin of some mighty drum. And between it and the driftwood fire on its raised hearth, the Chiefs and Captains of the Tribe were gathered.

Phaedrus, standing alone at the huge painted feet of the God, saw them only as thickened shadows, lit here and there with the blink of bronze or gold, here and there with the life-spark of an eye. The shadows, that had had deep-murmuring voices before his coming, had fallen silent, and even the wind had ceased for a moment its drumming on the entrance skins; only the sea pitching on the rocky foreshore still boomed and roared, flinging its echoes about the cave.

Then Gault, standing with his knot of household warriors a spear's length to one side, cried out in a voice which leaped back from the rock walls with the rough ring of war horns, "Here he is, then! Here is the Prince Midir, your true Horse Lord, whom the woman Liadhan would have slain seven winters ago!"

And among the crowding shadows below the fire, there was a stirring and an indrawn breath that was almost a sob.

Then a voice shouted back, "What proof can you give us that this is indeed Midir, and not some other with the look of him?"

"What is proof to do with myself or with Sinnoch the Merchant? We have found and brought to you the Prince Midir. The proof is for him to give, if it's more than the sight of your own eyes you're needing!"

"Let him give it, then!"

Phaedrus put his hands to the circlet of braided gold wires that pressed low on his temples, and lifted it off and flung it down ringing on the rock floor at his feet, baring his forehead to the torches. "Here is your proof! Come closer and look!"

A formless smother of voices answered him, lost in the boom of the storm wind as it swooped back, and the shadows parted and came crowding up past the fire, taking on the substance of living men as the flaring torchlight met them. An oldish man, whose hair showed brindled as a badger's pelt, thrust out from the rest, his voice, deep and glad, crashing through the bell-booming of the storm. "Midir! It is Midir, after all these years?"

"Seven years," Phaedrus said, and reached out to him, the gold and copper arm-rings clashing on his wrists. "It is good that they are over and I come back again!"

But the doubt lingered in some of them. A tattoo mark could, after all, be copied, and they had learned caution under Liadhan's rule. "You do not speak like us," someone called from the heart of the throng.

And Phaedrus dropped his hands and turned on him. "Set a wolf cub among the hound-pack, and he'll learn to bark like a dog. Great Gods, man, I have been seven years in the South!"

Then another spoke up. "Why did you not come back before?"

"Why does the mare not foal before she is mated, or the bramble ripen before the flower falls? What would have happened if I had come creeping to your hunting fires one night, or worse still, burst in upon you shouting war cries, before the time was ripe? Before you called me back? I heard no man call till now."

"We did not know that you yet lived."

And somewhere out of the knot of warriors a third voice rose, with others in support. "How does it happen that you did not drown as we were told? Tell us what passed that night and after."

The drumming of the wind about the cave mouth filled the expectant hush, but Phaedrus had a sense of silence. He had known that this would come, and come again and again; he had his story ready, so familiar that it seemed part of his own memory; but suddenly, every nerve on the stretch, he knew that this first time he must not tell it; that to tell in answer to a shouted demand would not have been Midir's way.

His head was up and his hand caressing his dagger. He laughed a little, but without mirth. "Ach now, did they not tell you that tale when they summoned you here? Did the messengers only whisper in your ear 'Midir is back from the slain! Come!' And you came, asking no question?"

"We would hear it from yourself, Midir."

"Would you so?" Phaedrus looked them up and down, then flashed out at them in a fine blaze of anger. "Now, by Lugh of the Shining Spear, to hear you a man might think the Prince Midir stood on sufferance, here among his own! Shall I come to you with my hands held out, and bend my neck and stand before you like a beggar before the master of the house, telling my story for a crust of bannock and a corner by the fire? It is not for you to wag your heads and take me in as the master of the house takes in a beggar of his charity; it is I, Midir the Horse Lord, who comes back to take the place among you that is mine; mine to me! I am the spearhead of this rising that shall drive the She-Wolf from the place that she has snatched, and free the Tribe to walk in the daylight again! I am the Lord of the Horse People as my father was before me; if you do not believe me, kill me for an imposter; if you do, then take me for what I am, and be glad of my coming!"

For a moment longer the hush endured, and then the badger-haired man broke it. "That had the true ring of Midir about it. There was never a shred of respect he had for his elders!"

And someone laughed deep in his throat, and the hush broke into the hubbub of slackened strain.

And in the midst of it all, Phaedrus was handfast with the badger-haired one, and saw in the torchlight the line of an old scar slicing through one eyebrow, and said, suddenly quiet, "What, Dergdian, no doubts at all?"

"None!" Dergdian said. "I knew you from the first moment. I am not like some fools who forget a face they have not seen for a week! Ah well, I set my mark on you, as I remember."

"And I on you! The scar still shows a little—but you made me pay for it! My back still smarts when I remember that day!" He hitched at his shoulders. "I still say it was a simple mistake; you were red as a fox in those days. Not so red now, Dergdian."

"Na na! I will not be called a fox! That is for Sinnoch. I am a hound growing gray about the muzzle." Laughter lines deepened about Dergdian's eyes. "But I am your hound as I was your father's." And still holding Phaedrus's hands, he got stiffly down on to one knee, and pressed his forehead against them, in the way of a tribesman swearing loyalty to his Chief.

One by one the others followed his lead, pressing about Phaedrus to take their allegiance. Their faces were alive with reborn hope. And suddenly Phaedrus wanted to fling the next man off and shout at them "Don't! In Typhon's name don't! I'm not Midir—if you want him go and look for a blind leather worker in Eburacum!"

And then behind the rest, with some kind of great fur collar round his neck, he saw a man holding back, taking his time; watching him out of eyes that seemed, even in the gloom beyond the torchlight, to be oddly set—one a little higher than the other. ...

Their gaze met, and Phaedrus saw in that instant that the fur collar had eyes too. A striped-gray-and-dark thing with eyes like green moons. The young man made a sound to it, and the thing rippled and arched itself into swift, sinuous life, became a wild cat, poised and swaying for an instant on his shoulder, and leaped lightly to the floor, advancing beside him with proudly upreared tail, as he came forward to take his place among the rest.

For an instant, as they came face to face, and the wild cat crouched at his foot, Phaedrus thought that this could not, after all, be the cousin born in the same summer, who had helped Midir to wash the blood from his back after that long-ago beating. Not this wasp-waisted creature with hair bleached to the silken paleness of ripe barley, who wore a wild cat for a collar, and went prinked out like a dancing girl with crystal drops in his ears and his slender wrists chiming with bracelets of beads strung on gold wires! But one of the man's eyes was certainly set higher than the other; and on the bright hazel iris was a brown fleck the shape of an arrowhead.

For a long moment they stood confronting each other and Phaedrus knew that this was indeed the danger moment. He saw a flicker of doubt in the odd-set eyes, quickly veiled, and something tensed in his stomach, waiting for what would happen next, while the men around him looked on.

The young man said "Midir." Just the one word, and his hands came out. Phaedrus, with an unpleasant consciousness of the wild cat crouched with laid-back ears on the floor, followed his lead so instantly that the onlookers could scarcely have said which made the first move. But next instant their arms were round each other in a quick hard embrace that looked like the reunion of long-parted brothers, but had actually nothing in it but a kind of testing, an inquiry, like the first grip of a wrestling bout.

The wild cat spat as though in warning, but made no move.

Then both stepped back, and stood looking at each other at arm's length.

"Conory—you have changed!" It was the only thing that Phaedrus could think of to say, and it seemed safe.

"Have I?" Conory said. "So have you, Midir. So—have—you," and the doubt was still in his eyes; indeed it had strengthened, Phaedrus thought, but it would not be there for anyone but himself to see. At any rate—not yet. What game was he playing? Or was he playing any game at all? Had he, Phaedrus, only imagined that flicker of doubt? It was gone now. Unless it was only veiled once more. ...

With Conory's grip on his shoulders, he discovered that there was more strength in those slender wrists than anyone could have expected. He made another discovery, too. He did not know, looking into those oddly set eyes that were so silkily bright, whether he and Conory were going to be heart-friends or the bitterest of enemies, but he knew that it must be one or the other; something between them was too strong to end in mere indifference.

7 | *The Road to Dun Monaidh*

THE CHIEFS AND CAPTAINS WENT THEIR WAYS, EVEN GAULT and Sinnoch were gone, and there was still a moon and a half to pass before the time of Midwinter Fires. But for Phaedrus, in his hide-out on the wild west coast, while the gales beat in from the sea and the days grew shorter and the nights longer and more cold, the time did not hang heavy for he was kept too hard at his training.

Gallgoid the Charioteer, who had remained behind (officially he was lying sick in his own hall under Red Peak) to captain the little guard of warriors who were left with him, took a large hand in the training. It was the month in the Onnum cock loft over again, but whereas that had been enclosed, a training of the mind, this was a thing of the open moors, a training in the skills of hand and foot and eye that the Horse Lord must possess. With Gallgoid and sometimes one or another beside, there were long days out in the hills, inland, always leaving and returning in the dark, and gradually he learned the things, strange to him, that Midir must have known since childhood; he learned how to move silently without loss of speed on the hunting trail, how to ride on the fringes of a flying horse herd and cut out one chosen colt from the rest, how to bring down game in full run with the three cord-linked stone balls of the hunter's bolus, even such small things as how to mount by vaulting on his spear instead of the more familiar steed-leap with one's hands on the horse's withers.

Then too, the Dalriadain were all charioteers. It was four years since Phaedrus had handled a chariot, and the first time that he took out Gallgoid's, he found with disgust that in growing used to the short sword and heavy Circus shield his hands had lost much of their old cunning. At least he was thankful that the master who had made him a charioteer before he sold him into the Arena had driven a British-built chariot, and not one of the graceful scallop shells that the Romans called by that name. At least he knew the kind of vehicle he was driving, with its greater weight and different balance, the wider-set wheels for stability on a rough hillside, its open front that gave one a sense of being almost on top of the flying ponies. And little by little, the thing came back to him, in the way of old skills that are seldom quite lost but only stored deeply away.

By the end of a month he and Gallgoid had grown so used to each other's ways that one day, up in the hills above the Loch of Swans, reining in from a sweeping gallop, Gallgoid said to him, "You'll do! Didn't I be telling you you'd make a driver one day, when you stood no taller than a wolfhound's shoulder—" and he checked, and they looked at each other and laughed, though the laughter was awkward in their throats.

Four days before the Midwinter Fires, they set out from the Cave of the Hunter, Phaedrus, in a rough plaid with his hair gathered up into his old leather cap, turning for the last time to salute the great horned figure with something of the same grim flourish with which he had been used to salute the Altar of Vengeance before going into the Arena, and headed South for the Royal Dun.

It was already dusk when they mounted the waiting ponies in the sheltered hollow inland of the sea ridge, but there was a young moon sailing behind the hurrying storm clouds when they came riding like a skein of ghosts past the Serpent's Mound at the foot of the Loch of Swans, and by the time the full dark closed down,

Phaedrus reckoned that they were the best part of ten Roman miles on their way. They found cold shelter for themselves and the ponies for what was left of the night among the woods of a steep-sided glen; and pushed on again at first light, across ridges where the thin birch woods grew leaning all one way from the western wind, round the heads of gray sea lochs where many islands cut the water with yeasty froth and the swirl of tide races. Toward evening, with the wind dying down, they were following a narrow track that snaked along the seaward slopes of the hills, hazel woods bare and black with winter rising sheer on the left hand—dropping like a stone into the broad firth on their right; and at dusk came down at last into the fringes of a sodden marsh country of reed beds and sere yellow grass and saltings that, in the failing light, seemed sinking away into the sea while one watched. And then, in what shelter a tangle of furze could give them, they settled down to wait for darkness. In all that way they had seen no one save a few herdsmen in the distance, and once a hunting band of the Little Dark People jogging along beside the track. But it was well to run as little risk as possible of being seen on the next stage; better that no stray onlookers should know of any link between the little knot of Sun People coming down from the North and the larger band heading from the South next day. Besides, they must wait for the tide.

It was a long wait, while darkness came—a black darkness, for tonight the moon was almost hidden—and then gradually a strange sound stole into the air, a distant wet roaring that was yet vibrant as a struck harp or a human voice, and Phaedrus, shifting one chilled and soaking knee from the ground, asked under his breath, "What is that?"

"That roaring? That is the Old Woman Who Eats Ships. She always calls when the tide is on the turn."

"And who—what is this Old Woman?"

"The whirlpool—out yonder where the waters dash between two islands. A coracle can pass safely at slack water, but when the tide turns, that is another matter. That is why they say that the Old Woman calls."

"The sound of death is in her calling," Phaedrus said.

"She's far out of your sea-road."

Phaedrus laughed, softly. "An old woman who used to tell fortunes outside the circus gates once told me that I should not die until I held out my own hands to death; so assuredly I am safe tonight, for I've no wish to go answering the call of the Old Woman Who Eats Ships."

Gallgoid turned his head quickly to look at him in the dark, as though he had said something startling. But he only said, "I've known a two-man coracle caught in the pull and escape, all the same. The seamen of these coasts are seamen and no mere paddlers about in pond water." And then, "Come, it is time that we were on our way."

Leaving the ponies and the rest of the band behind them, they went on alone, far out into the maze of sour salting and little winding waterways and banks of blown dune sand. Stranded on the tide line in the shelter of a sandy spur, a two-man coracle lay tipped sideways like an abandoned cooking pot, and to Phaedrus's landsman's eyes not much larger, and the black shadow of a man rose from beside it and stood waiting.

He and Gallgoid exchanged a low mutter of greetings and then, as the man picked up his small craft and heaved it into the water, Gallgoid spoke quickly to Phaedrus in parting. "Now listen, for there is always a chance of betrayal. We have seen no one likely to be a danger to us on the trail South, but that is not to say for sure that no such one has seen us. Gault may not come himself to meet you on the far side. If you do not know the man you find there, say to him that the flower of four petals is opening in the woods. If he replies that there is promise of an early spring, for the horse herds are growing restless, you will know that he is to be trusted."

"And if not?"

"You have your dagger," Gallgoid said meaningly. "Struan the boatman will wait for you a spear's throw off shore, until he knows that all is well."

"Sa. Then if I do not see you again tonight, I will be looking for you tomorrow in Dun Monaidh."

The boat man was squatting in the stern of the coracle now, and had got out the rowing-pole. "As I will be looking for you," Gallgoid said. "Steady! Don't rock her. It is easy to see that you have long been among inland folk!"

Phaedrus, splashing through the icy shallows, got himself gingerly over the side of the coracle without shipping more water than, say, a hound would have done, and settled into the bottom of the bowl-shaped craft. He had never been in any kind of boat in his life before, and with an eye on the yeasty water beyond the sand bar, blurring into the dark, he wished that he was a better swimmer.

The boatman grunted something, and pushed off with the rowing pole, and they were heading out across the mouth of the broad sea loch that ran inland to lose itself somewhere away eastward in the marshes and the peat moss below Dun Monaidh. The sea took the small crazy shell of stretched skins and wickerwork as she cleared the sandspit, and she began to dance. Phaedrus would have felt deadly sick, but that he was too numbed with cold to feel anything; it was bitterly cold, and the spindrift burned like white fire on the skin. But crouching there with his cloak huddled to his ears, feeling the little craft lift like a gull to each wave, and noting the skill with which the boatman handled her, he found after a while that he was beginning to enjoy himself. The man never spoke to his passenger, but had begun to sing to himself softly and deeply, in time to his rowing; to himself, or maybe to the coracle, as men will sing and shout and croon to a horse for encouragement and companionship. The crossing, which would have been only a mile or so direct, was made much longer by the run of the seas; and the unseen moon was down, leaving the world, that had been dark enough before, black as a wolf's belly when at last the seas gentled and they grounded lightly among more rushes and coarse grass and sand dunes on the farther shore.

Phaedrus scrambled out, landing knee deep in the shallows. The lightened coracle bounced high at the bows, and instantly, still crooning to himself, the boatman backed off. A figure uncoiled from among the broom scrub, a darkness on darkness. There was no possibility of seeing whether it was one that he knew or not. Phaedrus spoke softly, with his hand ready on his dagger.

"The flower of four petals is opening in the woods."

The voice of one of Gault's household warriors said as softly, "You wouldn't think it now, but there's promise of an early spring. Already the horse herds are growing restless."

"Sa, I have no need of my dagger. That is good," Phaedrus said.

"That is most certainly good!" replied the voice with a quiver of laughter. The man's shadow turned seaward again, and gave the whistling call of a dunlin, three times repeated. "That will tell Struan that all is well."

A few moments after, as they turned inland, the man asked, "Do you remember what he was singing?"

"How should I? I—I have forgotten our songs in the past

seven years—we sang other songs after supper in the Gladiators' School."

The other glanced round at him, surprised, but not suspicious. "It was the King's rowing song that keeps time for the oars when the King goes seafaring. I'd not think it had ever been sung in a two-man coracle before, but he must have been glad to be raising it again."

"What about the Queen's seafaring?"

"It is a song of the Men's Side; even Liadhan would be knowing that."

Again there was that faint note of surprise; and Phaedrus thought, "Typhon! I must not be making that kind of mistake too often!"

They walked in silence after that, cross country through birch and heather and bilberry scrub that was ill going in the dark, and maybe an hour later, hit the old trade road from the South and the mainland crossing. And a short way down it, came upon a small rath or a farm steading within its ring stockade, with a saffron flicker of firelight shining from an open doorway and three or four chariots squatting with yoke-poles cocked up against the house-place wall.

Someone was waiting to draw aside the dead thorn bush that stopped the gateway; somebody quieted the baying hounds. Coming in out of the midwinter night's cold and dark, the blast of firelight and warmth, and smell of warm animal skins and broiling meat, and the crowding of men in the small, rough hall met them like a buffet. There must have been a score of men there besides the lord of the house and his sons. Gault looked up from the pattern he was tracing among the hearth ashes with a bit of charred stick. "So, you come at last. Now we can shut the night out and fill our bellies."

One of the sons rose and went to slam the heavy, timbered door, and the lord of the house rose without a word and came and dropped to one knee before Phaedrus, and took his hands and held them to his forehead as the Chieftains had done in the Cave of the Hunter. His front hair, like that of every man in the house-place, hung in slim braids on either side of his face.

Next morning they slept late—not knowing when they might sleep again—and spent a good while in burnishing their gear and the bronze horse ornaments and whetting their short dirks to a final keenness. And when, well past noon, they headed North again by the old trade road, Gault had a new charioteer.

It was a fine chariot that Phaedrus found himself driving, not so fine to look at as that of the master who had sold him into the Arena, for it lacked all ornament that could add a feather's weight, but so finely balanced that one scarcely realized that it was heavier than Gallgoid's; like many British chariots, it was nowhere pinned or doweled but latched together with thongs of well-stretched leather, so that the whole structure was lithe and whippy, almost vicious underfoot, giving to every rut in the trackway, every hummock and hole and furze root when a stretch of track washed out by the winter rains turned them aside into the heather, like a living thing, a vixenish mare that one loves for her valor.

Phaedrus, shifting his weight on wide-planted feet to trim the chariot on the slope of a hill shoulder, felt the vibrating of the woven leather floor under him, felt the proud and willing response of the team flowing back to him through the reins that were like some living filament between them, hearing the wheel-brush through the heather, and the axle-whine, and the softened hoofbeats, and the shouts of the other charioteers behind him, and began to whistle softly through his teeth.

He heard a brusque laugh beside him, where Gault sat on the sealskin cushion of the Warrior's Seat. "It begins to be good?"

"It begins to be good," Phaedrus said, with only half his mind, steadying the team down once more to the track ahead. The countryside that had seemed so empty yesterday was suddenly alive with riders and chariots; even—well clear of the trails—little bands of the Dark People loping along, with paint on their arms and faces, and their full ritual finery of dyed wild-cat skins and necklaces of animals' teeth, and here and there a girl with green woodpecker feathers in her hair. And the track from the South, which had been bad enough before, was rapidly sinking into a quagmire under the passing feet and hooves and chariot wheels, as Earra-Ghyl gathered in to the Royal Dun and the Midwinter Fires and the seven-year King Slaying and King Making.

The gray light of the winter's day was fading into slate color when they came down from the low grazing hills, where the horse herds ran loose even in the coldest weather, into the sodden flatness of Mhoin Mhor, the Great Moss, and westward a faint chill mist, that had been kept at bay by the wind, now that the wind had dropped was creeping in over the marshes from the loch of last night's crossing. Northward, the hills rose again, and everywhere was the gleam of water, sky-reflecting pools like tarnished silver buckles, and winding burnlets that wandered down from the hills to join the broad loop of the river that flowed out through Mhoin Mhor to the sea. And on the near side of the river, not much more than a mile away, stood Dun Monaidh, on its fortress hill that rose abrupt and isolated out of the waste wet mosses.

At that distance, and in the fading light, Phaedrus could not make out much more than the crown of ramparts, and a haze of smoke that hung low over the hilltop. But as they drew nearer, the ramparts stood up high, timber faced, pale with lime-daub against the tawny winter turf; and the faint gleam of torches, strongly yellow as wild wallflowers in the way of torches at first twilight, began to prick out here and there, and the blurred freckling of things no larger than ants along the foot of the slope became chariot ponies grazing for the most part two by two as they had been loosed from under the yoke, in the narrow infields between fortress hill and the marsh. To judge by the number of teams, especially remembering that the horses of the Chiefs and Captains would be stabled above in the Dun, a huge company must be gathered already, for on the track that Gault and his party followed, and dim-seen on the track from the North, and on foot by the unseen paths of the marsh, men were still drawing in from the farmost ends of the Tribal hunting-runs to Dun Monaidh.

Their own trail ran on into the marsh, paved with logs over a bed of brushwood, winding to follow the firmest ground, to the foot of the fortress hill, giving better traveling than the hill tracks had done—so long as one did not overrun the side.

"Let them feel the goad, you're not driving a pack train now," Gault said. But Phaedrus had not waited for the words. If it had not been in his nature in the first place, the circus would have taught him the importance of making a good entrance; and on this entrance so very much might depend. For afterward men would remember, and say to each other, "That was the first that we saw of Midir at his homecoming."

He tickled up the flanks of the team with the goad that he had scarcely used before—he had never been one to drive on the goad—shouting to them "Ya-a-ya! Hi-a-hup! Come up now. Hutt, hutt, hutt!" And the ponies, snorting from the sting, sprang forward with stretched necks and laid back ears into a full gallop. The wind of their going ripped by, filling his dark plaid, the chariot leapt like a demon under foot, its axles screeching, and the rest of the little band, riders and chariots, came drumming along behind.

There was another chariot on the track ahead of him, and he misliked the sight. It was not for the Prince Midir to enter the Dun Monaidh at the tail of another chariot. He passed it going like an arrow, with an inch to spare between hubs and his off-wheel skimming the drop to the marsh; and when he was back in the center of the track again, Gault, who had not moved or spoken, said simply, "It's a fine thing to make a hero's entrance but I'll be reminding you that other lives hang on yours—and even on mine."

"It was not right that the Prince Midir should come home with his mouth full of another team's mud. There was no risk; you have good horses."

The black-browed warrior seemed on the point of choking. "And you know how to handle them. Nevertheless, if you fail as a king, do not you be coming to me, to be my charioteer!"

"If I fail as King, I'll have no need to come to anybody for anything," Phaedrus said, his eyes unswerving on the track that had begun to rise as they reached the first slopes of the fortress hill. He eased the team from their flying gallop, steadying them as the slope steepened. The track turned sharply back on itself where a small rocky stream came leaping down to join its lowest stretch, and yoke-pole and axles groaned as he gentled the team round it and urged them forward again. Not a good place to attack, Phaedrus thought; no reasonable way up, seemingly, save for this one steep hillside gully that looked as though it would be as much torrent as track, after heavy rain, and which, moreover, was angled so that in the last stretch the unguarded right side of any man making for the gate must be open to the spears of the defenders. He could see now why Gault and the rest of the

Council had been so decided that the rising must have its beginning within the ramparts.

The huge timber-framed gateway was close before him. He caught the dark glint of iron and bronze, saw the dappled red and white of the bull's-hide bucklers where the warriors and hunters thronged the turf ramparts to watch the latecomers in. The rest of the band behind him, the chariot that he had overtaken still caught among them, he drummed across the ditch causeway. The great carved gate timbers lurched past on either side, the iron tires howled on the broad lintel-stones, the sparks flying from under them as from blade on anvil. He swept through into the broad outer court of the Royal Dun, and brought the team to a plunging halt before the tall gray pillar-stone of the Horse Lord.

8 | The King Slaying

LATER THAT EVENING, PHAEDRUS FEASTED AMONG THE charioteers of the Chiefs and Nobles, in the foreporch of the great
round heather-roofed Fire Hall. They were not slaves after the
way of charioteers among the Romans, nor even servants; they
were sons and younger brothers, close friends, lesser kinsmen,
but there was quite simply no room for them in the Hall. There
was little enough room for them here, and they were packed like
spearheads in an armorer's basket; but that was a thing that had
its advantages, for little warmth reached them from the peat fire
that glowed on the central hearth, filling the high crown of the
roof with smoke, and small spiteful drafts that cut the ankles like
a fleshing knife hummed under the outer door; but close packed
as they were, their cloaks huddled about them, they had worked
up a steaming fug that was next best thing to the warmth of the
fire, and they ate whatever came their way, and filled and refilled
the mead horns from the bronze-bound vat with the boar's-head
handles just beyond the inner doorway.

Phaedrus, drinking as little as might be—the smell in the
foreporch was enough to make a man drunk without the help of
mead, and he would need a clear head later—was sharply aware
of the winter darkness beyond the smoky torch flare; the blurred
moon and the mist thickening over the icy marshes. Aware of
men crouching in that ghostly mist, among the furze and winter-
pale rushes, behind alder stumps and the tangle of hawthorn
windbreaks. Each man with his spear beside him—waiting for

the signal. ... Men within the Dun, too, gathered about the fires over which whole pig and oxen were roasting. Men here in the Hall itself. ...

He had managed to get a seat on the third rung of the loft stair from which, craning his neck, he could see most of the Hall through the open doorway, which was larger than any outer door could be. He saw the circle of seven great standing timbers that upheld the roof, and between the crowding shoulders of the warriors stray glints and flame-flickers of the fire on its central hearth. The pine-knot torches in their iron sconces on each of the seven roof trees flooded the heart of the place with a fierce tawny light, though it left the walls in crowding shadow; and letting his gaze wander, as though idly, from face to face, he saw many that he knew: Gault and Sinnoch, Dergdian, Gallgoid the Charioteer. Wherever he looked he saw men with red or dark, gray or russet hair, or the bleached locks that many of the young warriors affected, hanging in slender braids against their cheeks. But he saw too that they were outnumbered by men whose hair hung loose in the usual way. More than ever, he realized that their one real advantage was surprise, and that even with surprise on their side, in the first flare of the attack, the thing would hang by a thread. ...

Most of the Gate Guards were their own men, but everything would depend on whether, having raised the war cry, they could keep their feet with only the short dirks they had used for eating (for there was no certainty that they would be able to gain the armory before the Queen's Party) until the men from the outside dark could swarm in to their support.

A picked handful of the Bodyguard, the Companions, the only men who might carry weapons at such a gathering as this, stood leaning on their spears behind the High Place, and Phaedrus's questing gaze found Conory in their midst. Not that he needed much finding. He must have bleached his hair freshly for the occasion, because it shone almost silver against the brown of his skin; and his odd-set eyes were painted like a woman's. Under the dark folds of the cloak flung back from one shoulder he wore kilt and shirt of some soft fine skin, dyed green. There were fragile wire-strung bracelets on his wrists, and strings of crystal and gold and blue faience about his neck, and on his shoulders, arched and swaying to his every movement, the striped hunting cat, whose collar, like his own belt, was studded with enamel bosses. But it was something more than all this, Phaedrus thought, that singled him out from his fellows. Perhaps it came from the fact that in this hour, whatever was to happen later, he was the Chosen One, the King Slayer and the Young King. It was a kind of luster on him, a sheen such as one may see when the light strikes aright on the petals of certain flowers; the purple orchis or speckle-throated arum, the dark wild hyacinth. ...

Someone jerked an elbow into his ribs, and he found that the mead horn was being thrust under his nose. "Wake up, my hero! The man who sleeps when his turn comes round maybe doesn't get another chance!" It was a youngster with a mouth like a frog and a thatch of rough broom-yellow hair, the front locks doing their best to burst out of rather unsuccessful plaits.

Phaedrus took the mead horn, grinning. "I was not asleep then. I was taking a look at this new seven-year King."

And an older man leaned across to him from the other side. "A good long look, then. Aye well, he's worth looking at, and he knows it," he snorted, but there was a hint of admiration in the snort. "Ever since he came to manhood he's been one that women watch—aye, and men too—and there's times I think he makes a sport of seeing just how far he can go. He only has to come out one day with his cloak caught in a particular fold or a woman's earring in one ear, and next day half the young braves of the Tribe are doing the same."

Phaedrus drank and wiped the back of his hand across his mouth. "Someone else was saying the same thing—almost the same thing—a while since."

The other held out his hand for the horn and drank in his turn, still grumbling. "Now it's this new notion of plaiting their front hair. You can't expect sense from young fools like Brys"—jabbing a finger toward the yellow-haired boy—"who only Took Valor at the last Feast of New Spears and scarcely counts for a man yet at all; but when it's the grown men, the seasoned warriors who should be having more sense. ..."

But Phaedrus seemed to have lost interest in both the new seven-year King and his own sour drinking companion, and was craning his neck as he had done more than once that evening for a better sight of the woman seated on the piled crimson-dyed sheepskins of the High Place. The woman who had stood by to see Midir blinded.

Others of the Women's Side were moving to and fro to keep the mead cups filled, for among the Tribes, slaves did not serve in the Hall. But Liadhan sat to be waited on, for no man there, not Conory who would sit beside her in the King's place tomorrow at the Midwinter Feast, certainly not the dark silent man who sat there now, were her equals; she who was Goddess-on-Earth, the beginning of all things, without whom there could be neither sons to the Tribe nor foals to the horse herd nor barley to the fields.

She sat leaning a little back among the piled skins and pillows, one hand resting idly on the bronze-work branch with its nine silver apples that lay in the lap of her blood-red gown, relaxed as a great cat half asleep in the sun. Her pride, like a cat's, was huge, too complete in itself to need any outward showing. She must have been beautiful when she was young. The broad heavy bones of her face were beautiful now, framed in the braids of still-fair hair that were thick as a warrior's wrist, and her forehead was broad and serene under the tall silver headdress she wore. But looking at her, Phaedrus felt a little cold creeping of the skin that was not so much fear as a kind of physical revulsion such as some people feel for spiders—big female spiders who devour their mates.

The dark man beside her sat very upright, his stillness tense as hers was relaxed, his brooding gaze fixed on the torches as though he would drink the light of them into his soul. "The Old King has the Old Blood in him," Gault had said, that night in the back room of the Rose of Paestum. "For him it is the pattern. ..."

Logiore had accepted his destiny and there could be no saving him.

The feasting was long since finished; even the mead jars had begun to go round more slowly. The buzz of voices and bursts of laughter and the stray struck notes of a harp that had filled Hall and foreporch alike began to die down. There began to be a quietness and a sense of waiting. Phaedrus too was waiting for the thing to begin. He had been told what to expect, but something in him, even so, expected war horns—a clash of weapons—some kind of outcry to fill the place of the silver braying of Circus trumpets. And he was taken by surprise to find that waiting was over and the thing begun almost before he noticed it.

The curtain of heavy stuff over the doorway to the women's quarters was flung back, and a girl came stooping through and stood erect as the folds swung to again behind her. A tall girl, holding between her hands a wonderful shallow cup of worked amber. Her tunic of dark checkered stuff that seemed almost black in the torchlight was hung about with thin disks of bronze that kissed and rang lightly together as she moved; heavy gold serpent bracelets were on her arms, and her face, with the peat smoke curling across it, was like a ritual mask. There was a look of Liadhan in that mask, but it was lighter boned than Liadhan could ever have been, and the thick braids of hair that ended in swinging balls of enameled bronze were of a very different color, almost as fair, but warmer, with the gold softened and somehow grayed—dove-gold, he thought suddenly; dove-gold, and soft and unmanageable so that it was springing free of its braids much as the broom-yellow hair of the boy Brys was doing; hair that was almost living a life of its own in flat contradiction to the face that was only a mask.

Murna, the Royal Daughter, who, if tonight's rising failed, would be Queen one day in her turn ... if they failed—but they would not fail. He thrust the thought aside as unlucky.

The girl moved forward with small swaying steps. Her shadow, cast by the nearest torch, fell across Logiore as she stopped and gave him the cup. He took it without rising, without looking at it, and sat an instant, holding it in his hands, his eyes still full of the torchlight, then flung back his head and drank, and gave the cup into her hands again.

Phaedrus wondered if the drink was drugged.

For the first time, Liadhan turned to look at the man beside her, and it was clear that she was waiting. The whole crowded Fire Hall was looking to him now. It was he who must make the next move in the ritual pattern, and Phaedrus saw that he knew it, and perhaps had a last moment of dark laughter in making them all wait. Even Liadhan for this one time. But he would make the move, all the same.

Someone unseen had opened the outer door, and the cold mist blew in. And in the foreporch the charioteers were on their feet, crushing back against the dry-stone wall to leave a clear path, forcing Phaedrus further up the loft stair as they crowded the lower rungs, a few even slipping out through the open door.

Logiore got to his feet and stood an instant, then came walking stiffly across the paved central dancing floor, past the fire and through the foreporch, moving a little like a sleepwalker, and out into the winter night. Two of the Guard had stepped forward to follow him, each lighting a fresh torch from the fire as they passed, and behind them went two more, naked swords in hand, then Conory, his striped cat clinging lithely to his shoulder; behind him, the rest of the Guard with drawn swords and torches. Then the Chiefs and Nobles, draining out of the Hall like wine out of a cup, and leaving it to the women gathering onto the dancing floor.

The charioteers and armor-bearers had spilled outside, Phaedrus among them, but in the shadow of the doorpost he hung back until the squat bowlegged figure of Gault the Strong came by, then slipped out to join him.

Gault never turned his head or gave any other sign of being aware of him, only as they came to the gateway of the Citadel he muttered, "Pull that cap off; no time for fumbling later."

In a patch of dark between torch and torch, Phaedrus dragged off the close-fitting charioteer's cap and tossed it away, shaking his head as he felt his hair fall loose and the unaccustomed touch of the two slim braids against his cheeks. Then he pulled the hood of his cloak forward to shadow his face and the device on his forehead.

Sinnoch had come up on the other side, and glancing round as he walked, he saw Gallgoid, black-browed and grimly cheerful, close behind. Other faces that he knew caught the torchlight, and he realized without knowing quite how it had been managed that he was walking in the midst of a kind of bodyguard of his own.

The mist had thickened since he stabled the horses. It came smoking in over the turf and dry-stone walls of the Dun, smudging the torches into blurred mares' tails of flame. More and more torches as the crowds came thrusting in from feast fire after feast fire to join them. Surely, Phaedrus thought, Dun Monaidh could not seem more of a blaze from end to end if this were tomorrow night, the night of the Midwinter Fires.

So they went down, a growing river of men and torches and wreathing golden fog, from the Citadel, looping through one after another of the five courts of the Royal Dun, until each had been visited, and they came to the lowest and outermost court of all.

In the wide outer court, seven fires—the farther ones already blurred with mist—were blazing in a wide circle about the mighty upreared shape of the King Stone; and already the crowd was thickening between the fires, a crowd without visible weapons, and—strange among the Tribes—without dogs, for the hound pack, like the slaves, had been shut safely out of the way for the ceremony that was to follow. Phaedrus and the knot of warriors with him took up their places not far from where the Companions already stood leaning on their spears with Conory in their midst. Of Logiore there was now no sign.

And then they heard it, winding down from the Citadel—a wild wordless chanting of women's voices, and the thin white music of pipes wailing in and out through it. "I must be careful!" Phaedrus thought suddenly. "Gods! I must be careful or this music will draw me into it and I shall be lost! I must think of something else—think of the Arena sand underfoot and the swing of the parade march! Here we go, past the knackers' sledges and the Altar of Vengeance. If that woman on the third bench eats another honeycake she'll have a seizure. Typhon! This helmet strap's rubbing. I ought to have had it seen to after the last fight. Ah! Here's the Governor's box; *Ave Caesar! Morituri te salutant. ...*" The swaggering stamp and go of the parade march came to his help out of the world of familiar and daylight things, and he thrust it between him and the white wailing music that something in him understood rather too well.

It was very close now. Something stirred in the mist at the edge of the firelight, and Liadhan stepped into the circle of seven fires. The girl Murna, who seemed to be priestess of the rite, followed close behind her, and the women crowded after, bearing among them the crimson-dyed sheepskins of the High Place. They were chanting still, but the piping had separated itself, and while they piled the sheepskins into a throne it ran on in little thrills and ripples round the circle of fires. Phaedrus half saw grotesque shadow-figures that ran and flitted behind the fires and the torchlit crowd, the piping going with them; thin shimmers of sound, flutings and half bird calls that were as though they talked to each other on the pipes in some tongue older than human speech. Something made Phaedrus look over his shoulder, and he saw one of the shadows standing quite close to him. A man—a thing like a man—stark naked in the bitter cold that made men's breath smoke into the mist, save for the streaks of red ocher that daubed his body and the bracelet and anklets of shells and feathers and dried seed pods; a pipe that might have been made from the thigh bone of some big bird was in his hand, and on his shoulders, where his head should have been, was the snarling mask of a wild boar. For an instant the hair rose on the back of Phaedrus's neck, and then the thing crouched and raised the pipe to some hole hidden in the black shadow under the grinning snout, and he realized that there was a human mouth within the bristly hide. Masked priests, then, but priests of a very different kind from Tuathal the Wise. The man's long fingers moved on the pipe, and the shrill bird-twittering notes scurried up and down, and Phaedrus felt eyes upon him from somewhere within the mask and turned back to the lighted circle.

Liadhan had taken her seat on the piled sheepskins, between two of the sacred fires, with the women and the Companions of the Guard about her. She sat very upright now, still as the great standing stone that formed the hub of the wheel of light, her eyes going past it, out past the blurred fires of the farther side, into the darkness beyond. This was her hour, and the small still smile on her lips was such a smile as no mortal man or woman should wear.

The chanting had ceased now, and the fluting pipe calls had grown silent. Only the Royal Daughter sang on, a high white singing that had nothing human in it. She was moving from one to another of the fires, weaving an intricate dance pattern of swaying and shuffling steps, and at each fire she paused to feed the flames with leaves and herbs from a basket she carried on her hip.

A strange smell began to rise in the smoke, bitter and pungent, yet dangerously pleasant, bringing forgotten things hovering in from the edges of the mind. ... Somewhere in the drifting, milky dark beyond the flame light, the wolfskin drums began to throb, softly, like a sleeping heart, and something seemed to stir into wakefulness and run through the concourse, like the chill breath of wind before a thunderstorm.

Standing at Gault's side, his head bent and shoulders hunched into shapelessness under his cloak, Phaedrus stole a quick glance at Conory. His head was up, eyes and nostrils wide in his face, the look of a hound still in leash that scents the boar. One of the Companions had taken both spear and sword from him, and he had loosed his cloak and slipped it free from one naked shoulder; but the striped cat still clung to its accustomed perch. He could not be going to carry it into the actual fight with him, but meanwhile, everyone seemed to take as little heed of it being there as though it were a part of Conory, like his sword hand.

Murna, her circle of fires completed, had come to stand beside the Queen, and while the bronze disks on her skirt still clashed softly as they swung, Liadhan raised the slender branch with its nine silver apples and shook it once. The thin, sweet ripple of the little bells seemed to make strange echoes in the mist, and the throb of the wolfskin drums changed to a coughing roar that rose and rose—then ceased with a suddenness that left a woolen numbness in the ears.

Liadhan shook the silver branch again, and a long-drawn sigh, almost a moan, rose from the throng as something moved in the darkness where she looked, and out into the firelight stepped Logiore, the Old King.

It was an instant before Phaedrus realized that it was Logiore, this wild uncanny figure in the trappings of the Horse Lord. He was stripped to the waist, in warrior style. Heavy bronze arm-rings circled his upper arms, and about his neck hung collar upon collar of jet and amber beads and dark heron-hackles. Clay and ocher patterns had been painted on his skin, overlaying the fine blue lines of tattooing. On his head was a war cap that seemed to be made from the scalp of a red horse, the proud stallion crest still springing erect between the ears, the long mane tumbling on his shoulders; and out of the death-paint on his face, his eyes blazed on the world like those of a man who has taken nightshade. The naked knife in his hand caught the firelight and became a tongue of flame, as he came forward with a curious high stepping walk to stand before the Woman on the throne of piled sheepskins.

Conory flung off his own cloak, and under it he also was stripped for battle. He drew his own dagger without haste, and took the one long pace forward that brought him to the Queen's side and face to face with his adversary. The drums had begun to throb again; the smell of the strange smoke drifting from the fires seemed at once to heighten and confuse the senses. And still the striped cat clung to its lord's shoulder, its eyes enormous and fur fluffed up along its arched back until it seemed to bloat to twice its normal size. In the last few moments, Conory had been murmuring to it, its furry cheek against his, but now—surely he must have forgotten it was there. Others thought so too. One of the Companions spoke to him, pointing to the creature, putting out a hand to take the leash.

Conory answered with a sound in his throat that was for the cat alone, and the small fiend laid back its tufted ears and with a splitting screech of fury, the unsheathed claws plowing red furrows in Conory's bare shoulder, it launched itself and sprang straight for Logiore's face.

In the same instant, so that both flashes of movement were one, Conory flashed round with his dagger upon Liadhan the Queen.

But in the same instant also, there happened one of those small unforeseeable mischances that can tear an empire down. It was no more than a hound, tied up in the stable court, that had chewed through its leash and come to find its master. Nobody, certainly not Phaedrus who had his back to it, saw the wolf-shadow in the mist, poised on the crest of the broad dry-stone wall and searching the crowd with anxious tawny eyes. But in the barest splinter of time before the cat leaped screeching at Logiore's face, the hound gave a joyful bark of recognition and sprang out and down. He had leapt for a gap in the crowd, but something—maybe the grotesque figure with the boar's head—made him swerve in mid-air. He was no mere herd dog but one of the great wolfhounds of Erin, feather heeled, and for size and weight almost the equal of a yearling pony colt. His swerve brought him crashing full into Phaedrus, and flung him headlong, full into the light of the nearest torches. The hound landed on top of him, driving most of the wind from his body, and went bounding on across the circle to join its master on the farther side. Best-part winded as he was, Phaedrus was up again with a speed learned in the Arena; but the hood of his cloak had fallen back, and there on his forehead, plain for all to see, was the Royal Pattern of the Dalriadain, the Mark of the Horse Lord.

Time seemed to go slow, so that there was space for many things to happen between one leap and another of the great hound. Liadhan, perhaps already half alerted by something that had been in the air all evening, had whipped round to face the sudden small tumult, and the lightning stroke of Conory's dagger that should have ended in her heart gashed her side instead. With a furious cry, he struck again, but the girl Murna had flung herself between them, dashing the dark folds of her cloak across his face, muffling and blinding him as she did so. The Queen herself had sprung clear, and as the whole scene dissolved in howling chaos, Phaedrus saw, in the very act of regaining his feet, her terrible eyes fixed on the mark on his forehead. Then she screamed, and in screaming, raised the agreed war cry, *"Midir!"*

The women, their knives out, were swirling in upon Conory, and Logiore, his face now a streaming mask of blood, the wild cat still clinging to him, came crashing in with the shrill fury of an angry stallion.

Phaedrus, plunging forward with no thought save to reach Conory before it was too late, heard Gault beside him take up the war cry, raising the terrible bull-bellow that was the signal for those waiting in the outer darkness. *"Midir! Midir!"*

The perfect timing on which so much might depend had been lost to them, but there was no help for that now. All around the pillar-stone and among the seven fires, the warriors were reeling to and fro, as the men of the braided forelocks ripped out their dirks and hurled themselves upon the Queen's followers. But for the moment all that was lost on Phaedrus; in the heart of that hideous struggle before the High Place, he was fighting back to back with Conory. Fighting for his life and something more than his life, for no man likes the idea of being torn to pieces, against a screaming throng of women, whose weapons, besides their knives, were the wild beast's weapons of teeth and claws. He did not know what had happened to Liadhan or the girl Murna, not even what had happened to Logiore; there was nothing in this world but the screaming furies about him, and the feel of Conory's back braced against his. A knife gashed his shoulder, claws were at his throat; if no help came, it could not be long before he and Conory went down, and once that happened. ...

Suddenly the press was slackening, breaking up, the blood-screams of the women changing to howls of baffled fury, as a solid wedge of the Companions, heads down behind cloak-wrapped forearms, came charging through to their support.

The fighting had spread through into other courts by the sound of it. Someone shouted, "They're fighting for the armory!" and from somewhere in the heart of the Dun, a tongue of flame leaped up, blurred and wavering in the mist. Men were pouring through the great gate that had been opened to them, swarming in over the ramparts, men who carried each a spare weapon with him. Phaedrus, with one such sword in his hand, Conory racing beside him with his own again, was storming forward at the head of a swelling band against the main mass of the Queen's Party, who, after the first moments of random fighting, were gathering in closed ranks before the gateway to the stable court. They too, had weapons now; seemingly some of the Queen's people had reached the armory first. Away to his right he heard Gault's bull-roar, and yelled the war cry in answer: "Midir! *Midir!*"

Another band of men and women, headed by the wild figure of Logiore with his horse mane flying, came charging in across their path. They also were fully armed, for by now weapons were springing into every hand; and in the light of scattered fires and guttering torches, Phaedrus thought he glimpsed in the midst of the battle-throng around the gateway the moon-silver gleam of the Queen's diadem. Others had seen it too, for a new shout went up: a baying of hounds that sight the kill. Gault bellowed, "There she is! The hag! The She-Wolf!" as they crashed together with Logiore's band, hell-bent to come at the gleam of that distant diadem. The patterns of the fighting were changing and reforming so quickly that everything was shapeless as a dream; and now Logiore's band had been flung back, and they were at reeling grips with the warriors about the gate, locked knee against knee, blade against blade, snarling faces and flying hair.

And now the Queen's Party were falling back. Slowly, stubbornly, battling for every inch of the way. Somehow, the outer court was cleared, and then the Horse Court, and they were falling back on the gate gap of the King's Court, the Citadel itself. There were men on the crest of the rocky outcrop that formed part of the King's Court wall, and stones and spears came whistling among the attackers. And still, somewhere ahead in the swirling press, like a flicker of moonlight between racing storm clouds, the gleam of a silver headdress came and went.

They were back to the gate again now, and every foot of the outcrop wall had become a reeling battle line. The mist was red about them, for somebody had fired the heather thatch; and in the fiery murk, Phaedrus had come together with Logiore the Old King.

And then a strange thing happened, for the rest of the fight surging all about them seemed to fall away a little on every side, and in the space so cleared they fought, as Old King and Young King were fated to fight according to the ancient custom: Phaedrus still in the rough dress of a charioteer, his red mist-wet hair flying about his head, and the man in the trappings of the Horse Lord, the terrible burning eyes in the terrible painted and blood-streaked face. Even Conory held aloof from that fight and found plenty of work for his sword elsewhere; and in this isolation they crouched and thrust and parried, with the sparks from the burning Hall falling about them. Logiore was a fine swordsman; Phaedrus the Gladiator, used to the quick judging of an opponent, knew that, but knew also that, thanks to Autome-don's training, he was a better.

The struggle for the Citadel did not last long, for the Queen's Party was by now heavily outnumbered, and though the numbers were equal enough in the actual gateway, they were too few to hold the inner wall against those who swarmed over. They made their last desperate stand, while before the flamelit gateway Old King and New fought the ancient ritual fight that was ritual no longer. Both were bleeding from gashes on breast and arms and shoulders; no space to maneuver, no springing back out of touch; they fought where they stood, close-locked as battling stags. Phaedrus could see the mist drops in the horse headdress and the sparks of the burning thatch that died among them, the other-world glare in his enemy's eyes. He saw the eyes change, as he had once seen Vortimax's do, and parried the deadly lunge, turning the other's blade at the last instant, and lunged in his turn past the open guard. He felt his own blade bite deep, and saw those eyes widen and had time to wonder at the triumph in them, before the Old King staggered back and went down.

Everywhere the line of the defense was going, and the followers of the Horse Lord were crashing in through the gate and over the broad low walls. Hounds were baying and the screams of terrified and angry horses tore the air. But in the Citadel itself there seemed for the moment to be a strange silence. Logiore, with his headdress torn off and most of the death-paint washed from his face by blood, lay like any other dead man—and there were plenty—crumpled against the right-hand gate stone where he had been trampled and kicked aside in the break-through. But the look of triumph was still in his eyes.

And Phaedrus knew the reason for it now, as he stood leaning on his crimsoned sword, drawing his breath in great whistling gasps, and looked at Murna the Royal Daughter standing between two of the Companions on the threshold of the burning Hall. Murna with blood on her ripped and tattered tunic, and a little smile that echoed Logiore's triumph lifting the corners of her lips. And on her head the tall silver moon headdress of the Queen.

9 | "I Stand with My Friends"

GAULT SAID IN A RASPING VOICE, "WHERE IS LIADHAN?"

"The Queen, my mother, is in a place where you will not find her—Gault the Traitor!"

Gault shrugged his bull shoulders. "I have other things to do than be playing hurly with evil names for a ball." Then to the two Companions, "Take her away and lodge her safely—remembering that she is the Royal Daughter, and not to be mishandled."

"Sa sa, I have to thank you," the girl said. "Would you have given my mother the same cause to thank you, if you had taken *her*?"

"*When* we take her, you will have the answer to that question." Gault jerked his chin at the Companions, to take her away. She half turned in obedience to their hold on her arms, then checked, and looked back full at Phaedrus for the first time. A long, strange look, completely unreadable, and meeting it, Phaedrus wondered if she knew how her mother had in truth disposed of the real Horse Lord. If she did, she must know, even as Liadhan must have known it when the first shock was over, that whoever else he might be he was not Midir. And like Liadhan, there would be nothing that she could do about it. He returned the long, cool stare, and in a few moments she turned away between her guards.

The fiery fog seemed to get into Phaedrus's head after that, and everything became like a dream in which there was no ordered sequence of events. He heard Gault shouting orders, and was aware of men tearing off the burning heather thatch and beating out the flames that had spread to the timbers, aware of fighting still going on in odd corners of the Dun, with now and then a cry to tell how some fight had ended. There was a search going on, swift and desperate and very thorough, among the mist-shrouded buildings and the huddled dead. He was bleeding from a score of gashes, none of them serious, and beside him, Conory was cursing softly as he tried to staunch a deeper wound in his upper arm with a strip torn from a dead man's kilt; and somewhere a cat was raising its wild squalling cry. Stupidly he looked about for it, and saw in the dying flame-light a striped shape with eyes like green moons and blood dripping from a gashed flank, clinging to the edge of the foreporch roof and singing a triumphant song that might have been made by all the fiends in Ahriman's deepest pits of torment. Conory left off cursing long enough to call "Shan" and the thing leaped to his shoulders and settled across his neck, singing still, the shreds of its leash trailing behind it.

A man was panting out some message to Gault, and then there was a time of running, in the midst of which Phaedrus stumbled on the body of an almost-naked man with an otter's mask for a face. And then he was in the outer court again, over in the far angle away from the gate, staring at the place where the overflow from the spring that formed the Dun's water supply disappeared into a narrow gully and dived under a rough-cut lintel stone through the rampart wall. Three men with braided forelocks lay dead there, each tangled as though from a distance into the thongs of a hunting bolas, and stabbed where they lay. Someone was holding a torch low to the dark mouth of the tunnel, and the light showed the gleam of silver apples under the running water. Someone else fished it out. The Silver Branch.

"So that's the way she went," Gault said, chewing at a lower lip that was chapped and red-raw.

"She will be heading for Caledonia, and her own kin," Conory said. He had knotted the rag round his wounded arm, and save for the blood on him he looked as unruffled as the striped cat who had dropped from his shoulder and was now sitting a little way off, unconcernedly licking its flank wound. "Can we stop up the runs before she gets clear away?"

Gault shook his head. "I doubt it. The People of the Hills will stand her friends, and no one save the red deer know all their runs. Nonetheless, we must try it, for she carried maybe the life or death of the Tribe in her keeping." He swung round on the young warrior with the torch. "Brys, find me your Lord Gallgoid, and Dergdian if the life is still in him—and that horse smuggler Sinnoch; there are few men know the border hills as he does."

Phaedrus had not recognized the boy for his cheerful neighbor of the crowded foreporch; his face was so gray and old, with the laughter all gone from it. "My Lord Gallgoid is dead."

"Cuirithir then. Those three—quickly."

The boy went, running. And presently Dergdian was there, and Sinnoch, and Cuirithir hard on his heels, and Gault was speaking quick and harsh. "The She-Wolf is away—you'll all be knowing that—and she must be heading for Caledonia by one way or another—there's nowhere else for her unless she takes to sea. Sinnoch, you know the border hills better than any of us. How many trails into the Cailleach's country at this time of year?"

Sinnoch thought a moment. "As many as there are fingers and thumb on my right hand."

"One to each of us here, then."

"There are six of us here," Dergdian said, hackles up, and with a glance at Phaedrus.

There was an instant's pause, and then Phaedrus said, "It is a long while since I was in the border hills. I will ride behind one of you."

"One to each of us here, then," Gault said, as though there had been no interruption. "Conory, take what men you can raise quickly—two score should be enough—and follow the track up Loch Fhiona, the Royal Water, and across the mountains into the Glen of Baal's Beacon. Not beyond; it will not profit the Tribe that you run wild into the Cailleach's hunting runs and never come back! Dergdian, and you Cuirithir, make for the great Gap of Loch Abha, and divide there; take one of you the Glen of the Alder Woods and the other the Glen of the Black Goddess."

"She will not be taking *that* way," Cuirithir said. "Ach now, it is close on twice as far, and the trail runs a full two days through the very heart of Earra-Ghyl."

"She will not likely be taking that way," snapped Gault, "but if the Little Dark People choose to be her guide and cast their mists about her, for the very reason of its unlikeliness she might take it, and we'd be fools to leave it alone. Myself, I will be for Rudha-Nan-Coorach, and the fisher folk shall lend me their coracles to cross Loch Fhiona. The trail down the Glen of the Horns keeps hard enough at this season, and with fisher folk all down the far shore to see her across the Firth of the War Boats, I'm thinking that's the trail she might choose. That is four. Where runs the fifth trail, Sinnoch?"

"It is in my mind that I miscounted. There are two more trails—two more at the least, between the Royal Water and the Firth of the War Boats. But it is all wild country, and the Caledones hunt over it almost as often as we. It is hard to be sure in one's head, without seeing the state of the trails; there have been heavy rains in the past moon."

"Go and look, then. Those trails I leave to you. Take the best hunters with you; you'll need them."

"Sa, that means my old Vron for one. Some of the best hunters in Dun Monaidh are hammering from within on the slave-house door at this moment."

"Men of the Little Dark People?" Gault interrupted.

"The Little Dark People are the best hunters in the world." The dry smile was in Sinnoch's voice, though his face was lost now in darkness. "And as for those in the slave-house, Liadhan's slaves do not learn to love her—even for Earth Mother's sake."

"So be it then, hunt your little dark hounds."

"Those and others—a mongrel pack, shall we say—open to any who are not too proud to hunt with it."

"I will hunt with your mongrel pack," Phaedrus said, and decided, by the moment of sudden silence about him, that that had been a mistake. But to change now would have been an even worse mistake, and besides—surely even a prince of the Dalriadain need not dance always to other men's piping. "Unless I am too out of skill as a hunter," he added, pretending to misunderstand the silence.

And Sinnoch said with that dry amusement out of the darkness, "You are the Prince of the Dalriadain. Surely you may hunt with any pack—even the Hounds of Hell—that you will."

For four days Phaedrus hunted with Sinnoch's mongrel pack, on foot or on one of the small mountain ponies they had rounded up beyond the heather hills and steep forested glens between the two great sea lochs. But if Liadhan had passed that way, she had been too swift for them, and left no trace behind her. And on the fourth evening, when they foregathered with Conory and his band, far up the Glen of Baal's Beacon, they too had had bad hunting.

They were fog-wet and bone-weary, and their wounds had had little chance to heal. The dried meat that the Tribes carried with them on trail had begun to run short and there had been no time to hunt for themselves, and so they were hungry. They made camp dourly, on the strip of turf and heather between the river and the forest that seemed to reach its hands toward them in the gathering shadows as though it too were hungry; and tended and picketed the rough-coated ponies—they dared not let them graze loose with the trees so near.

And meanwhile Phaedrus and Conory had come together, and as though the thing were arranged between them, gone down river a short way toward the head of the loch. The rest of the camp had seen them go without surprise or remark; they had always been best content with each other's company as boys.

They did not speak at once of the thing that both knew had brought them out from the camp. Indeed for a while they did not speak at all, but simply stood looking across the river to where the great hills of Caledonia caught the last red of the winter sun, while the striped cat, who had stalked after them through the heather and bog myrtle, sat down for another lick at the healing wound in her flank.

"So—the She-Wolf is safe away into her kinsmen's hunting runs," Phaedrus said moodily, at last.

"Unless Gault or Dergdian have had better hunting than we."

"They will not."

"No, I am not thinking it likely."

"Was it my doing? Or the dog's? Or the chance fall of the dice?"

Conory shrugged. "Can the dice fall chance-wise from the Gods' hands?"

"I have wondered that, before now. It is the way they cast for pairs of fighters in the Arena. What will happen now?"

"Nothing now, in the black of winter. You know what the tracks are like, and not even Liadhan can move a war host over these mountains and mosses when the high passes are deep in snow and there's no grass for the chariot ponies. But when the birth buds thicken and the burns come down in spate from the melting snows, then there will be a great hosting among the Caledones."

Phaedrus looked round quickly. "It will really come to war?"

"She is the King's kinswoman. And do you think that the Great Mother—the Lady of the Forest, they call her—will not rise up in war paint to protect her own? Have you forgotten that the Caledones follow the Old Way, too?" Conory turned his head slowly, and the mocking, veiled gaze was on Phaedrus's face. "You have forgotten many things in these seven years."

"There is time to forget many things in seven years."

For an instant gaze held gaze, carefully blank.

Conory's cloak had fallen back from his left shoulder, and glancing down, Phaedrus saw that the rags about his upper arm were dark and juicy. "That wants rebinding," he said.

"I'll see to it, by and by."

"Better now, while there's still enough daylight to see by. I'll do it for you." Then at something he saw on the other's face, "It is not the first time that you and I have bathed each other's hurts."

There was a small, sharp silence, empty save for the rush and suck of the water and the sudden desolate calling of some bird among the winter-black heather. Then Conory said slowly and deliberately, "Is it not?"

Phaedrus's heart gave a small sick lurch under his breastbone, but there was no shock of surprise in him. This was the thing between them, the thing that had brought them down here away from the camp. He tried once more, prepared to fight it to a finish, all the same. He forced a laugh. "There is one time that sticks in my mind above all others—but you did not have the beating. So there's less reason for you to remember helping me wash the blood off my back after Dergdian had thrashed me for half braining him with a throw-stone."

Conory whirled round on him. "Who told you that?"

"Who should tell me? It was I that had the beating, and I remember well enough without being told."

"Oh no, you don't," Conory said, silken-soft. "It was Midir who had that beating, and *you are not Midir.*"

"You are out of your wits! It must be that you have the wound fever," Phaedrus said.

"Both the wound and my wits are quite cool."

"Very well then, tell me who I am."

The other's hands shot out and clenched on his shoulders with that unexpected strength that he had felt before in the Cave of the Hunter. Conory's face was thrust into his, the odd-set eyes narrowed under the traces of paint that still clung to the lids. "*You* shall tell *me* that!"

Phaedrus made no attempt to break the other's hold, though with Conory's arm wound he could have done it without much trouble. For one thing, the cat had stopped licking its flank and was crouching ready to spring, with laid-back ears, and mask wrinkling in a silent snarl. It made no sound, it did not move, but he knew that at the first movement of his that looked hostile, it would fly at him. The added complication of being attacked by a wild cat, he felt, was more than he could handle just then.

But another kind of recklessness took him like a high wind. He did not know whether or not this was the end of the trail, but he laughed in the other's face. "Sa sa! I will tell you! My father was a Greek wine merchant, and my mother was his slave who kept his house for him. I was born a slave and bred a slave—you can see now how suitable was my choice of pack to hunt with!

I was bought and sold, bought and sold, until I came into the Corstopitum Circus, and was a slave still. Most gladiators are slaves, did you know? *That* is what you cried 'Midir!' for, five nights ago!"

"And so Sinnoch saw you in your circus and saw the likeness— and opportunity. Well may men call him 'Sinnoch the Fox!' What price did he pay you?"

Phaedrus asked quietly, "Was that meant for an insult?"

"If it seems so to you, then yes. But chiefly I was asking a question."

"One that I cannot answer. I gained my Wooden Foil on the day he first saw me—that means freedom with honor for a gladiator. I was free for a whole day after they had pushed me out, until the howling boredom of it drove me into a street brawl, and my freedom ended in the town jail. If you would know how much it cost in bribes to get me out, you must ask Sinnoch—or Gault."

"I am not interested in the cost of unbarring a prison door. What was *your* price? And in what kind? Did they buy you, or force you? Or did you come because anything was better than this howling boredom?"

"Something of all three. Also they called in Midir to their aid. He—was a master of persuasion."

The hands on his shoulders gave a little jerk, and released their hold. Conory let them drop limply to his sides and half turned away. "Midir ... yes, of course. Nobody but he could have told you about washing off the blood of that beating ... and the other things—all the other things. He was always thorough." Phaedrus saw him swallow. "Will you tell me something. If Midir still lives, why did they need another man to take his place?"

"He is blind," Phaedrus said.

"Blind!" Conory's voice sounded sick in his throat, and he

made a strange little gesture, pressing the heels of his hands into his own eye sockets as though for a moment he felt them empty. "So that was how she made sure of him. ... Where is he?"

"He went back to the man he works for, a harness maker in a Roman city far South of the Southern Wall."

"How long have Gault and Sinnoch known all this?"

"Three years, I believe."

"And who else beside?"

"Tuathal the Wise, Gallgoid—but he's dead." (It was odd that it had hardly struck home to him until he said the words.) "Two or three more."

"And never told me; even when the She-Wolf sent me her token last Beltane and the time came to begin sharpening our swords, I that was closer to him than most brothers."

"There was a great while still to wait. They are all gray-muzzles, except—Gallgoid, and maybe they feared that you might do something hotheaded."

"Did they fear the same thing at summer's end, when they told me the same tale as the rest of the Tribe, concerning the Prince Midir come back from the dead?" Conory's voice had a bite to it.

"It seemed to them good that you should be the test. If you did not know that I was not Midir, then nobody would know it. But you knew, and so I have failed."

They had come a long way from the dangerous mood of so short a while before.

"No," Conory said absently, "I'd not be saying that, for the test was not a fair one." He looked round at Phaedrus with his gentle, almost sleepy smile. "This arm of mine begins to ache. Is there light enough, do you think?"

A few moments later, they had scrambled down the bank and were kneeling among the tangled alder roots at the water's edge, and Phaedrus had begun easing off the filthy rags that left dark stains on his fingers as though he had been picking over-ripe blackberries. Conory squinted down to watch him. "Ach no, I would not be saying you had failed at all. Unless you make some glaring mistake, you will pass well enough—with everyone else."

"What mistake did I make with you?" The last clotted fold came away, and Phaedrus stooped to cup the icy water in his palm and bathe the stale blood from the wound before he could see how it did.

"More than one, small things enough. When Gault was ordering away the hunting bands, it came to you that you did not know these hills, and there was an instant when you did not know what to do. You covered up well, though; to choose Sinnoch's mongrel pack to hunt with was just the kind of thing Midir would have done. He was always one to take a devil's delight in seeing how far he could go in outraging the gray-muzzles and the customs of the Tribe."

"As you do in seeing how wild a fashion you can make the young braves follow for their own befoolment?"

"It is always amusing to see what can be done in that way," Conory said, and caught his breath a little at Phaedrus's probing fingers on the wound. He glanced up at the striped cat, who had remained at the top of the bank and was now crouching there with her face a little above his. She was staring into some inner distance of her own, but when he put up his hand she rubbed her broad furry head into his palm. "They will tell you it is not possible to tame a wild cat, and most times it will be true, but not—quite always. I found Shan as a kit, before her eyes were well open. Her mother had been killed by an eagle—aiee, a great fight that must have been—and the rest of the litter were dead for lack of her. But there was still a spark of life in this one, and so I took her.

She bit my thumb to the bone in the hour that she first had teeth enough to bite with, but now—you see?" He smiled reflectively, and Phaedrus knew that he was taking refuge from the thought of Midir alive and blind, until he had had time to get used to it.

"You had best take *this* to the Healer Priest, when we get back," Phaedrus said, "but it will do for now. ... Well, she proved her ancestry when you flung her in Logiore's face. Did you think to see her again with the life in her striped hide?"

Conory gave a small one-shouldered shrug. "It was a risk we all took. She is a fighting animal, as we all are. But it was good to hear that wicked triumph song of hers, afterwards."

He returned to the thing they had been speaking of before Shan came into it. "Only small mistakes. But I would not be needing any mistake at all. Way back in the Cave of the Hunter—what name did you answer to, before you answered to Midir?"

"In the Arena, they called me Red Phaedrus." He was tearing a strip from the end of his cloak. It would make a better bandage than that foul rag, anyway.

"Then, Red Phaedrus, tell me—in the Circus, were you wont to draw your weapons from some common store, or did you each have your own?"

"You do not have anything of your own in the Gladiators' School, save the clothes you stand up in, and the geegaws that your patrons and admirers give you; but as far as may be, you stick always to the same sword."

"Sa. Then you will know how it is with weapons: to the eye they may be as like as one grain of sand is like another, but each comes from the armorer a little different in balance, with some nature of its own that no other weapon has, and your hand grows to know it, so that if you take up another in its stead, though there is no difference to the eye, your hand knows."

Phaedrus nodded.

"Midir and I were two halves of the same nut when we were boys. I was not sure at first, that night in the Cave of the Hunter, but when we put our arms round each other and made a show for all those onlookers, *then* I was sure. The balance of the blade was not right."

"Why did you not speak out, then?"

"It was in my mind to see what would happen—to learn what you were, since you were not Midir. Also it was not in my mind to wreck the uprising we had waited and planned for so long, and perhaps be the death of many friends."

Phaedrus was binding up the wound, and his eyes and Conory's were very close together. "And now? If you denounce me now, you will split the People of the Horse from top to bottom, and Liadhan will walk back unchecked into the red ruins of her queendom."

"If we needed the Prince Midir in throwing off the She-Wolf's yoke—we will be needing the Prince Midir still."

Phaedrus tied off the knot. "You will stand with me, then?"

"When a man binds up a gash in my hide for me, I must be counting him as a friend. And most times I stand with my friends. Is it so with you?"

"Ach, don't you be putting overmuch trust in my friendship— we learn to take such trifles easily, in the Arena," Phaedrus said, lightly and harshly. "The only man I ever counted for a friend I killed in winning my Wooden Foil."

They looked at each other an instant, and then Conory said, "It's a chance I'll take."

They went back toward the camp, with their arms lightly across each other's shoulders. And this time it was not altogether for show. The striped cat stalked ahead, tail uplifted like a banner.

Gault and his band had just ridden into the forgathering as they got back to the camp. Well on into the night, Cuirithir and a knot of horsemen came with word that Dergdian would be in next day. None of them had any success with their hunting. And later still, when the meager food had been eaten in dulled silence, and the weary men were already huddling into their cloaks and the heather windbreaks close about the fires, Gault gathered the leaders about him and kept them waiting until he was ready to speak; then he looked up from drawing in the ash with a bit of stick and said abruptly, "We have two moons—three if the spring comes late, but assuredly no more—to have our swords whetted before the Caledones take the war trail. It is time enough but no more than time enough. Therefore the sooner we bring the King to the Crowning Stone, the better, for when that is done"—the wolf-yellow gaze whipped round, singling Phaedrus from the rest, so that for the first time Gault's words were directed for him— "The sooner that is done, and he has taken the Princess Murna for his woman, the sooner we shall be free for the whetting of our swords."

Phaedrus had sprung up before the last words were spoken. "The Princess Murna?"

The wolf stare never wavered. "Who else?"

"It was not in the bargain!"

"What bargain?" Gault's voice had the ring of iron. "If Liadhan had not escaped to her left-hand kin, the thing might not have been so direly needful, at least not so urgent. As it is, you must take the Royal Daughter for your woman, even as your great-grandsire took the Royal Woman of the Epidii, that the two people might become one, and you must take her as soon as you are crowned King. The Little Dark People, the Women's Side, all those who make their foremost prayers to Earth Mother will accept you the more readily if you hold by the ancient right, as well as by the right of the Sun People, and you must make your claim strong, before any rise to question it."

Phaedrus was seeing inside the darkness of his head the white masklike face under the silver moon headdress, with the look in the eyes that he could not read. The face of Liadhan's daughter. "How if I refuse?" he demanded, his voice thick in his throat.

The dark brows lifted a little. "You will not refuse. You are the King."

Phaedrus made one desperate effort to beat down the tawny wolf's gaze that would not leave his face, but he was trapped, and he knew it; and he knew also, raging inwardly, that he was hamstrung in this battle of wills by the fact that he had been a slave too long, trained to obey as a thing that had no right to any will of its own, and the training had left scars and weak places in him like an old wound that lets you down when you least expect it.

He turned the thing into an ugly jest. "So, I will take Liadhan's daughter for my woman. But 'Like mother, like daughter' they say. Will you promise not to let her eat me and choose another King, seven Midwinter Fires from now?"

He dared not meet Conory's eyes, lest he should see scorn in them, or worse still, the look of a man making allowances for a friend.

10 | *The King Making*

PHAEDRUS OPENED HIS EYES INTO COMPLETE DARKNESS AND lay for a while trying to remember where he was, trying to pierce back through the black sleep that had come down like a curtain between him and some strange shadowy half-world on the other side of it. Three days, they had said—someone had said—three days and three nights for the Horse Lord before he came back to life. But surely it had been longer than that, whole years longer than that. Or had there perhaps never been a beginning to it, and would there never be an end?

He made a sudden panic movement, and the pain and stiffness of his body seemed to tear apart the feeling of nightmare that had begun to rise in his throat, so that he remembered where he was and what was happening to him. He turned his head cautiously and saw a little way off the few red gleeds of a dying fire. There had been many fires in this place when the Little Dark People had laid their dead chiefs away, when they were the lords of the land; he had seen the dark scars of them on floor and roof, at the start when there were torches to see by. The Place of Life, they called it, this place where now the boys came at their initiation mysteries, and the Horse Lord must lie for his three days and nights among the dead.

He had not been alone in the tomb-chamber. Vaguely he could remember now the Sun Priests coming and going about him; silent figures in horsehide cloaks and aprons, their heads shaved save for the broad center crest. The strange-smelling herbs that they had burned in the fire, the ritual patterns of sound and movement that they had woven round him. Dreams there had been, too, that seemed to come from the smoke of the fire, dreams of having four legs and a heart like flame, and running with a four-legged herd of kindred, in a thunder of hooves and a sky-wide flying of manes and tails. Strange wild dreams of freedom such as no mortal man had ever known.

He moved again, carefully, testing out his body, and the stiffened smart of the new tattoo marks on breast and shoulders brought him fully back to himself with a rush, and to wondering why, in the name of all the Gods that ever man had prayed to, he had got into that fight at the wine booth. Why hadn't he simply hitched up his bundle and turned South, the moment the gates of the Gladiators' School closed behind him? He might have been in Londinium, a free trainer in some other school, perhaps, by now; his own master among his own kind. Even when Gault came, why hadn't he pretended to agree and waited his chance and run as though all the fiends of Tartarus were after him? He supposed he had grown so used to thinking no more than one day ahead that when Gault and Sinnoch had put the scheme to him, and when he was with Midir, it had only seemed like a wild adventure to set out on, and he had not realized that it was for all the rest of his life.

To the end of his life, he was Midir the Horse Lord, and when he came to the end he would be laid in much such a place as this, with a sword to his hand and a pot of heather beer to cheer him on the dark journey, and be remembered by a name that was not his, by a people who were not his, either.

Meanwhile, wasn't it time that somebody came? How much longer? Soon the last gleeds of the fire would dim and go out. Suddenly the darkness was bearing down on him with all the weight of piled stone and turf between him and the world of living men, suffocating and engulfing him, crushing him out of existence. There was a drumming sound all about him, quicker and quicker, and a strange animal panting that seemed to echo back from the unseen walls, and he did not realize that he was hearing his own heartbeats and his own hurrying breaths. He thrust back the soft skin rug in which he was wrapped and struggled to an elbow, then into a sitting position, groaning as every stiffened fiber of his body protested.

There was a stir and a flicker of torchlight far off at the entrance to the tomb-chamber, as though someone on watch there had only been waiting for some sound of movement to tell them he was awake, and figures came ducking in along the low tunnel. After so long in the dark, the sudden light of the torches they carried jabbed at Phaedrus's eyes, half blinding him so that it was a few moments before he could see that the foremost of the torch bearers was Conory, for once without his cat, and with two more of the Companions at his back.

"It was a good sleep?" Conory asked the ritual question.

And Phaedrus gathered his wits to make the ritual answer. "A good sleep. And a good waking."

The Companions were setting their torches into the makeshift stands of crossed spears that stood ready for them against the walls, and the light, flaring upward, splashed the great incurving stones with honey color, till they ran in to meet at the great fire-blackened lintel-stone high overhead. It was like a giant beehive, Phaedrus thought suddenly; easy to imagine the wild bees nesting up there, filling the chamber with their deep song—would the rib-cage of a dead Chieftain make a good framework for a honey-comb?

"It is time to be making ready," said Conory's voice in his

ear. And he pulled himself together and straightened his mind from its wandering with an effort. There were so many things he wanted to ask. So much could have happened during these three days and nights that he had been shut away from the world of living men. He wanted to know if there had been any word of Liadhan, and what had happened to her priests—those that had not died in the fighting—how many of the Tribe had died on either side, how the rising had fared in the further parts of Earra-Ghyl. But all that must wait. He had been well drilled by Gault in how he must behave during this time of being made ready. So he drank the dark bitter-tasting brew in the bronze cup that Conory gave him and got stiffly to his feet, the floor dipping under him until whatever was in the drink took effect, and the world steadied somewhat; and he stood to be decked out for his King Making—like a sacrificial bull for the slaughter, he thought, and had a moment's insane desire to laugh.

In silence, Conory and the Companions combed his hair and bound it back with thongs as though for battle, and dressed him in breeks and tunic that they had brought with them. They hung round his neck an ancient clashing necklace of river gold, amber and cornelian, and a broad collar of heron-hackles; sheathed a leaf-shaped dagger with a gold pommel mount at his side and sprang onto each arm a pair of coiled bronze arm-rings that he seemed to have seen before. It was a few moments before he remembered when and where, and that it was not the arm-rings alone; and then, looking down, he saw the dark clotted patch where Logiore's blood had sunk into the heron-hackles.

They gave him a spear with a collar of black horsehair. And lastly, they set on his head the great maned and crested headdress of the Horse Lord. He felt the scalp cap gripping from his brows to the nape of his neck, and the side fringes with their little gold disks that swung against his cheeks and chimed at every move-ment of his head; felt the heavy balance of the great arched stal-lion crest and the sweep of the mane between his shoulders; and for the last time before they faded altogether, he remembered those dreams of racing four-legged among the horse herd.

He crouched his way down the arched tunnel followed by the three Companions, his head ducked low between his shoulders to keep the great crest clear of the roof, and stood erect on the threshold, between the huge stone entrance posts; then he stalked forward into the flare of pine-knot torches, where the rest of the Companions waited for him, and beyond the standing-stones of the forecourt, horses were being walked to and fro in the bitter dark. After the still and heavy air of the tomb-chamber, the thin wind of the winter night seemed to whine through his very bones, and the torchlight was flecked with spitting sleet. The warriors raised a great clamor at the sight of him, drumming their spears across the rims of their bucklers. Then someone—Phaedrus saw that it was the boy Brys—brought him a red horse with a mealy mane and tail, and he made the steed-leap on his spear, and was away, the others mounting and pounding after him—Conory a bare half length behind, lest at any time he should be uncertain of the way.

Down every narrow side glen as he headed South, from every rath and village among the snow-puddled moors, mounted men came in to join them, many carrying torches until the whole countryside was speckled with flame; herdsmen on little sure-footed hill ponies ragged-fleeced in their winter coats, men in their best cloaks and carrying their finest weapons; here and there a knot of men on fine horses with the Arab strain in them; once a fat man with a flame-red beard, riding a mare with twin foals at heel. More and more, until Phaedrus found himself riding at the head of a fiery cloud of horsemen that churned the glen trails to a puddled slush; and his ears were full of the soft rolling thunder of hooves and the exultant throat-cries of the riders.

It was midnight when they set out on that wild ride, and dawn was not far off when they came in sight of Dun Monaidh across the marshes, dark-humped against the half-thawed, half-frozen snow that pooled and pale-dappled Mhoin Mhor, and crowned with torches. The men set up great shouts at the sight, heels were struck into horses' flanks, and the whole mass drummed forward into a gallop, strung out along the looping causeway track, splashing through the paved ford, and sweeping left-hand-wise to come at the fortress track. A flying skein of horsemen came out from the Dun itself, sweeping down to meet them at the foot of the fortress hill; and all around him was a great shouting above the smother of hooves; saffron and black and crimson cloaks flying in the torch flare and the spitting sleet, weapons tossed up and caught again.

So with a great riding of horsemen before and behind him, Phaedrus swept on up the steepening track and in for the second time through the gates of Dun Monaidh, and reined in before the tall pillar-stone.

The Sun Priests were there, and their chanting rose into the pallor of the winter dawn, full voiced and strong in the invocation to Lugh of the Shining Spear; and there also were the elders of the Kindred, to receive him as he swung down from the red horse. Tuathal the Wise stood foremost among his priests, wrapped in his horse-hide robe, with the amber sun cross on his breast: he came forward and put a stone-hilted dagger with a strange leaf-shaped copper blade into Phaedrus's hand. A knot of young warriors were bringing up the sacred white stallion.

Midir, and later Gault, had warned him that he would have

this to do, this making of the Horse Sacrifice before the pillar-stone of the Royal House. "I am no priest and no butcher," he had said angrily. "I have killed men but not horses; I shall bungle it." And Gault had said, in the tone of one giving an order he will have obeyed, "You will not bungle it! A clumsy killing is taken as an ill omen, and there will be no room for ill omens that day."

And he did not bungle it, or not much. A clean kill enough, though the white horse reared up, screaming defiance as a stallion screams in battle, when he felt his death upon him, tearing at the ropes and swinging the men who held them from side to side. For one moment he towered over Phaedrus like a great wave before it breaks, ready to come plunging down and engulf him. Then the powerful haunches gave way and the great horse crashed side-ways to the ground, gave one convulsive shudder, and lay still. Tomorrow there would be a new Lord of the Sacred Horse Herd.

There was a smell of blood mingling with the smell of burning that still clung about scorched timber and blackened thatch, and a great wailing rose from the watching crowd. The old High Priest dipped his finger in the blood and made a sign with it on Phaedrus's forehead, above the Mark of the Horse Lord. And the wailing of the Women's Side was taken up and engulfed by a triumphant roar from the men, and that in turn was drowned in the deep booming splendor of sound that seemed to loosen the very thought in one's head, as two of the priests raised and sounded the huge curved bronze trumpets of the Sun that had not been heard in Dun Monaidh for seven years.

The torches were quenched and the gray light of dawn was all about them, as Phaedrus was led up through the Dun, the Sun Priests going ahead, the Companions and Kindred and then a great comet tail of people following on behind, until they came to the court next below the Citadel, where the Rock of the Footprint jutted up from the natural outcrop; the Crowning Stone of the Dalriadain.

There were more things to be done, but they were short and soon over: mare's milk to be drunk from a battered black pottery bowl that was never used save at the King Making; a ritual washing of hands and feet in the bowl-shaped depression at one end of the same great rock slab, where the gathered sky-water was more than half-melted sleet; the priests with short prancing steps making sacred patterns of words and movement that passed him by like a dream. They had brought the freshly flayed hide of the King Horse and spread it across the end of the stone opposite to the bowl depression, so that it covered the third thing that was cut there—the wild boar beloved of warriors.

Sleet was still spitting down the wind, but the yellow bar of a low dawn edged the eastern sky; and as Phaedrus mounted the Crowning Stone, and with his left foot on the hide of the King Horse set his right into the deep-cut footprint that had held the right foot of every king of the Dalriadain since first they came from Erin across the Western Sea, the first sunlight struck the high snow-filled corries of distant Cruachan.

Gault brought the spear of Lugh, and put it into his hand in place of the other that he had brought with him from the place of Life. Conory knotted the sheath thongs of the King's sword to his belt. Now they were loosening the bindings of the stallion headdress, lifting it away. Tuathal the High Priest was standing on the horsehide beside him, holding up a narrow circlet of fiery pale gold that caught the morning light for an instant in a ripple of white fire like the leaves of the white aspen when they blow up against the sun. Phaedrus bent his head to receive it and felt it pressed down onto his brows.

The bronze Sun Trumpets were sounding again; the deep

earth-shaking note booming out over the marshes and the hills and the high moors, to be caught up from somewhere on the very edge of hearing, and passed on, carrying the word from end to end of Earra-Ghyl that there was a Horse Lord again in Dun Monaidh.

11 | *Royal Hunt*

THE NEXT TIME PHAEDRUS WOKE, IT WAS TO THE FLICKER OF firelight through eyelids still half gummed together with sleep, and the morning sky milk-silver beyond the smoke hole in the crown of the King's-Place roof. He lay for a few moments basking in the sense of well-being that lapped him round; the aching stiffness and the leaden weight of exhaustion all washed away by that black warm tide of sleep. Then gradually a weight of some other kind settled on him in its place as he remembered. Yesterday he had been crowned Horse Lord, but today was the day of his marriage to the Royal Woman.

He opened his eyes and came to one elbow with something between a groan and a curse; and a small rhythmic sound that had been going on all the while without his noticing it stopped abruptly. The young warrior Brys, squatting by the great fire that glowed warmly in the center of the big square hut, looked up alertly from the great war spear with the black horsehair collar he had been burnishing across his knee.

Phaedrus scowled, startled for the moment at finding he was not alone. "What in Typhon's name are you doing here?"

"I was burnishing your gear and weapons while you slept, Lord. Gault bade me come to serve you."

"Gault!" Something in Phaedrus seemed to snap. "Gault bids this thing—Gault bids that thing—Gault will choose me my armor-bearer, *and* my wife. ..." He checked at sight of Brys's face, and quietened his tone somewhat. "You have served me well;

that spear blade looks as though it had this morning come fresh from the armorer's hands. Now go back to your own Lord, and if you should be seeing Gault on the way, tell him I thank him for his care of me but I will choose my own armor-bearer."

There was a moment's pause, and then Brys said, "My own Lord is dead."

And suddenly Phaedrus was remembering the place where the fortress stream dived through the outer wall, and Brys holding the torch that called that gleam of silver apples under the water. Gault had said, "Your Lord Gallgoid," and the boy had said "My Lord Gallgoid is dead." He rubbed the back of one hand across his forehead, trying to clear the confusion that still blurred all the edges of that night. "Of course. You will be—you will have been Gallgoid's armor-bearer."

"His armor-bearer and his charioteer."

"It is in my mind that to suit Gallgoid a charioteer would need to be good at his trade."

"I am," Brys said with conviction.

"Sa—and modest as well. And now you would be mine?"

"I am of the Kindred," the boy said proudly, stating his claim. "You would not be remembering; I was only in my first year in the Boys' House when you—when the bad thing happened. But I am of the Kindred."

"Gallgoid had no one with him all that moon and more that he was with me in the Cave of the Hunter."

"He left me behind in his Hall, until the time came to join him here in Dun Monaidh. There had to be those that he could trust, while he was supposed to be lying sick in his own place."

"And you were one that he could trust."

"Nobody found out that he was not there."

Phaedrus looked at Brys with fresh eyes, noticing the good

straight look of him, and the stubborn mouth. "Sa sa—it may be that I shall need someone to trust, one day. ... I will take Gallgoid's charioteer after him."

"In spite of Gault the Strong?" Brys said slowly.

"In spite of Gault the Strong." Suddenly Phaedrus laughed. "If Gault had sent me Cuchulain himself this morning to be my armor-bearer and drive my team, I would have spat in Cuchulain's eye if I could not be coming at Gault to spit in his." Then as the slow smile broadened on Brys's face, "Now leave that burnishing and go and find me something to eat, for my belly's cleaving to my backbone."

The unpegged curtain of skins across the doorway had scarcely fallen behind him when voices sounded outside; the heavy folds were thrust back once more, and Conory, with Shan draped across his shoulders, strolled in. "A fine and fortunate day to you," he said pleasantly, and deposited on the low stool by the fire a gaming board and a carved wooden box. "Since there's no going out for the bridegroom until they summon him out to his marrying, it was in my mind that a game of Fox and Geese might serve to pass the time."

Phaedrus flung off the bed-rugs with a sudden violence and sat up. "Conory, it's madness! I can't be going through with this marrying!"

Conory had settled onto his heels and taken up the gaming box to open it. He said very softly, "Midir, it is in my mind that you have no choice."

"She will know!"

"Keep your voice down, you've a King's Guard outside. Here—let you put that cloak round you and come to the fire."

"Fiends and Furies!" Phaedrus swore, but he picked up the heavy saffron cloak that lay tumbled on the bed-place and flung it round him over the light under-tunic which was all he had on, and came to squat beside the fire, facing Conory across the checkered board on which he had begun to set out the pieces of red amber and narwhal ivory. *"She will know!"* he repeated desperately.

"She will not. She was only ten—eleven summers old when it happened. A babe who will scarcely have begun her weapon training." (To Phaedrus, it still seemed strange that the women of the Northern tribes shared the training of the young warriors, becoming as used to the throw-spear as to the distaff; and unconsciously he frowned). "You have nothing to fear on that count. She will not know the balance of the blade."

Phaedrus had just drawn breath for one more furious protest, for indeed it seemed to him a horrible thing, not only on his own account but on Midir's also, that he should take this She-Wolf's daughter for his woman; but at that moment Brys returned, with a beer jar in one hand and a bowl piled with cold pig-meat and barley bannock in the other, and the protest must be left unmade. Instead, while they ate together—Brys had brought more than enough for two—he turned to the questions he had longed to ask yesterday. And Conory answered him as best he could, while Shan, springing down from his shoulder, pounced on and played with and tormented a lump of pig-fat that he had tossed for her beside the fire, until she wearied of the game and stalked out, tail erect, in search of better hunting elsewhere.

By the time they had finished eating, it was all told: the number of the dead, and how many women were among them, the success of the rising that had swept like heath fire through Earra-Ghyl, freeing the Dalriadain of the dark bondage that had held them for seven years; the flight with Liadhan of the Earth Priests not killed in the fighting.

"Now it will be for the women once again to make the Mysteries of the Mother, as they have always done," Conory said.

"Those furies!" Phaedrus gave a small shudder, thinking of the women with their knives and their rending claws, and Conory and himself fighting for life in the middle of them.

Conory flicked a faint, warning glance toward Brys, who was standing by to take up the bowl and beer jug. "Do you ever remember them like that before, save when a man intruded on the Women's Mysteries? And any man who does that has himself to blame for the thing that happens to him, as any woman would have only herself to blame, who spied on the boys' initiation ceremonies. Ach no, that night was Liadhan's doing, and the dancing in the Fire Hall, and the flute-magic of the priests."

When Brys had departed with the empty bowl, Phaedrus, looking after him with his mind full of the things that they had been talking of, found that his thoughts had slipped sideways for a moment, and he was discovering that the Princess Murna could not be more than a year older than Brys himself. For that one moment he was thinking of her as a person, wondering how it had been with her in the days since Liadhan had fled, and where she was held captive, and if she also had woken to a weight on her heart this morning—supposing that she had slept at all.

Then Conory said, "Shall we begin? Amber plays first."

They played three games, and Conory won them all.

"Since you have my kingdom," he said, when he had made the winning move for the third time, "it is only fair that I should have the games."

There was a laugh from the direction of the doorway, and looking up, Phaedrus saw that several of the Companions had entered and were standing just inside, watching the end of the game.

Yesterday they had been no more than strange faces and chance-heard names, these men who had been boys with Midir. But now, after the wild ride down from the Place of Life that they had shared, and last night's feasting that they had shared also, names and faces had begun to join together. Lean freckled Loarne, and Diamid of the somber eyes and devil's-quirk eyebrows; Comgal and Domingart who were brothers and seldom apart; the little dark one, probably with Earthling blood in him, whom they called Baruch the Grass Snake. And in a vague, tentative kind of way, they were beginning to take on a friendly look.

"The day be fortunate to you," Diamid said, "and may the ill luck have gone into the gaming board."

"Fox and Geese was never your game, my Lord Midir." That was Domingart, shaking his head regretfully as he surveyed the board before Conory began to gather up the pieces. "And still it would seem that it is not."

"I am seven years out of practice," Phaedrus returned. The excuse was unanswerable.

Brys had come in behind them, and began taking many-colored garments from the big carved chest against the far wall, gravely proud to be the King's armor-bearer, so that Phaedrus thought if he had had a tail like a hound's it would have been lashing slowly from side to side behind him.

Time to be moving, then. He flung off the saffron cloak and got to his feet and stood ready for them.

When he was once again clad in the ritual dress of the Horse Lord, from the brogues on his feet to the great stallion headdress that had been brought from the hut where the priests kept the sacred objects, he went out with the Companions to the Horse Court beside the Court of the Footprint, where the horses stood ready for them, and they mounted and rode down into the great forecourt.

The forecourt was already alive with men, and growing more so every moment, as others came in from all over Dun Monaidh. There were few women among them, for the Women's Side were for the most part gathering in the same way to the Royal Court. A shout greeted Phaedrus when he appeared with the Companions riding about him, and they were caught up in the general movement and swept across toward the gate gap which gave onto the Court of the Footprint and thence into the Citadel.

"The King rides hunting!"

Somebody raised the shout and suddenly it was running through the great gathering, taken up from end to end of the Dun.

"The King rides hunting!" And then, "Who rides with the King?"

Conory and the Companions crashed out the answer. "*We* ride hunting with the King!"

They were close before the inner gateway now, jostling and jostled; the ponies stamped and snorted, puffing clouds of steam from their nostrils; the colors of cloaks and fringed riding rugs and the glint of bronze from brooch or bridle bit were darkly brilliant in the gray light of the winter's day that was already far past noon. "What quarry for the King's hunting?"

For a moment there was no answer, and the crowd fell silent, watching the gate. Then from within that last inner circle of rock walling rose the low wailing of the Women's Side, making the ritual lament for a maiden carried off from among them against her will. Phaedrus, on the red horse with the mealy mane, ignored Gault's dark face among the nobles in the forefront of the crowd and glanced aside under his red brows at Conory; saw that Conory looked amused and politely interested more than anything else, and could have hit him. There was a little stir among the waiting tribesmen, and then the dead thorn bush that closed the inner gateway was dragged aside. He could glimpse movement within, and the glint of colors, and the Princess Murna came walking slowly through the gate, with the women of the Kindred behind her and on either side. She walked looking neither to right nor left, down through the Court of the Footstep and out into the wide forecourt. Her head was held very high, and the soft springing hair, loosed from its braids and drawn forward over her shoulders, hung in thick falls of dove-gold down over the breast of her many-colored gown. The last time Phaedrus saw her, she had been wearing the silver Moon Diadem; now she was crowned only with a narrow headband of crimson stuff, strung about with shining wires and hung with disks of gold and coral; but under it her face was covered by a mask of red mare's skin, that gave her the look of something not belonging to the world of men, so that looking at her, Phaedrus felt the skin crawl and prickle at the back of his neck.

"What quarry for the King's hunting?" the men shouted again, and the women flung back the answer: "A Royal Quarry! A Royal Quarry for the King's hunting!"

Down at the foot of the outer court, where the timbered gates stood open, two men had just flung a fringed riding rug across the back of a young black mare, who looked, as Phaedrus had thought when he first glanced down toward her past the pillar-stone, to have been ridden already today. He had said as much to Conory, and Conory had smiled that gentle smile and said, "A sad thing it would be if the quarry should outrun the hunter."

The Princess was level with him now. She turned her head once in passing, and he caught the flicker of light behind the eye-slits of the mask. Then she passed on, the men parting to let her through, until she reached the gate and the black mare waiting there. She seemed to come to life then, and scooping up a great fold of her skirt, drew it through her belt and made the steed-leap as lightly as any boy.

A strange high cry like a sea bird's floated back to them as she wheeled the mare toward the gate and, with a jab of the horse-rod, urged her from a stand into a canter.

She was out through the gate, and under the chanting of the Sun Priests invoking Lugh of the Shining Spear, they heard the hoofbeats trippling down to the outer gap, then bursting into the drumming rhythm of full gallop. Phaedrus saw in his mind's eye that steep rocky track down to the marshes—and she was riding it as though it were a level practice field. His hand clenched on the whipping horse-rod of green ash, and unconsciously he must have tightened his knees. The red stallion stirred and buckled forward under him, and instantly Conory's finger flicked up, warningly, on his own bridle rein. "Not yet."

There was a general laugh all about him. "See how eager he is! This will be a fine fierce hunting!"

The drum of hoofbeats was very faint now, almost lost. The chanting of the Sun Priests died on a last long glowing note, and again the finger flicked on Conory's bridle rein. Phaedrus raised the small bronze-bound hunting horn that hung from the stallion's pectoral strap and, putting it to his mouth, set the echoes flying; then while the notes still hung on the winter air, heeled the red horse from a stand to a canter in his turn. The Companions were close behind him, Conory as usual just to his right, as he bore down on the great gate. Behind him he heard cries of "Good hunting!" Gault's bull-roar topping the rest. "Good hunting to you, Midir of the Dalriadain!"

They were out through the gates and across the ditch causeway, the track dropping before them toward the moss. For a moment there was no sign of horse or rider. Then Conory pointed. "There she goes!" And away northward, Phaedrus saw the flying figure, already dimming into the sere gray and tawny of the marshes.

"She's not going to be easy to follow, once the light begins to go."

They took the plummeting track at breakneck speed, down from the hill of Dun Monaidh, from the inpastures where that year's colts scattered as they drummed past, and out into the great emptiness of Mhoin Mhor.

The Companions were stringing out like a skein of wild geese threading the winter sky. The red horse snorted and stretched out his neck, and the foam flew back from his muzzle to spatter against Phaedrus's breast and thighs; the mealy silver of the mane flowed back across his bridle wrist as the land fled by beneath the pounding hooves. Excitement rose in them all; laughter and hunting cries began to break from the men behind him. He guessed that in the ordinary way of things, the girl's flight would have been only a pretense, like the wailing of the Women's Side. But this was different; if he wished to catch the Princess Murna, then he would have to hunt her in good earnest; and pity twinged in him, not for her, the She-Wolf's daughter, but for the weary mare she rode.

The track was pulling up now, out of the great flats of Mhoin Mhor, and the quarry, striking away from it, was making north-eastward for the hills around Loch Abha head. And the wild hunt swept after her, hooves drumming through the blackened heather, skirting little tarns that reflected the sword-gray sky, startling the green plover from the pasture clearings. Far over to the West the clouds were breaking as they came up into the hills, and a bar of sodden daffodil light was broadening beyond the Islands, casting an oily gleam over the wicked swirling water of the Old Woman, while away and away northward, the high snows of Cruachan caught the westering beams and shone out sour-white against the storm clouds dark behind.

But now the chase was turning tail to the sunset, and all at once Conory let out a startled curse and, urging his horse level with Phaedrus's, shouted, "By the Black Goddess! She's making for the Royal Water and Caledonia!"

And his words were caught up in a startled splurge of voices and echoed to and fro behind him.

"The vixen!" Phaedrus said, and laughed. "You were saying it would be a sad thing if the quarry were to outrun the hunt. The Sun's warmth forever on the shoulders of the man who rode that mare today!"

After that it was a hunt in deadly earnest, and shouting to the rest, Phaedrus crouched lower and dug his heels and settled down to ride as he had never ridden in his life before. The ground began to be cut up; soon they were into a maze of shallow glens, wooded in their hollows, and tangled with stone-brambles and bilberry and sour jumper scrub along the ridges between; and once they thought they had lost her—until Baruch the Grass Snake pointed across the glen, yelling, "There she goes!" and on the crest of the far ridge, the flying shape of horse and rider showed for an instant against the sky. They wheeled the horses and plunged downhill after her, fording the little burn between its snow-puddled edges, and stringing out in a beeline up the opposite hillside. When they gained the crest, she was nowhere to be seen, but a few moments later she came into view again, heading up the glen toward the high moors; she had doubled northward, in an effort to throw them off her trail, relying maybe on the fading light to cover her. But there was just too much light left, and in turning North, she had missed the ford a short way downstream, and was left with a tiring horse, and fast water running between her and her way of escape.

Conory was riding almost neck to neck with Phaedrus, a little in advance of the rest. He leaned toward him and said quickly, "It is seven years since you were in these hills. Will you let me give the orders?"

Phaedrus nodded, and Conory fell back a little, shouting over his shoulder to the smother of horsemen that followed after. "The mare is tiring East, and if we can hold her in sight a while longer, she's ours! Baruch, Finn, Domingart, you three ride the lightest of us all—back to the ford with you, and come up the far side. If you can reach the glen head before her, you can turn her back while we keep her from breaking away on this side, and we'll have her before the last light goes!"

The three young men wheeled their horses and plunged away, while the main chase swept on after their desperate, flagging quarry. But in a short while they appeared again, deliberately showing themselves on the skyline and going like the Blue Riders of the West Wind. Phaedrus saw the black mare flinch sideways flinging up her head, as though the hand on her bridle had involuntarily jerked at the bit; the rider snatched a glance over her shoulder; he could almost feel her despairing moment of indecision, then she wheeled about and took to the open hillside, swinging West again.

It was not quite a hunt now, more like rounding up a runaway colt. The Companions were not only behind her but creeping up on either side, heading her back the way she had come. The light was going fast as they dropped down from the hills onto lower ground. What still lingered of it lay over the wide levels of Mhoin Mhor stretching gray and dun and dreary-pale toward the sea; but on the left, behind the down-thrust tongue of the hills, the gathering twilight could not yet quench the one stretch of full color in all that winter evening, the luminous, wicked green of bog between its islands of half-thawed snow.

The distance between them and the wild rider was lessening steadily, the mare, despite all her valiant efforts, rocking in her gallop and almost done. Then the girl snatched one more glance behind her, as though judging the distance that she still had in hand, and wrenching the mare round in her tracks, sent her plunging down into the hazel woods that sloped southward into those luminous green shadows.

Conory cried, "Thunder of Tyr! She's heading straight for the bog!"

So she would take even that last hideous way out! Ahead of them as they crashed after her, heads low against the whipping hazel twigs, the bog lay smooth and deadly, and the girl was heading straight toward it, crouched over the mare's straining neck, drumming her heels into the poor laboring flanks. Her voice blew back to them, crying endearments and encourage-ment. Phaedrus, driving in his own heels, had somehow flung the red stallion out before the rest; he was circling to ride her off as the herd lads rode to turn a breakaway. The divots of soft black earth that spun from the mare's hooves flew past him like a flight of swallows; behind him the muffled hoof-drum of his Companions, ahead and to the right, the mare floundering and swaying in her stride; and the livid greenness of the bog rushing nearer—nearer, in the evening light. The cold rooty smell of it was all about them. A few moments more, and they would be into it. ...

Shouting would be no use. Desperately, Phaedrus flung the horse-rod point over butt like a dagger and saw it arch spinning past the mare and plunge into the bog myrtle just ahead of her and to the left. That was one useful trick learned in the Gladiators' School. Startled, she swerved aside, snorting, and plunged on, but no longer straight toward the fringe of the bog. Now the red horse's muzzle was almost level with the dark streaming tail, as the Princess struggled to head her mount back to the waiting greenness of the bog that was now so hideously close. But the mare was just about done, and Phaedrus clamped in his knees and hurled the stallion forward, and they were neck and neck. And with only a few strides to go and the ground softening at every hoof-fall, he wrenched round and deliberately took the black mare in the shoulder, all but bringing her down. She screamed with fear, and lashed out, but the crash had spun her in her tracks, away from the deadly verge. In the same instant Phaedrus felt his own mount side-slither under him, as one great round hoof slipped into the black quaking ooze beneath the green. For one long-drawn sickening moment the red horse lurched on the brink, and it seemed that in the next they must be over into the bog, but his own speed carried him on, and the next flying stride found solid myrtle tussocks underfoot again.

The girl had turned with a cry of fury and lashed him across the face with her horse-rod; but he had her reins and they were racing along the flank of the bog, perilously locked together, floundering in and out of solid ground and sinking pocket, but drawing steadily away from the livid greenness of the hungry mire. Then with a sound between a laugh and a sob, Phaedrus had an arm round the Princess Murna and dragged her across the red horse's withers. The wild-eyed mare, lightened of her load, sprang away and went streaking back toward the hills, with a couple of the Companions in pursuit. And Phaedrus, still riding full gallop, was clamping the Royal Woman against him with his free arm, while she struggled to break free and fling herself off.

Then quite suddenly the fight seemed to go out of her as they slackened pace from that wild gallop to a canter. Phaedrus freed one hand—he was controlling the panting stallion with his knees now—and caught at the red mareskin mask.

Just for an instant, as his hand touched the hairiness of the hide, he wondered if it were the Moon Diadem trick over again, and the face beneath it would not be Murna's. Wondered with a little shiver of cold between his shoulder blades whether it would be a human face at all, or something else, something that was not good to see. ... Then he pulled away the mask and flung it behind him among the following horsemen. It was Murna's face looking up at him, gray-white and somehow ragged, as though in pulling off the bridal mask he had torn holes in something else, some inner defense that she was naked and terrified without. And for that one instant, despite the dusk, he could look into her face instead of only at the surface of it. Still feeling rather sick from the nearness of the bog, he laughed in sudden triumph, and bent his head and kissed her.

Surprisingly, she yielded against him and kissed him back. But as she did so, he felt her hand steal out, light as a leaf but not quite light enough, toward the dagger in his belt.

His own hand flashed down and caught her wrist, twisting the weapon from her grasp before she well had hold of it, and sent it spinning into a furze bush. "Softly, sweetheart! Maybe we shall do better if we are both unarmed," he said, gently dangerous. She could have no other weapon about her, or she would not have gone for his dagger.

She gave a sharp cry of baffled fury, and became a thing as rigid and remote as one of the stocks of wood, charmed into human shape, that the People of the Hills left behind in its place when they stole a child of the Sun Folk. And yet the odd thing—

Phaedrus knew it beyond all doubt—was that the kiss she had given him had been as real as her hand feeling for his dagger.

It was long past full dark by the time they came back to the Dun, and all down the steep track and massed in the gateways the warriors were waiting, with pine-knot torches in their hands, so that they rode through a ragged avenue of light. Midir of the Dalriadain, with the Royal Woman conquered and captive across his horse; and after them the Companions, Conory triumphantly bearing aloft the red mareskin mask on the point of his spear, as though it were a trophy.

The King was home from his hunting.

12 | *Golden Plover's Feather*

WHEN IT CAME TO GETTING AWAY BY ONESELF FOR A WHILE, Phaedrus decided, the Lord of the Dalriadain was in much the same case as a gladiator with his town leave stopped. All the past two days up here in the hill horse-runs, watching Sinnoch's leggy two-year-olds in the first stages of their breaking, the Companions had been with him, friends and bodyguard in one, alert and willing to go anywhere and do anything as a knot of hounds at heel, and as difficult to get rid of.

In the end he had simply gone to the garbage pits—at least they let him go there alone—and from there strolled round by the back ways of Sinnoch's steading to the stable huts, and bidden Brys, whom he found there playing knucklebones with three other charioteers, to bring out the dun colt for him.

"Do I ride with you?" the boy had asked.

And Phaedrus had said, "Neither you nor anyone. If Conory or any other of the Companions ask where I am gone or seek to follow me, tell them I've gone to find better company than theirs."

And he mounted and clattered off by the lower gate where they brought the colts up to the practice yards. They would probably think that he had gone off after some girl glimpsed yesterday in one of the herdsman's bothies. Well, they'd not be surprised. The Horse Lord's month-old marriage had only been a form, and nobody would be fool enough to think there was anything in it to keep him from going after other girls, or that the Queen would care or even notice if he did.

She had not changed since the night he brought her back to the Dun, with Conory carrying the red mareskin mask on the point of his spear. The torn defense, whatever it was, was whole again, and she still seemed like some cold thing magicked into human-seeming that the Dark People might have left behind in the stealing of the real Murna away. Once he had said to her, "If I strike you with cold iron, will you fly up through the smoke hole, or turn back into a log of wood?"

And she had said in a tone of complete indifference, "Try it, and see."

He had been half minded to do it, too. But in the end—he had not quite dared to, in case what he had said in angry jest was true. And yet there had been the moment when she kissed him back, even while she felt for his dagger. That had not been a clay-cold changeling's kiss. And sometimes he wondered if the real Murna were there inside her all the while, looking out at him as he had so often looked out at the world through the eye-slits of a gladiator's helmet. Well, it was not anything to him, either way; he simply visited the Queen's Place as seldom as might be, and thought about her very little the rest of the time.

And he had better stop thinking about her now, because he had only been this way once before, and if he let his wits go wandering off down every gust of wind, he would almost certainly miss the half-dead birch tree where one left the glen track.

But he found it easily enough in the end, and the little white thread of a burn that came chattering down from the high moors.

It was sere dark country that he climbed through after that, leading the colt now because it was too steep to ride; outcropped with rock and picketed with wetness. It would be fair in its own wild way, when the new fern came thrusting through the sodden wreck of last year's bracken and the ancient hawthorns were in flower along the burn; but now, in the dark end of winter with spring still a long way off, it was desolate enough. That was why it was left to the Little Dark People, Phaedrus supposed, the dispossessed, whose place was always the rock screes and the waste wet mosses that were no use to the later-come lords of the land.

It was all strange country to him, since leaving the track, and he had no idea how far he had to go. ("Away up the burn—that way," Sinnoch had said yesterday, when they passed the birch tree on the way to the outland horse-runs, and that was all.) And he had begun to think he must have missed the way when suddenly between one step and the next—there it was.

No more than a tumble of stones and turf laced together with brambles, that might have been only a natural hummock of the hillside, save for a dark opening in its side that was just too large and just too regular to be the mouth of a wild thing's lair. Midway between the hummock and himself, as he checked to look, a great flat stone cropped through the blackened heather. Nothing moved or sounded but the hill wind and the burn water, and a golden eagle swinging in mile-wide circles far overhead.

He had heard before of places such as this, where one left something that needed mending, together with a gift, and came back later to find the gift gone and the broken thing mended; it was one of those things no one talked of very much, the places where the life of the Sun People touched the life of the Old Ones, the People of the Hills. Like the bowls of milk that the women put out sometimes at night, in exchange for some small job to be done—like the knot of rowan hung over a doorway for protection against the ancient earth magic—like the stealing of a Sun Child from time to time. Save for the few who were their slaves and bond folk, the Tribes had little else to do with the Old People;

certainly they were used to taking less account of them than they did of their chariot horses and beef cattle, when it came to casting up the chances of war. Yet assuredly it was by the aid of the Little Dark People that Liadhan had escaped to her Caledonian kin. Gault had said as much, and now, with the war horns sounding over the edge of spring, Phaedrus, with the common sense of his Roman upbringing, felt that the time was come when the Dark People must count at least for as much as ponies and beef cattle. Sinnoch had said that this mender of worn and broken things, who had his lair and his leaving-stone up here, was the Old Man, the Chieftain of his village. A king in his way, and it seemed to Phaedrus that a visit to him was probably the best chance he would ever get of making contact with any leader among the Dark People.

The colt had begun to fidget, and Phaedrus quieted him and hitched his bridle over a hawthorn bush, then walked forward and, pulling a good serviceable strap of tanned leather and three barley cakes from the breast of his tunic, stooped and set them on the flat stone.

Then he retreated downstream to where he had left the pony, and turned again to face the dark hole in the turf hummock, that might almost have passed for the mouth of an animal's lair save for the betraying wisp of smoke that rose from the briar tangle above it.

Slowly and deliberately, knowing that his every movement was being watched, he laid his spear on the ground, the blade pointing away down the glen, and his dirk beside it. He held out his hands, showing them empty, and called, "Old Man of the Green Hillocks—let you come out to me."

Nothing moved but the thin hill wind. Phaedrus waited—waited—then he walked back slowly, part of the way, and checked again, feeling suddenly how little he knew of the Dark People, wondering what he should do about it if the man did not come. "Chieftain—see, I carry no cold-iron blade; let you be coming out to me."

And from just within the dark mouth, a voice answered, speaking the tongue of the Tribes in the lighter, softer tone of the Old People, "You have left me a gift, but nothing that needs my skill to make it whole again. Why should I come out to you?"

"Because I have brought you the gift; and the thing that I ask for it is not the mending of a worn brogue or a spring rivet in my dagger hilt, but that you should come out and speak with me."

"So—o, that seems fair enough," the voice said consideringly. But still nothing moved beyond the mouth of the dark hole. And then—Phaedrus realized afterwards that he must have glanced away, but at the time he could have sworn that he never took his eyes from the door hole under the briar-tangle—suddenly a man was standing on the far side of the stone. A small, slight-boned man in a kilt of otter skins and with gray hair bushing from his narrow skull, and eyes that seemed at first glance like jet beads until one looked again and saw that they were not black at all, but the dark furred brown of a bee's back. Phaedrus made the sign of the Horns behind himself, and then had an uncomfortable feeling that the other knew it. But he only said, looking at the forehead mark that was like a four-petaled flower, "What is it that you would speak with me about, Midir of the Dalriadain?"

"I would speak with you because it has been told me that you are a chieftain among your own people, and because the war horns are sounding across Druim Alban. When the spring comes, the hosts of King Bruide will take the war trail, and at such a time it is surely good that the Horse Lord should know something of all those within his hunting-runs, not of his own Tribe alone."

The little man gestured to Phaedrus to sit himself on the flat stone, and then squatted down at his feet. "You have more than one of our people among the slaves in your Dun. Why not ask *them* what you would know of the Dark People?"

"Because a slave answers as a slave, and it is the answer of a free man that I am wanting."

The other nodded. "Ask, then."

Phaedrus knew that it would be no good trying to come at the thing slantwise, not with this little man who would understand slantwise methods all too well, so he made his question as direct as a dagger thrust. "When the fighting comes, this fighting that will not be only for cattle or boundaries, but for deciding whether the Dalriadain shall be a free people any more, and what kings shall rule us, and what Gods we shall follow—have we to fear your little blue flint daggers in our backs while our shields are turned to the Caledones?"

"If you had, should I tell you?"

"No," said Phaedrus promptly, "but I have fought for my life to amuse a Roman crowd too often not to be able to judge men's faces. I had hoped that your face might tell me before you were aware of it."

"And it does not? See now, I will be telling you myself, and I will be telling you the truth. We count for nothing, we, the people of the dark-blue flint; since the Horse People took our hunting-runs, we count for nothing, and we know it. But the Tribes come and go like wind-waves through the heather, and we bide in our hills and let them pass. It is no concern of ours when they fight each other. We shall always be here as long as there are wolves on the hill. Kill and be killed as you choose, it is nothing to us."

"Yet you helped Liadhan to escape into Caledonia."

"Surely. She was the Mother, the Lady of the Forests. She was ours to us, and we were hers. Yet because she fled from it when her own Call came—aiee, though we helped her in her fleeing—I do not think that many of us will stir from our own fireside for her sake again."

"When her own Call came?" The phrase caught at Phaedrus's attention, and he was puzzled by it.

The other's dark gaze was on his face, and the burn sounded very loud in the silence. High, high overhead, Phaedrus heard the thin, sharp yelp of the golden eagle. Then the Little Dark Man said softly, "The Horse Lord, of all men, should be knowing what that Call means ..." and then as though changing the subject, he reached out and took up one of the barley cakes, and broke a long piece of crust from one side. "Lord, do you see what I am holding?"

"Surely," Phaedrus said, surprised.

"What is it, then?"

"A crust of barley cake."

"Are you sure?"

From being surprised, Phaedrus was puzzled, and somewhere deep within him was a flicker of warning that he did not understand. "I am quite sure. It is a crust from one of the barley cakes I brought you."

"Look at it well," the man said.

And Phaedrus found himself obeying, his head bent over the crust as though it were something strange and wonderful that he had never seen before.

"Are you still sure?" said the soft, insistent voice.

And suddenly he was not so sure. Not sure at all. The thing in the narrow dark hand was growing blurred, losing its outline, changing into something else. Something—something—

"What is it, then?" said the voice.

"It is—it is *like* a feather."

He could see it taking shape, the strong slender line of it, as it were, filled in with mist—but the mist was thickening, taking on substance and color. He could see the almost blackness of the strong pinion barred with gold—in another moment. ... But something in him had begun to resist.

"What kind of feather would it be?"

"A golden plover's ..." he began, and checked. "No feather at all!" He forced the words out, his eyes fighting for the lost outline of the barley crust. He could see it now very faintly like a shadow—showing through the feather that was growing misty again. For what seemed an eternity of time the two images hung equally balanced, so that he could see them both, one showing through the other. "It is only a barley crust—*a barley crust!*"

The feather was no more substantial than a wisp of wood smoke, and with a supreme effort of will he snuffed it out, the dark slender shape and the golden shadow-bars, and there was nothing in the other man's hand but the strip of crust with the grains of parched barley scattered on top.

He looked up with a gasping breath and drew the back of one hand across his forehead. Despite the little chill wind, it was wet. "Why did you do that?"

There was sweat on the Little Dark Man's forehead too, as he set the barley crust back beside the cake that it had come from. "That? It was no more than a small piece of Earth Magic, such as may be made between the eyes of one man and the eyes of another. I made it—for the answering of a question that was in my mind." He looked up from fitting the crust back into place with a craftsman's care, and his eyes rested consideringly on Phaedrus's face. "It is strange; I could have sworn that there was not one among the Sun People that I could not have made to see that golden plover's feather and forget altogether the barley crust, until I bade them remember it again."

There was a little pause, and then Phaedrus said, "I have spent seven years in the Romans' world, which is a different world from ours; maybe that is why you could not work your magic on me perfectly."

"Maybe," the other said, but his eyes still brooded on Phaedrus's face.

And meeting the question in them, Phaedrus conjured up the old swaggering Arena smile that he had learned as he learned his sword strokes. "Na now, do you think that I am not Midir of the Dalriadain, not the Horse Lord after all, but another wearing his forehead mark?"

"I do not know," the man said slowly, "but when you see that golden plover's feather again, you will be the Horse Lord; and the forehead mark your own."

"Read me the riddle, Old Man."

"Time will do that. But this I will tell you, that you may be knowing I speak true: within three days one of the Old People will reach out to touch your life again, but it is in my heart that he will be already dead."

So—Phaedrus had his answer; it was only the horses and the beef cattle that need be reckoned, after all. The People of the Hills were part of a different world, and no more to be counted as strength or weakness than the glen woods on the snows of Cruachan. ...

Next day he rode back with the Companions to Dun Monaidh, and after that there was little time for remembering the scrap of Earth Magic that was already fading in his mind like a dream or for thinking of the things that Old Man had foretold. Little time for anything save the matter in hand. And the matter in hand was war! War when the wild geese flew North in the spring.

In Dun Monaidh, as in every other Dun and rath and steading

of Earra-Ghyl, the smiths and armorers, the horse breakers and chariot builders were at work. All day long from the huddle of blackened bothies in the outer court came the red lick of flame and the roar of the sheepskin bellows, and the ding of hammer on anvil, as here the fresh iron tires were fitted to chariot wheels, and there the dints were beaten out of the rim of a dappled oxhide shield; and every warrior sharpened and resharpened his weapons on the great pillar-stone.

And then on the second day after his return, Phaedrus came out of the long chariot shed with a couple of the Companions behind him, and heard somewhere over toward the northern rampart a sudden worry of sounds that were all human, and yet made him think of the moment at the end of a hunt when the hounds close in and make their kill.

The small tumult died out almost as he began to run, the other two at his heels, and when he came out between two store-sheds into the clear space just within the dry-stone curve of the rampart, the little group of warriors he found there were quite silent, their dirks still in their hands, looking down at a body that lay crumpled on the ground among them. One of them was turning it over with his foot as Phaedrus arrived, much as a man might turn over a dead rat, and as it fell all asprawl, he saw that it was the body of one of the Dark People, stabbed in four or five places about the breast and belly.

"What has happened here?" he demanded.

And the man who had turned the body over answered him, "A rat hunt, Midir."

"It seems that you have made your kill. What was he doing in the Royal Dun?"

Another man shrugged. "Spying. We found him hiding in the wood-store yonder. He must have come over the wall in the night."

"Or up by the way that the She-Wolf went."

A small crowd had begun to gather; someone came cleaving his way through them like a strong swimmer in a rough sea, and Gault stood there, arms folded on barrel chest, looking down with hard wolf-tawny eyes at the slight dark body in its blood-soaked deerskin. "A spy, most assuredly." He bent forward abruptly for a closer look. "Aye, he's out of the Caledonian hunting-runs, by the patterns on his hide. Doubtless if you had not found him he would have been out over the wall again tonight, and away back to King Bruide with word of how many chariots Dun Monaidh can muster." He straightened and half turned away as though, for him, the thing was finished. "Make a fire on the eastern slopes beyond the outer wall—good and high, for the blaze to show far across country—and burn me this rat."

There was a sharp, half-surprised silence, and then little Baruch said, "Why do more than tip him into the bog—or throw him out for the wolf-kind?"

"Fire is the fitting end for rats."

Phaedrus, his eyes narrowing under the red brows, suddenly took command. "Why are you so firm set on this burning, Gault the Strong?"

"His litter-brothers will come to know of it. It will maybe serve for a useful warning."

"They will come to know that he is killed. Will that not serve for warning enough?"

"I am doubting it," Gault said harshly. "The Old Ones are so close to Earth Mother that death is to them no more than a short journey."

And so, the fire. ... Phaedrus had been long enough out of the foursquare Roman world to have some idea of what all this was really about. To the Sun People it made little real difference whether earth or fire took their bodies when they were done with them; but with the children of Earth Mother it was very different. Grain thrown into the fire would never quicken, and for them, burning took not only the body but the life that had belonged with it. Gault in fact was proposing to destroy whatever this little dark creature had of a soul, for a warning to his kind. Phaedrus had never cared overmuch for the laws of men, but this was another thing, and the laws of men had nothing to do with it. Until now, feeling his way in a new and unfamiliar world, he had left the real leadership to Gault and the inner Council. But now he knew, suddenly and with absolute certainty, that he had come to the end of that.

"But to my mind, the killing is enough," he said, "and Gault, it is *I* that am the King! Whatever he was doing, his death settles the score. *There will be no burning!*"

Gault's wolf gaze whipped round to meet his, and Phaedrus read in the other's frown that he too knew the time had come for a trial of strength between them. "You are the King, but it seems that you have forgotten much of your own world in the Arena. And until you remember, best be leaving such matters as this to those of us who will better understand what we do."

"I have forgotten much," Phaedrus agreed, "but I learned some things too. Even in the Arena, we count the fighting ended with the kill, and do not seek to carry it beyond the death stroke."

The knot of onlooking warriors was growing moment by moment, but no one attempted to take any hand in this odd quiet battle of wits. It was a thing between Gault and the Lord Midir, with the body of the little dark hunter lying between them.

"You speak like a gladiator—a mere bought butcher," Gault said at last.

"There might be worse things to be than a gladiator."

"Such, for instance, as Lord of the Dalriadain?" It was easy enough to read the meaning behind that: "I made you and I can break you. No need to be Lord of the Dalriadain another hour, if it displeases you."

Phaedrus's mouth lifted at the corners in the faint insolent smile that his fellow sword-fighters had come to know. "Surely it is a fine thing to be Lord of the Dalriadain; and Lugh Shining-Spear himself forbid I should forget it was you who took me from Corstopitum city jail and set my foot on the Coronation Stone." He let Gault see the meaning behind that, too: "You made me and you can break me, but you will be broken with me, if you do."

There was a feeling of battle in him, under the quiet surface. He had again the old sense of life narrowing and sharpening its focus until there was nothing in it but himself and Gault and both of them knowing that the thing they fought for was the leadership of the Tribe.

So they confronted each other, eye looking into eye, neither speaking again nor moving, until the silence between them drew out thin and taut so that Phaedrus felt he could have plucked sparks from it like notes of a harp string; and he heard his own voice break it, saying very clearly, each word separated from the next, "There will—be—no—burning."

Something flickered far back in Gault's eyes, and he shrugged his bull shoulders. The fight was over and the victory to Phaedrus. "You are the King, the thing must be as you choose. But the Gods help you and all of us, if you choose wrong." But there was no enmity in his tone; indeed his dark frowning gaze held a new respect.

On the surface, it had been such a small battle; it had not even concerned a warrior of the Tribe, only one of the Little Dark People, who, in the eyes of the Dalriadain, were half animal and half uncanny. Yet it was now, and not in the moment of his King

Making, that Red Phaedrus felt the Lordship of the Dalriadain come into his hand.

"Take him away and throw him out for the wolves," he said to the men who had done the killing. The wolves did not matter; it was only the fire that mattered.

It was only then, watching them dragging the little body away, that he remembered the Old Man's foretelling, of just three days ago.

That night, when the evening meal was over and the harping silent in the Fire Hall, and Phaedrus went to the King's Place to sleep, he checked on the threshold with a caught breath of surprise. Beside the central hearth, where Brys should have been waiting for him, sat a woman. She had drawn his own stool to the fire, and sat there, with her loosened mantle dark about her. Her face was hidden from him by her hair which she had unbraided and begun to comb, as though to pass the time while she waited, but the falling curtain of it was unmistakable, the soft, dove-gold, mouse-gold hair of the Royal Woman.

"Murna! What is it that you do here?"

She flung back the mass of hair and turned her face to him. "May the Queen not come to the King's quarters when she chooses?"

"Surely. But has the Queen chosen to come so often?" He pulled off his heavy cloak and flung it across the piled skins of the bed-place, and came to stand beside the fire, and look down at her, his shoulder propped against the roof tree.

"I was wishing to have word with you," she said, "and so I sent your armor-bearer out for a while."

"Yes?" Phaedrus's guard was up.

"You gained a victory today."

"In the matter of the spy? So you have heard about that?"

"There is little that the Women's Side do not hear about," she said, and the cool hazel eyes that he suddenly realized were like Conory's, for all that they were set level, rested on him consideringly. Then, as though making up her mind to something, she added, "But he was not here for spying."

"No? For what then?"

"He came to get speech with me."

"And did he get it?"

"Yes. He brought me word from my mother, and a gift—for you."

Phaedrus's red brows flashed up. "For me? I'd not have thought she loved me so greatly."

"There are gifts and gifts," Murna said.

"And this one? Are you going to give it to me?"

For answer, she laid down the ivory comb she was still holding, and brought something from the breast of her gown and held it out to him.

He took the thing and looked at it warily: a leather flask so small that it lay like a chestnut in the palm of his hand, plugged with a bone stopper carved into the likeness of a tiny snarling head—human or animal, there was no telling which. The thing had an almost palpable smell of wickedness, and he took care not to interfere with the waxed thread that kept the stopper in place.

"What is it?"

"Death," Murna said.

"Poison?" He had been half prepared for that, but something twisted coldly in the pit of his stomach all the same. He stood for a few moments turning it over and over, and looking at it. Odd to see one's own death lying in the palm of one's hand. "Why have you told me this—shown me this?"

She held out her hand for the thing's return. "Because I do not think I will be using it, after all."

"After all?" Phaedrus, surprised and amused to find what a fool he was, gave it back to her.

She sat cradling it in her hands and looking up at him between the falls of mouse-gold hair. "You have changed in seven years. The Midir I knew when I was a child would have let Gault have his burning without another thought—unless it seemed to him amusing to pit his strength against Gault's and he chanced to be in need of amusement just then."

"And how do you know that I did not chance to feel in need of amusement today?"

For the first time there was the shadow of a smile in her face.

"Did you?"

"No."

"And most assuredly, if it had been like that, the Midir I knew would not have troubled himself to lie to me."

"I was a boy, seven years ago. Boys do change, growing into men."

"It is more than that—another kind of change."

"You have said 'the Midir I knew' twice, but in truth you were little more than ten when your mother put an end to that Midir. You were never knowing much of him, were you, Murna?"

Her face tightened, and for a moment he wondered if she was going to fly out at him for that word of her mother. But she let it pass. "I knew maybe better than others guessed at; more than you remember. But you were never one to care much what you broke, or even remember the breaking of it, were you, Midir?"

"Was I not? If I was never one for remembering, what use to ask me?" He dropped the light hard tone. "Tell me—if your mother's messenger had escaped, and so the thing between Gault and me today had not happened, would you have used the poison?"

"In the day that I have a use for poison," Murna said simply, "I have no need that my mother should send it to me."

She snapped the thread and pulled out the bone plug; and poured the contents of the tiny flask into the heart of the fire, then dropped the flask itself after it. The fire spat like an angry cat, and a bluish flame leapt up, wavered, and slowly died out.

As it did so, Murna picked up the ivory comb and rose, wrapping the folds of her cloak about her. "Sa, there is no more that I came to say. Brys will be within call, I do not doubt, like the good well-trained hound he is."

And she was gone.

Phaedrus did not at once call his armor-bearer, but stood staring after her, a frown bitten deep between his brows, trying to make sense of many things that he did not understand, his own feelings among them.

13 | *War Dance*

THE SNOW WAS SHRINKING IN THE LOWER CORRIES OF Cruachan, and the nights were alive with the green sounds of running water and the mating calls of curlew flighting in from the high moors, when the Caledonian Envoy came.

The Lord of the Dalriadain received him and his escorting nobles seated on the High Place of black ramskins in the Fire Hall, with a group of the Companions about him; made them welcome, feasted them as honored guests, and afterwards bade his harper play for them. The pretense must be kept up that the green juniper branch in the Envoy's hand really meant that he came in peace.

But the knowledge of what was going forward, and the presence of the Caledonian nobles in their ceremonial cloaks of wild-cat skins was like a thin dry wind blowing round the Hall, and a mood was rising in the young men that needed more than harping. The Companions had begun to make another kind of music of their own, little Baruch beating out the rhythm with an open palm on one of the cooking pots, others taking it up from him, clapping and stamping it out on the beaten floor where they had kicked the fern aside. And six or seven of the young warriors spilled out onto the paved dancing space and began to crouch and stamp in a hunting dance, among the very fringes of the fire.

Diamid of the devil's eyebrows was the hunted, the rest were the hunters—men or hounds, it made no difference. The quarry fled from them, and turned back to them to dance, as it were, with his own death, and fled from them again, drawing them after him; and the hunters followed, miming the chase to that wild throbbing rhythm of stamping feet led by the strangely bell-like drumming of Baruch's open palms on the cooking pot, until the Old Magic filled the Fire Hall and Phaedrus could have sworn that the roof had become the interlaced branches of forest trees, and the shadows of the dancers, spun outward by the fire, were the shadows of a flying stag and a pack of hounds. They danced the kill, the rhythm rising to fever pitch, closed in about the panting quarry and pulled him down, and ran in with their spears. The drumming ceased, as though cut by the spear thrusts, and the dancers stood laughing and breathless, the mystery dropping from them like a cloak so that they were no more than young men, who had been letting off some of the pent-up strain in the air.

But now the mood was on them, and soon the dancing began again, the dancers constantly changing, until the whole night seemed to dissolve into stamping and whirling figures, and even the older men were adding their bit to the heady rhythms beaten out for the dancers.

But presently, in a pause for breath, Forgall the Envoy, seated beside Phaedrus, turned to him with an air of scarcely veiled boredom and said, "Tell me, is it not the custom with the Dalria-dain, as it is with us, for the women to dance also?"

"It is, when it pleases them," said Phaedrus.

"It is in my mind that I would gladly see your women dance. It would be interesting to me to see how they compare for skill with the women of my own people. Will you send word to the women's quarters, that maybe it will please them now?"

Phaedrus was suddenly furious at the cool demand so thinly masked as a request. The Women's Side did indeed dance when it pleased them, but for a stranger within the gates to demand it of them was an insult, and he very much doubted if this Caledonian noble with the full mouth and insolent dark eyes was ignorant of the fact. But before he could speak, Murna, who had led the other women all evening in keeping the mead horns filled, and now sat at his other side, erect and indrawn as usual under the moon headdress, said in a clear high voice, "It is not for my Lord the King to send such a message to the women's quarters. But since our guest would have it so, I will send the word." She looked across the great round Hall to where the few women who yet remained—old ones for the most part—had gathered in a little knot before the doorway. Grania, one of the women, came at her call, and was given some murmured instructions, and went out. And the young warriors lounged back to the places and pastimes they had left earlier, to fondle a hound's ears or start a game of knucklebones with a comrade. Phaedrus sat coldly raging under his best Arena smile. That this Envoy should have dared. ... That Murna should have made it impossible for him to thrust the insult back down the man's throat. ... But of course she would have been eager to avoid that; she was Liadhan's daughter, part Caledonian herself; probably the man was her kin.

There was a sound of women's voices and running feet outside, and a knot of girls came in through the foreporch, flinging off hastily donned cloaks. Their skirts were already hitched knee high, and each girl carried a dirk in her left hand and another thrust into her belt or girdle. The woman whom Murna had sent had returned with them, and she also carried two dirks; but clearly she was not going to dance, for her gown still fell in straight folds to her ankles, and in her free hand she held a long elder pipe.

Murna rose in her place, and called in a clear hard tone to the girls by the door. "The guests in our Hall would have us dance for them, my sisters. So—let us dance."

One of the girls, a dark, fierce creature, laughed as though sharing a harsh jest that their hearers did not understand as yet. "We will dance for them, Murna the Queen—as we used to dance when we called ourselves the wild cats, and went to the practice grounds together."

And as they came forward between the crowding warriors, Murna walked out, kilting her skirts through her bronze studded belt as she went, to join them on the dancing floor.

For a long moment the silence in the Hall was so intense that all men could plainly hear the faint chiming of the row upon row of tiny hanging silver scales that, stitched onto the tall leather headdress, made up the Moon Diadem. She held out her hands, and the older woman came and put the two dirks into them, before she moved aside with her pipe and settled down with her back against one of the seven great roof trees.

The dancers formed a wide-spaced ring about the fire, each girl with the blade of her left-hand dirk lying across the blade of her neighbor's right, and as the first notes of the elder pipe thrilled out, began to move slowly round the fire, with little short weaving steps. So far it all seemed very childish and pretty, Phaedrus thought, still coldly angry, though one might have expected the girls to be linked by a garland or a colored ribbon rather than by crossed daggers, and he wondered why every man in the Hall caught a quick breath and sat more upright; why Conory muttered, "Gods! The wild cats indeed!"

At first there had been no sound but the piping and the light pad of the dancers' feet on the flagstones; then, one after another, the men began to pick up the rhythm as they had done before, and the rhythm itself was changing from white to red, growing fiercer, more urgent. The dirk blades pointed now up, now down, began to nuzzle each other, blade licking round blade as though each had a life of its own. Faster and faster, the blades flickered and leaped, the shadows spun ... and then the circle seemed to break off its own spinning, and instead of a ring of dancing girls, there were seven pairs of young warriors. And Phaedrus understood the sudden tensing in the Hall. He was watching a war dance of the Women's Side.

He was watching, too, a Murna whom he had never seen before, whom he had never known existed. Murna with her face come to life, and a tense laughter in every line of her, dancing out her mimic battle with the dark girl, so close to where he sat that he could have reached her in one stride and pulled her out of the dance. He wondered for a passing moment if she would turn those leaping daggers on him if he did, then knew that far more likely she would simply change back into the Murna he knew, the cold, unreachable Royal Woman, between his hands. And another kind of anger sprang up in him, a raging helplessness that he did not understand; but then he understood scarcely anything to do with Murna.

All round the circle the long knives whirled and darted, flashing their deadly interlacing patterns in the flame light; the pipes shrilled higher and higher against the throbbing rhythm that the men were stamping out from the shadows, and the ring of blade on blade. And then at last, in each pair of warriors one girl dropped to her knees and flung herself round and backward, to lie with outspread arms, radiating like the petals of some great dagger-tipped flower from the fire that was its heart, while the other made the victory leap high across her body, and the dance was over.

The vanquished sprang to their feet again, the dark girl picking a stray bracken frond out of her hair. And Murna tossed her two dirks back to the woman who had piped for them, and left the dancing floor without a backward glance, freeing her skirts as she did so. She was the cold Queen again; even the Moon Diadem, held secure by the thongs that knotted it into her braids, was not a hair's breadth out of place. To the Envoy she said, still breathing quickly, "Can your women do better, across Druim Alban?"

The Envoy also was breathing quickly, and there was a curious line of whiteness round his nostrils. "Beyond Druim Alban it is not usual for women to dance the war dance for a guest who comes in peace."

"And on this side of Druim Alban it is not usual for a guest to demand that the women should dance for him at all," Murna said gently.

"There are those, among my people, who might count such a choice of dance for an insult." The man rose to his feet, drawing his catskin mantle about him, and stood flicking the peace bough of green broom as an angry cat flicks the tip of its tail.

But Phaedrus was up in the same instant. "An insult for an insult, shall we say, and cry quits?" and before the man could answer, he reached out and caught Murna by the wrist. "Come, my Queen. It grows deep into the night, and we must remember that our guests have had long journeying and will be taking the home trail tomorrow. My Lord of the Green Branch, may you and your Companions have sound sleeping in the guest huts; we meet here again in the morning."

With the general sound of rising and breaking up behind them, he said again, "Come, my Queen," though indeed there was little need of the order for his hold was still on her wrist; and for the first time since he had pulled the red mareskin mask from her face, they left the Fire Hall together, and by the curtained doorway giving on to the huddle of linked huts that made up the women's quarters.

In the empty Queen's Place, when he had roughly ordered out the Queen's bondwomen who waited for her there, Murna said, "And now, will you be letting go my wrist, Midir?"

She had left the Hall with him as though his hold on her wrists had been only the lightest touch, and he had not realized until that moment that he was still gripping it, and gripping it with an angry strength.

He let go instantly, and as she drew away, he saw in the light of the seal-oil lamp the darkening bruises that his fingers had left. Any other women, he thought, would have been cherishing her wrist, but not Murna. And most of his anger went out, leaving only the baffled helplessness behind.

"I am sorry," he said, "I did not mean to hurt you."

"Did you not?" she said, without interest, and turned from the subject. "There is something you would be saying to me?"

"Murna, why did you do that?"

"Make our dance for the Lord Envoy?"

"Yes."

"Because he called for the Women's Side to dance. Would you have me refuse the demands of an honored guest within the gates of Dun Monaidh?"

"Maybe not. But need you dance yourself? You who are the Queen?"

"I could not be asking the other women to dance at his call, and myself refuging behind my queenship."

"Sa, you have an answer for everything. But why in the name of Thunder choose the war dance?"

Her eyes widened gravely. "Oh, my Lord, would you have me accept his insult for the Women's Side? 'An insult for an insult.' You said as much yourself. Ah now, it will make no difference to the terms they offer. The Caledones do not bargain. That man will have come over our borders already knowing to the last word what it is that he will say tomorrow." Her voice was scornfully consoling. "We have nothing to lose, my Lord of the Horse People, by spitting an insult or so back at them."

"That I know well enough; no need that you should speak me gently like a child afraid of the dark. However long they talk tomorrow, with spring, they will take the war trail, and so shall we." He laughed. "Na, it was a fine war dance, and you are as skilled with the dirk as your mother with poison. I did not know the danger I was in, when I pulled the bridal mask from your face, my Royal Woman!"

Maybe that would get through her guard, make her drop the mask again. But nothing moved behind her face; only a waft of blue peat-smoke, side-driven by the wind through the smoke hole, fronded across between them, and she avoided his jibe with the cool skill of a swordsman. "I was afraid that the skill would have left me, for it is long since I danced the dirk-dance with my wild-cat sisters. But it came back to me well enough. None the less, it is in my mind that I shall go down to the practice grounds again tomorrow."

He looked at her, frowning, not quite sure of her meaning, and she half smiled. "There will be many of the Women's Side brushing the rust off their spear-throw, in the next moon or so. Did you not say that when the spring came the Caledones and the Dalriadain would both be taking the war trail?"

"The war trail is for the Men's Side," Phaedrus said quickly.

"When there are men enough. The Caledones are a great tribe and the overlord of other tribes; we are a small people still. You will need the women on this war trail."

"None the less, we shall ride without them as long as may be. If a warrior chooses to take his own woman with him into battle, that is his affair, and hers; I shall not call out the wild cats, or any other of their kind."

"Why?" she demanded. "Why go against the custom when you have most need of it?"

"In the world I come from—" Phaedrus began, and caught back the slip. "In the world where I have been these seven years, war is men's work, and the women bide at home."

"You allow them to bear the sons for it, of course? That is generous of you. But otherwise—the sword for you, and the loom and the cooking pot is all that concerns the women. How glad I am that I do not belong to the world where you have lived for seven years!"

She had begun to unfasten the thongs that secured the moon headdress, and it seemed that she had only half her attention to spare from the fastenings. Phaedrus, watching her, thought, in the way that one does think of small unlikely things in the middle of something else, that they must have cut the thongs on the night that she took the diadem from her mother and wore it in her stead. And the thought of that night hardened him against her. He said, "Be very sure of this—if the time does come that I must send the Cran-tara among the war bands of the Women's Side after all, still I shall not call for the Royal Woman—remembering that she is *Liadhan's daughter!*"

Her eyes dilated, like Shan's when she was angry, became enormous, and full of light. "How *dare* you speak so to me!" she whispered. "To me, the Queen!"

"Do not be forgetting it was I that made you the Queen."

"Was it? To me it seemed rather that by marrying me, the Royal Woman, you gained the Kingship that you could not have held without me!"

Phaedrus's hands shot out to catch and shake her. "You cursed vixen. ..."

But he never began the shaking. She stood quite still, the cool brilliant stare meeting his. "Yes, that is much better, much more the man I should have expected to flower from the Midir I knew!"

And Phaedrus dropped his hands to his sides, and turned with a curse, and strode out of the Queen's Place.

Next morning, in the Fire Hall, the demands of the Caledonian Envoy were clear and simple. Liadhan the Queen was to be set back in her rightful place, to rule as Goddess-on-Earth over all Earra-Ghyl. Conory, the Chosen One, was to take his rightful place also, at her side. The Tribe was to turn again to the Old Ways and the Old Worship.

"And myself?" Phaedrus inquired, interested. "Liadhan the She-Wolf and Conory the Captain of my Guard have both their places made ready for them; what place then, in all this, for me?"

"For yourself, the word of King Bruide is this; that you go free, so long as you go far from here. If you set foot again in the hunting-runs of the Dalriadain, then death, for you and for those who raised you to the place where you sit now," the Envoy said insolently.

Phaedrus wondered with a detached interest just how far he would get on his way into exile before he met with a fatal accident or simply disappeared. He looked Forgall in the eyes, and laughed; it was a laugh that surprised himself, short in the throat, and cold. "For myself, I am the Horse Lord! I have seen enough of wandering these past seven years, and have no mind to turn wanderer again. For Conory my Captain, if he chooses, he is free to go back with you to this Goddess-on-Earth and be her seven-year King; but he shall not be seven-year King among the Dalriadain!"

Conory, standing just behind him, with Shan in her favorite position curled across his shoulder like a fur collar, bent forward with lazy grace and spat into the fire, and the cat, startled at the sudden movement, dug in all her claws, her ears laid back and her pink mouth open in a soundless snarl. "Sa sa, we are generally of one mind, you and I," Conory murmured to her, gently detaching a claw that had drawn blood.

"As for Liadhan, once the Royal Woman of the Tribe, who without right calls herself Queen: death on the day she sets foot in the hunting-runs of Earra-Ghyl." Midir's anger was rising in Phaedrus's throat, and he had lost all sense of playing a part, as he leaned forward to stare contemptuously into the dark face before him. "That is the answer that you may carry back to Bruide your King—and to the She-Wolf who calls herself Queen of the Dalriadain!"

The eyes of Forgall the Envoy were dark and opaque, as those of the Old People, whose blood ran strong in the Caledones; but little red sparks glowed far back in them, and his face was beginning to have the same pinched whiteness round the nostrils that had been there last night in the Fire Hall. "The claim of Liadhan the Queen holds good according to the Ancient Law. It is yourself, Midir Mac Levin, no more than the son of a son of a son, who sit where you have no right to be! You have forsaken the Mother and the True Way to follow strange Gods, and the curse of the Cailleach lies on such as you—on all the Dalriadain who would seek to drive her from her rightful place in the heart of men!"

"Listen," Phaedrus said, "listen, little man, for the Epidii, and the Old People before them, the way was the Old Way; but it is we, the Dalriadain, who rule now in Earra-Ghyl, and for us the way is a different one. Before ever we came over the Western Seas, we made the Noon Prayer to Lugh Shining-Spear, and called to him on the trumpet of the Sun; and our kings were the sons of kings, and not merely the mates of Royal Women. For us, that is the way. Shall we therefore come to you and say, 'You shall turn away from the Mother—you shall cast out your King Bruide who rules only because he wedded the Queen's daughter, and set in his place Conal Caenneth, who is your last King's son; and you shall follow our way because it is *ours*?' The Caledones are a free people, and so are the Dalriadain, and being a free people they ask no leave to breathe under the sky, from the dwellers beyond Druim Alban!"

"Bold words," the Envoy said, "bold words from a small people to a great one!"

" 'Whoever came away whole by bowing his head to the wolf,' " Phaedrus quoted roughly. "Listen again—it would be a fine thing for the Caledones that you set your kinswoman back in the High Place of the Dalriadain and keep her there with your swords, and a fine hold it would be giving you over this tribe for so long as the Sun rises in the East and the wheat springs in the ground. You have gained other vassals so. But the Dalriadain are not minded to be vassals of yours, and we are a stubborn people, little like to change our minds."

"And that is the last word you have to say?"

Phaedrus had meant to consult with the Council and the Kindred before making an end. But he scarcely remembered even that they were there in the great Fire Hall. "That is my last word. Yes."

There was a long silence. Then the Envoy took one step back, and ceremoniously broke the branch of broom, and threw the pieces into the fire.

"Whet your spears, then, Midir of the Dalriadain."

"The spears are already whetted."

14 | *Chariots in the Pass*

THE STORM THAT HAD BURST UPON THEM IN THE NIGHT HAD cleared the air, and high overhead the clouds drifted against a sky of clear rain-washed blue, trailing their shadows after them across the mountains. But here in the low-lying stretch between the river and the alder woods, with Beinn Na Stroine heaving its slow height out of the woods ahead of them and Cruachan still white-maned with snow in the high corries, filling all the world northeastward, the air barely stirred. The heat shimmered over the ground, though spring had scarcely turned yet to summer, and the gadflies fidgeted weary men and still more weary horses unbearably. Head after head was tossed impatiently, hooves stamped and tails swished all down the chariot line. Brys spoke soothingly to his team, holding them on a light rein. "Softly! Softly my children! It will not be long—soon there will be a wind of our going that shall blow the biters clean over Cruachan! Softly now! Softly I say!"

Phaedrus, squatting on the warrior's seat to the left of the charioteer, longed to fling off the stifling plaid fastened on his sword-shoulder with the huge buckler-pin of gilded bronze and blue enamel that was the war brooch of the Horse Lords. But the Lord of the Dalriadain, though he might go stripped to the breeks under it, did not drive into battle uncloaked like a mere foot-fighter. At least the heavy folds were some protection against the biters. Phaedrus thought that he as well as the fidgeting team could do well with the wind of their going; and meanwhile sweltered on, the sweat pricking on his forehead and lip, and the war paint running on his face.

His hand opened and shut, opened and shut, on the shafts of the three light throw-spears he held in the hollow of his bull's-hide buckler. It was two full moons since they had sent the Cran-tara through Earra-Ghyl, summoning the warriors to the hosting-place, more than one since they had taken the war trail; but in the first weeks, the fighting had been little more than a breaking surf of skirmishes and cattle raiding among the high moors that lay between Royal Water and the Firth of the War Boats, and through the steep Druim Alban glens. But today's fighting would be no mere skirmish, and Phaedrus, feeling the throw-spears in his hand, had again the old familiar sense of waiting for the Arena trumpets.

He had been in the South with the main war host, turning a thrust of the Caledones who had seized on the few hours' darkness at the black of the moon to swim their horses across the narrows of the War Boat Firth and coracle-float the light chariots over, when the word had come. Word brought by a wounded man on a foundering horse that a vast chariot horde was swarming through the Druim Alban passes, heading for the glens of the alder woods and the Black Goddess, and the ways down to Loch Abha. The light chariot bands led by old Dergdian who were on guard there would hold them—ah yes, to the last man—but it could not be long, if help did not reach them, before that last man went down. Aye, the man said, another rider had set off at the same time as himself for Dun Monaidh; they would have the word before this, for the old chariot road made swifter traveling than these accursed hills. ... Then he died.

Chariots. That would mean the Glen of the Black Goddess, steep as it was; there would be no way for chariots through the crowding alder woods. The leaders had taken hurried council, almost while the teams were being harnessed, and Gault had remained with a strong force, including all the foot-fighters, to finish with the southern thrust; and Phaedrus and Conory had taken the flower of the horsemen and chariotry and flung them northward like fighting geese, spare chariot horses harnessed as wheelers for extra speed and to fill the places of any yoke horses that foundered on the way.

The distance was less than it would be from Dun Monaidh, but, as the messenger had said, the old chariot road made swifter traveling than these accursed hills. And the storm, bursting on them last night, maddening the horses and bringing down all the hill burns in sudden spate, had held them up still further. Three days they had been on that desperate ride, and at least seven horses they had killed with the merciless speed of it. But when they had come down through the pale storm-spent dawn into the low wet country of the Loch Abha Gap, the scouts sent on ahead had found the light chariots still holding, with the reserves that had reached them yesterday, still holding but cut to pieces, and the fight already joining again after the few hours' darkness.

No time to rest the men and horses, as he had hoped to do; no time for any council. Phaedrus remembered looking over at Conory, the question and the agreement passing between them unspoken, and then giving the needful orders. He remembered the sharp trampling of hooves as the scout wheeled his pony and was off again with word to old Dergdian and the hard-pressed and dwindling chariots far up the Glen of the Black Goddess: "I send horsemen to cover your flanks; be ready to fall back when they come. We stand ready to catch you."

And almost on the heels of the messenger, the weary horse-band had been away, riding into the early mists, each man eating his morning barley bannock from the bag tied to his horse's pectoral strap as he rode.

Now, with their own morning bannocks eaten and the horses tended as best they could be, there was nothing to do but wait, here in the glen mouth, with the wide woods and marshes running to Loch Abha behind, the river guarding their left flank, and ahead of them the bare rocks and plunging bracken slopes of the Glen of the Black Goddess, shimmering in the heat.

Phaedrus had no experience, before this past few weeks, of leading a war host, but his gladiator's training and a natural trick of leadership had stood him in good stead; and now he glanced along the chariot line, taking in the placing of the rough-riding cavalry with the eye of one who had at least a fair idea of how to place his men to the best advantage. The gaps left in the chariot ranks were there to let the hard-pressed squadron through, the little companies in the rear standing ready to swing forward and close them before the enemy could follow. Phaedrus, used to the disciplines of Rome and the ordered sham fights of the Arena, had given the order for that battle-move; but the Tribesmen had never heard of such a way of fighting, and now he knew that in trying to carry it out with an undisciplined horde of chariots he was running the most hideous risk. What would happen if the gaps did not close in time was a prospect that sickened him to think of, but unless they were going to leave valiant old Dergdian and his squadrons to their fate, it was a risk that had to be taken.

A gadfly stung his wrist, and he swore and cracked his hand down on the place, and brushed the small crushed body away. And went on waiting. There should be some sign of them by now. He was straining his whole attention out ahead of him up the rocky sweep of the Glen, for any sign of movement—any sound. ...

With the air full of the soft wet rush of the river, it was hard to be sure when the first rumors of sound came at last. Suddenly, far off from the slopes of Beinn Na Stroine, a curlew rose, crying its alarm note, thin and small with distance. And away down the chariot line a pony flung up his head, and another pawed the ground, snuffing the eddy of cool air that came down the glen from the high hills of Druim Alban. A faint, formless murmuration that seemed to drift on the little stir of wind died with it into the fern, and then came again. Then clear on the heat-bloomed air broke the sound of a hunting horn. Someone still in command up there was calling back the survivors of that first heroes' stand, as a huntsman calls off his hounds.

Something—a kind of boiling and thickening of the heat haze—was gathering far up the glen; and out of it came a blink of light, and then another, sunlight on weapon or wheel hub or glittering horse-pectoral. Darkness was growing under the dust cloud, and a sound muttered out of it like thunder among the hills. It grew to the rumble and drum of wheels and hooves, the clash of war gear and the shouting of men; all the ragged turmoil of a running fight. Phaedrus, on his feet now like all the rest, could see their own chariots falling back—back. The war horn of the Dalriadain boomed hollow from the skirts of Beinn Na Stroine; and suddenly the bracken slopes below it were alive with running figures with long spears in their hands, while the cavalry came sweeping down to join their fellows covering the flanks of the hard-pressed chariot band.

They were so near now that Phaedrus could see through the dust cloud how in every chariot that still carried two men the warrior rode faced about to the pursuing enemy, spear still in hand, and shield up to guard both himself and his driver's back. They were pouring in through the gaps, like the squadrons of some terrible ghost army, tattered and bloody; chariots with only one man in them, chariots with driver and warrior slumped against the wicker side or dragged askew by one wild-eyed and wounded horse, with the harness dangling where a dead teammate had been cut free. The wild cavalry was swinging right and left toward either flank of the war host. The weary horses in the chariot line, roused by their comrades and the tumult and the smell of blood, had forgotten their weariness and were fighting for their heads. Conory, next in line, was looking to him, but Phaedrus, sweating with more than the heat now, set his teeth and held the whole war host in leash that one moment longer, until the very last of the retreating chariots were safely through; while the enemy behind them, maybe in fear of a trap, reined their horses in and swerved aside for a few moments from their charge, and the waiting bands in the rear were whipping forward to close the gap; waiting one racing heartbeat of time longer, and then, with the Caledones on the very lip of spilling forward again, raised the bronze ox horn to his lips and winded one sharp blast that flung to and fro among the hills until the high corries of Cruachan caught and flung it back, startling every shore bird in Earra-Ghyl.

But long before that last echo had died into the wild crying of curlew and sandpiper, the chariot line of the Dalriadain was away at full flying gallop to meet the onrushing hosts of the Cailleach. Phaedrus heard himself raise the war cry: "Cruachan! Cruachan!", heard it taken up and hurled back by the long-drawn battle yell of the enemy. He flung his first spear as they came into javelin range, and one of the leading charioteers went down, his plunging team bringing confusion on those behind him, and almost in the same instant the two chariot hordes rolled full tilt together, with a great shouting of men and a screaming chaos of horses; a ringing crash that seemed as though it must shake the very roots of the mountains.

How long they struggled there in the mouth of the glen, the whole battle mass swaying now this way and now that, Phaedrus never knew. Time was not time any more, it passed with the speed of a lightning flash, and yet it seemed to him that they had been fighting here all their lives, to hold the Caledones back from Loch Abha levels and the way into the heart of Earra-Ghyl.

The battle had long since lost all pattern and broken up into a swirl of scattered fighting. The whole glen was full of dust now like a vast threshing floor; the chariots careered and circled, wheel locked in wheel, while the horsemen hung on the fringes of the battle, driving in a thrust of their own wherever the chances opened, and everywhere the foot-fighters swarmed with daggers reddened to the hilt. It seemed to Phaedrus that many of these on foot were women, but he had no time to think of that just then.

Ahead of him in the smother of flying dust and flung weapons, he saw a chariot covered with black oxhide, whose team of bright duns flashed back fire from their gilded pectorals in the dusty sunlight, and whose half-naked warrior, daubed with the woad and red ocher of the Caledones' war paint, wore about his neck the broad golden torque of a chieftain.

His throw-spears long since spent, the broad infighting spear in his hand, he shouted to Brys. The boy laughed and crouched lower, and the red team sprang forward from the goad, scattering blood-stained foam from their muzzles. The splendid chariot rushed nearer on Phaedrus's sight, almost broadside on. He nerved himself for the shock, catching one searing sight of the horses' upreared heads and flying manes, and the blue-eyed snarling face of the Caledonian Chieftain, as the darting spear just missed his shoulder; and then in the instant before the crash, the enemy team plunged away left-hand-wise and Brys wrenched the reds aside, and as one chariot hurtled across the hind-flank of the other, with no more than a thumb's breadth between wheel hub and wheel rim, for one splinter of time the enemy driver's back was exposed as he fought to get his plunging team under control. And Phaedrus drove home his spear, and dragged it out again with a satisfied grunt, and was past before he could see the man crumple forward on to the haunches of his team. *That* was a battle-move that the Tribes knew well enough. He hated the killing in the back, the first time, but he was used to it now.

A shout from Brys brought him round to see a second chariot charging down upon them. But the boy was a better driver, or maybe more fortunate, than the other had been. Almost at the last moment, he dragged the reds back on their haunches and brought them plunging round toward the onrushing team. The chariot leaped and twisted like a live thing in pain, and from somewhere under the floor came an ominous crack. They were scraping the side of the enemy war car, and it seemed that in the next instant the wheels must lock; and then, somehow, they were clear, while the other swept by and turned to charge again.

It was the driverless dun team, whose warrior, like many of his kind, had sprung down to fight on foot, that cut across and fouled the onsweeping enemy, bringing all into confusion; and in the instant before the sweating charioteer could get clear, the warrior, with a yell of rage, drew back his spear-arm and flung the great broad-headed war spear as lightly as though it was no more than a javelin. Arching high, it took Phaedrus on the temple as he flung up his shield, and sliced downward, laying his left cheek open, and tore its way out through the young red beard along his jaw bone.

For one terrible moment, as half his sight went out in red darkness, brought to his knees and clinging to the chariot rail, he thought his left eye had gone. Then as he freed one hand and flung it up to his face, he realized that he was only blinded by blood.

He heard Brys shouting something, and he spat blood, and shouted back above the tumult "Na—I am well enough," but from the feel of it, the chariot was far from well enough; some vital lashing had given under that terrific strain, and it was little fit for more fighting that day.

Phaedrus had got himself to his feet again, wiping the blood out of his eyes with the back of one hand as strength came back to him. "Only a gash. Much mess but little matter. Try to keep near me, but above all, hold the horses out of trouble," and drawing his sword, he sprang down to meet the Chieftain in the gold torque, who came roaring in on him again.

The battle had swept them closer to the river than he had realized, and on the bank above the yeasty water, they met and locked in combat, while the battle swung to and fro about them. They fought close, each with his back to his own hunting-runs. The Chieftain attacked with the courage of a wild boar, but against his tremendous strength and two good eyes, Phaedrus could set those four years of the Gladiators' School. The two things canceled each other out and made the fight an equal one. And the fierce joy rose in him, and with it a kind of fever-haze, so that he was scarcely aware of making his kill at last, only of a different enemy before him, a younger and lighter man who sprang in and out like a dancer as he fought, making the Horse Lord suddenly aware that his own feet were growing slow and his sword arm heavy. He knew that deadly creeping weakness from an earlier time, and the shouting and hoof thunder and the clangor of the war cars all about him blurred for an instant into the roar of the Circus crowd. He shook his head to clear it, and saw the steep fall of the river bank almost beneath his feet; and the dark flash of his enemy's blade coming at him like death made visible—and dived in under the man's guard, driving his point up under the buckler rim.

The Caledonian's eyes widened suddenly, with a puzzled look in them, his guard flew wide, and with a choking cry he crashed backward down the bank, almost dragging Phaedrus with him by the sword still in his body. Phaedrus flung himself back on his heels, and the blade came clear with a grating of metal on bone and a gush of blood, and as the man disappeared with a splash, he stumbled round, his sword reeking to the hilt, to face whatever came next.

A knot of enemy horsemen was bearing down on him. In the shifting patterns of battle he had long since become separated from the Companions, and Brys was nowhere to be seen; and in all the dreamlike chaos, he realized with a small cool certainty that this was the end of his fighting, and prepared to take as many of his new assailants with him as might be when he went down.

And then with a thunder of hooves and a whirling clangor of wheels, and a yelling that might have come from the dark throats of devils, three war cars of the Dalriadain were sweeping toward him. He turned and stumbled to meet them. He saw a hand with bead bracelets on its wrist like a woman, and caught it—or was caught by it—as the foremost chariot swept by, and half scrambled, was half dragged aboard, the horses scarcely slackening their wild career.

The wind of their going cleared his head somewhat, and he realized for the first time that the eternity of surging to and fro over the same ground was over, and the tide of battle had set all one way; up the Glen of the Black Goddess, away from the Loch Abha levels, and back—back—toward the hills that bordered Caledonia!

The Caledones were breaking almost everywhere, falling back and streaming away, save here and there where some knot of warriors cut off from their fellows turned to go down fighting. There were broken chariots among the fern and the trampled wreck of young foxgloves; dead horses, dead men, and the pursuing chariots swept over the bodies of friend and foe alike. It was Phaedrus's first experience of driving at speed over a spent battlefield; the wheels lurched and bucketed over corpses in the bracken, and came up with the iron tires wetly red, blood splashed up at the axletree and even forced its way between the leather straps of the floor, and he wanted to lean over the chariot rail and be sick; but he swallowed the vomit in his throat and got to his feet, holding to the side of the chariot. He was the King, the Horse Lord, leading the victorious pursuit that spread behind him and on either side. He shook the blood out of his eyes and looked around at them, and it seemed to him that there were fewer than he expected.

There was another sound in the air; the screeching, venomous war song of a wild cat, and looking down, he saw Shan, her tufted ears laid back and tail lashing behind her, crouched along the yoke-pole, where she always rode in battle. Conory himself was driving, crouched low on wide-planted feet, with the reins knotted round his body, as many of the charioteers drove, so as to have a hand free for his spear.

Phaedrus demanded thickly through shut teeth, "Where is Brys my charioteer?" But in his heart it was all those others he asked for as well.

"Somewhere behind us with a spear hole in his thigh," Conory said. "Mine is dead. You must be making do with me for your charioteer this time," and he crouched lower yet over the haunches of the team, calling to them by name. "Come on now, Whitefoot—Wildfire! They run now; keep them running! Drive them as the wind drives the storm clouds from Cruachan crest—so shall thy mares be proud to bear thee many sons!"

It became a kind of song in Phaedrus's head, a triumph song that rose and fell with the hideous war song of the great cat. The fog of unreality was thickening all about him, so that he knew nothing very clearly any more, save for the smell of blood and the fiery throbbing of his wound. Certainly not how the hunt ended, or who gave the order to call the hunters off.

But suddenly there was no more tumult, no more lurching chariot floor under him; and he was sitting on the stinking yoke-pole, while the spent horses with hanging heads and heaving flanks were led away. Someone was bending over him, holding a cold wet cloth to his face, and a voice said, "He's left his beauty behind him up the glen, I'm thinking." And another answered, "The bleeding has slacked off, anyway, and that will be the chief thing." And then a third voice—he thought that both it and the hand holding the wrung-out cloth were Conory's—said, "Gods! He's come near to losing that eye!"

And he wondered, as though he were wondering it about someone else, what would have happened if he had. Did one eye count the same as both, where the kingship was concerned?

Someone was holding a flask of mead to his mouth. The rim jolted against his teeth, and he raised his head and tried to suck the drink between them. His face was set rigid as though with a grinding cramp, and a little of the fiery stuff came out again through the great torn place in his cheek. But he managed to swallow a few mouthfuls, and the fog seemed to roll back a little.

He looked about him through the sick throbbing that seemed to pound inward from the wound and fill his whole head, and saw that it was evening, the shadows lying long across the woods and marshes; Cruachan towering sloe-dark against the sunset, with gold and purple storm clouds flying like banners from its crest. Across the level toward Loch Abha the shadowy scrub was alive with camp fires, and between the fires the horses were tethered to their chariot rails. But again, it seemed that there were surprisingly few of them, fewer of everything, chariots, horses, men—many fewer men. ...

Phaedrus made to struggle to his feet, but someone pushed him down again by the shoulders. "Bide still, the Healer Priest is coming."

He shook his head, and put up an exploring hand to the ruins of his left cheek. "It is scarcely bleeding now. Let you give me that clout to take with me, and I'll do well enough." The words came thick and slurred between his teeth, for his throat and even his tongue were swollen.

"Wait for the Priest."

"That can come later. I've other things to do now—and so has he."

But the hands were on his shoulders still, and he was too weak to rise against them. Instead, he asked after a moment, "What of Dergdian's chariot bands?"

And the voice of Dergdian himself answered him. "Here in the camp, and wolfing stirabout—those that are left of us."

Phaedrus heaved up his head—it was so heavy he could scarcely lift it—and saw the old warrior bending over him. "We—came as fast—as we could."

"Surely," the other nodded.

"And the rest of us? There—seem so few."

There was a small, leaden silence, and then Conory said with an odd gentleness quite different from his usual silken tone, "It is in my mind that the Caledones have their wounds to lick, too—more and deeper than ours."

"Ours are deep enough, seemingly! Na, I must—see for myself—" Phaedrus gathered whatever strength was still in him, and lurched to his feet. "Take your hands away—I must—see. ..."

They let him go, and he never knew that Conory was close behind him as he stumbled away toward the nearest fire.

Before he reached it, a voice called weakly, "My Lord! My Lord Midir!" and he checked and looked round. Only a few paces away, his red horses were tethered to the rail of what remained of the Royal Chariot, a few armfuls of cut grass piled before them, and close beside them lay young Brys, straining up on to one elbow, blood still seeping through the strips of someone's cloak that had been bound about his thigh.

Phaedrus turned unsteadily in his tracks and doddered toward him. "Lie still, you'll start bleeding—like a pig again if you—writhe about like that. And—we've lost enough men as it is, seemingly."

"My Lord, I—" the boy glanced at his bandaged thigh. "I got this, and—when I could get up again, I had lost you—and I wasn't good for much more, save to get the horses out of harm's way."

"You did that finely, and there was—no more you could do. Ach now, lie still, will you—I'll be wanting my charioteer another day."

He tried to grin, but his whole face seemed set rigid as though clay had been plastered over it, and pain clawed at the wound, almost blinding him again, and he turned away quickly, so that the boy should not see.

The sudden turn set the world spinning round him. For a moment the camp fires swam into a bright sun wheel, and a roaring cavern seemed to open in his head. And then straight in front of him, but a long way off, he saw a face. A face that was curd-white under the colored streaks of war paint, with the eyes in it so dark that they seemed to cast a shadow over all. And he saw without the least surprise that it was Murna's.

He did wonder vaguely why she looked like that, not knowing what he looked like himself, blood-stained from head to foot, and with that terrible torn face like a ragged crimson mask. Without knowing what he did, he started toward her, and the ground tipped under his feet and began to slide away. Somebody caught and steadied him—and in the same instant Murna was there, and above the roaring in his ears, he heard her say, "Give him to me." Her arms were round him, and he felt her brace herself under his weight as his knees gave under him and he slipped to the ground. She was kneeling beside him and holding him as he leaned against her with his broken and bloody face in the hollow of her shoulder.

The world steadied again, and he pulled his head up with a great effort, leaving dark stains on the shoulder of the boy's tunic she wore. And then a thing happened that seemed surprising afterward, but at the time did not surprise him any more than finding her there had done. She took his ruined face between her hands and kissed him. And this time she did not feel for his dagger afterwards.

He mumbled thickly, "Now you have blood on your face as well."

"It will wash off with the war paint," she said.

15 | *"Begun among the Spears"*

PHAEDRUS LAY IN PILED BRACKEN IN THE LITTLE BRANCH-woven bothy, covered by his cloak with the worst of the blood washed out of it, and watched Murna burnishing his weapons by the light of the fire that burned before the opening. Outside, he could hear the voices of the Companions—not Loarne's voice or Domingart's, or Ferdia's,—they had gone with so many others onto yesterday's death fires, in the Glen of the Black Goddess, and their voices would not sound among the Companions again. He could catch a glimpse of Conory leaning on his spear, and Shan beside him playing some small self-contained deadly game with her own leash.

He stirred uneasily, made restless by the fever in him, though the salves of the Healer Priest and the life that he had driven into the wound through his forefingers had eased some of the pain; and Murna checked in her burnishings and looked up, her eyes anxious and questioning. It was strange how different her face looked, now that it had come to life. The same shape as it had always been, the same color, and yet even in the firelight the difference was there.

He said, "If you burnish my weapons, who will burnish yours?" It was still hard to talk, and the great wad of salve-soaked cloth that covered all the left side of his face did not make it easier. But there were so many things that he wanted to say to Murna, and he could not wait any longer.

"I lost my spear in the fighting; I've only a dirk like the foot-fighting women."

"So you called out your wild cats."

"When the word came to Dun Monaidh, we knew that there would be need of everyone who could hold a weapon."

"Even the Queen?"

"I could not be asking the other women to make the war dance, and I refuging behind my queenship," she said, almost exactly as she had said it on the night the Caledonian Envoy came. And suddenly there was a rather piteous twist to her mouth. "Not even though you forbade me because I was my mother's daughter, and not to be trusted."

Phaedrus watched in silence as she turned his shield to come at the other half of the rim. "Don't be holding that against me, Murna," he said at last. "Murna—*she is your mother!*"

"And so? Did I give you the poison at her bidding?"

"That is one thing, but to take the war trail against her is another."

"How if I say to you that the Caledones have always hated us, because they fear that one day we shall grow strong? That when Liadhan my mother fled to her own kin among them, they saw their chance and took it, and that I take the war trail against them, because I would not have them trailing their catskin cloaks lordly-wise through Earra-Ghyl?"

"I should say that you spoke the truth—but not all the truth."

"I will try again, then—I am my father's daughter as well as my mother's. Do you remember how big and warm and golden he was, before she drained him out until he was only the poor hollow husk of a man? Just such a husk as Logiore was at the end?"

"Yet it was your cloak that saved her from Conory; and you stayed behind, wearing the Moon Diadem, that she might escape."

"She was the Goddess-on-Earth."

"You believe that?"

"I did not have to believe it. She *was* the Goddess-on-Earth. I do not have to believe that you are the Horse Lord. I saw you crowned."

"Then how is it different now? If she was the Goddess then—" He checked, not knowing quite how to go on.

Murna did not answer him for a long moment, then she said in a voice so low that he could scarcely catch the words, "Maybe she lost that, when she fled—when the time came for her and she—would not make her own sacrifice."

The words made a kind of echo in Phaedrus's mind as though, somewhere, he had heard them—something like them—spoken before. But he could not remember where, or when. "If so, it is small loss," he said. "She made a somewhat ungentle Goddess."

She said patiently as though she was explaining something to a small child, "What has the Great Mother to do with gentle or ungentle? She does not *do*, she only *is*. She is the Lady of Life and Death. When a man and a woman come together to make a child, she is in it, and when a polecat finds a thrush's nest and tears the young to shreds while the parents scream and beat about its head, she is in that, too."

"And when a boy is—made away with, that another may take what is his?" Phaedrus wished that he could stop this probing, but something in himself could not stop. There were things that he must get unsnarled between himself and Murna.

She ceased her burnishing, and laid the shield aside before she answered. Then she said, "Let you believe me. I knew nothing of that until the night you came back. I knew only what all Earra-Ghyl had been told; that you were drowned in the river that runs by Dun Monaidh, and your body carried away."

Still he could not stop. "That I believe but, Murna, you were knowing, when you would have knifed me on the night I pulled the bride-mask from your face."

"What does a hunted wild thing do when the hounds bring it to bay? It turns and uses whatever weapons it has of teeth or claws or antlers."

"As simple as that," Phaedrus said, after a surprised pause.

"As simple as that. You hunted me and I was—very much afraid." Suddenly and surprisingly, she laughed, but it was laughter with a little catch in it. "No, you still do not understand, there is so much that you do not understand, Midir. Listen—my mother loved my father, and she loved Logiore, until she had sucked out all that there was in them to love. And—she loved me."

Phaedrus, a tiny chill shiver between his shoulders, reached out in the half dark and caught her hand without speaking, and she turned it over inside his until they came palm to palm and fitted.

"I can scarcely remember a time when I did not know that I must keep her out, and—I do not know how to be explaining this—I learned to go away small inside myself, where she could not reach me. I made walls to keep her out, and all these years that I have done and said and maybe even sometimes thought as she bade me, I have been safe from her behind my walls. Only, to be strong enough to keep her out—they had to keep me in. ... If I had passed, that would have broken them down, you see."

Phaedrus's hand tightened on hers. "I am trying to see. Go on, Murna."

"And then you came back and turned the world to red fire, and when you stood leaning on your sword and looked at me, after the fighting was over, I knew that presently you would come breaking through my walls, and find me, however small I had gone away behind them."

"And was that such a bad thing?"

"It is frightening, to come to life. I do not think I should be so afraid to die as I was when I knew that I must come to life."

"Does it seem so bad now, Murna?"

"No, not now. I think maybe I should have been a little less afraid if I had known—how much you have changed."

There it was again, this talk of the change in him. Phaedrus was brought up with a jolt, and found himself on the edge of dangerous ground. But he had to know. "Murna, you said before that I had changed, you said that I did not care what I broke and did not remember afterward. Murna, I *don't* remember. Tell me what I did."

There was a little pause, and then Murna said, "In the early times I had one chink in my wall. Just one. It was a tame otter. I found him abandoned when he was a cub—maybe his mother had been killed—and I reared him in secret, lest my mother should know. You found him and set your dogs on him one morning when you had nothing better to do. He didn't know about being hunted, so he was very easy to kill. Too easy, you said; there was no sport in it."

Phaedrus felt sick. "I couldn't have known! I must have thought it was a wild one," he said after a moment. "Murna, *I couldn't* have known he was yours!"

"Oh yes, you knew; I was there. But I was not ten then, a girl child of no account, and you hated and feared my mother. Maybe you did it because I was the nearest thing to her that you could hurt. But my otter was the only thing I had to love, and after, I closed up the chink, and never dared to love so much as a mouse again, for fear of what might happen to it."

So Midir had done that, and not even remembered afterwards, or he would have told him during those lessons in the cock loft at Onnum on the Wall. But though the story sickened Phaedrus, it did not hit him with any feeling of discovery about Midir, nor make him feel the bond between them any less close. Instead, he felt a sudden rush of pity for the boy who had been so much afraid—and he'd had good cause to be. And fully and freely he took the weight of that long-ago piece of wicked cruelty onto his own shoulders, not only because he had to, but because in some odd way it seemed as though by doing so he could lift it from Midir's. "Oh, Murna, I'm sorry—so sorry! It is in my heart that I deserved the dirk!"

"No," she said. "No, I know that, now. It was because you—because that boy was so afraid. We were both so afraid."

"You're not afraid any more?"

"No."

"But you're shivering—I can feel you."

"Only because I am tired." Murna made a little sound that was almost like a whisper. "I am so tired."

Phaedrus flung back the folds of his cloak with his free hand. "Then come and lie down, there's room for us both," and when she was lying in the piled bracken, he pulled his cloak over both of them, and sleep gathered him in like a tired hound after a hard day.

The wound-salves of the Healer Priest did their work, and before many days were past, Phaedrus was out with the war bands again, as sound as ever save for the great half-healed scar that dragged the left side of his face askew. He had most assuredly "left his beauty behind him up the glen"; and he knew it and did not like it, for he had been good to look at—the Arena had taught him that; a gladiator's good looks, if he had any, were part of his stock-in-trade—and now he was only good to look at if he stood with the left side of his face turned away. He caught himself actually doing that one day, and for the rest of the day the Companions wondered why he was in such a vile temper. Only Conory, whom he had been speaking to at the time, knew why. He never did it again.

But indeed he had other things than his lost beauty to think of in the months that followed.

All summer, though there were no more full battles, the fighting went on, now dying down like a fitful wind into the long grass, now flaring up in some new place, or in many places at once, as the People of the Cailleach drove in thrust after thrust, now down the Druim Alban glens, now across the fords and narrows of the Firth of the War Boats. But gradually, as summer wore on, the scattered fighting began to draw in to one point, narrowing into the country round Glen Croe that ran up northwestward from the Firth. It started with a skirmish there, no greater, as it seemed, than a score of others that had gone before, but where the Caledonian war bands had been driven off, others, many others, came spilling back. Quite suddenly it seemed that the country for half a day's trail up and down the Firth shore was swarming with them. And always there was enough going on elsewhere to make sure that Phaedrus could not concentrate his whole war host to the one task of driving them out. The dwindling war bands of the Dalriadain swept down on them again and again, but even when for the moment they were driven back, almost before the defenders of Earra-Ghyl could draw breath they were flooding in again, more and always more, until it seemed to Phaedrus and Conory and grim bowlegged Gault, struggling to hold the whole coast line of the Firth against them, and close the narrow lands between the Firth-head and the loch of Baal's Beacon, that they were springing out of the ground like the war hosts magicked from puffballs and thistle stalks of which the ancient legends told.

The whole glen was theirs now, and the heights on either side, and they held the old forsaken strong point of Dun Dara on the high shoulder of Beinn Na Locharn that commanded the pass through the mountains to Royal Water. Soon, when they were just a little stronger, they would come pouring over that pass, and now that they held the coast all about Glen Croe mouth, there was little to stop them from bringing over every warrior they had.

The leaders looked at each other with one question in their eyes. How much more strength had the enemy still in reserve? It was as the Envoy had said: the Caledones were a great people and the Dalriadain a small one; the Caledones had other tribes to call on, while the men of the Western coasts and islands had only themselves, and had come to the end of their reserves, even the boys and women. Yet surely even the Caledones must come to the end of their strength one day. ...

But for Phaedrus, that wild and bitter summer had a kind of broken-winged happiness of its own. All through the long night rides and the swift bloody fighting, while the rowan trees blossomed and the blossom fell into the hill burns running low with drought, Murna rode with him and Conory among the Companions, proving herself as hardy and as skilled with the throw-spear as any of the young warriors. And at night among the steep glens and wooded hollows of the moors, or in some hill dun long since cleared of cattle and all else that could be driven or carried away, when the warriors slept with their spears beside them and their shields for pillows, she spread her own cloak on the ground between the wheels of the chariot for Phaedrus to lie on, and lay down beside him with his cloak to cover them both. And there were times when they would laugh together at some foolish jest; and once when there was a night attack on the chariot ring, they fought together behind one shield.

But as summer drew on toward its end, and the heat-parched

heather began to fade, Murna had a look about the eyes that Phaedrus did not understand—and he knew the looks of her well enough by then. He wondered if the sword-cut she had taken across the ribs a few weeks back was troubling her. But when he asked, she laughed and showed him the place, and he could see that it was cleanly healed.

He told himself that he was imagining things, and turned his whole mind toward gathering the remains of the war host for what all men knew must be the last battle.

Through those last crackling, drought-baked days of summer, they gathered in from the scattered ends of Earra-Ghyl; war bands brought up to strength with men who were too old for fighting and boys who were too young, hastily mended chariots drawn by unmatched horses, each the survivor of some other team. They gathered in the steep glens northward of Dun Dara, and in the midst of them the Horse Lord and the men of Dun Monaidh made their great chariot ring on the grassland slopes of Green Head.

And then one morning, with the last battle, as it were, already brewing, Murna disappeared when the scouting chariots were being harnessed. And Phaedrus, going in search of her, found her crouched beside the low-running hazel-fringed burn, being very sick. He squatted down and held her head for her, just as he would have done for Conory or young Brys, and waited until the spasm was over and she was gathering up palmfuls of the cold peat-brown water and bathing her face. Then he demanded urgently, "What is it? Are you ill?"

She turned to look at him, with the color creeping back into her face, smiling at him a little behind her eyes. "No, I am not ill. But it seems that I must turn to women's work after all. I am carrying a child for you, Midir."

•

It was a time of lull, one of those uneasy lulls that come on the edge of fighting, or he would have sent her away at once. As it was, there were a few hours more, and the scouts reporting no signs of movement from around Glen Croe, Phaedrus was even able to leave the war host for a little while, to set her on her way.

And so at about the same time next day, they stood together on a ridge of high moors a mile or so westward of the main host, to take their leave of each other, while the small escort of Companions who were to take her back to Monaidh waited at a little distance. Early as it was, the sky arched, cloudless and already heat-pearled, over hills that were shadowed with fading heather or tawny as a hound's coat; a warm dry wind went blustering across the moors, making a sea-sound in the dark glen woods below, and Phaedrus remembered afterwards that there was a scattering of late harebells among the furze.

Murna said almost accusingly, "Why did you come seeking me yesterday? If you had not come then, you need not have been knowing. Not yet, not for a few days more. It was only a few days more I hoped for."

And the warm wind through the furze and the impatient harness-jingle of one of the horses were the only sounds again.

A few days more. ... In two or three days now, the thing would be settled, one way or the other, and she knew it as surely as any of them, and had tried to keep her secret long enough to share the last battle with him; and part of him wished sore that she had been able to keep it; she had been a good fighting-mate.

"Let me stay, then," she said, as though she knew what he had been thinking. "Just three more days."

"They might be three days too many." He looked her very straight in the eyes. "Murna, this one time *you will obey me!*"

"Sa; this time I will obey you." There was a small wry attempt at a smile on her mouth. "I am not wanting to—but the babe is stronger than I am. And he wants to be born and live."

"He? You are sure, then, that it will be a manchild?"

"Of course. A son to lead the Horse People after you." She flung up her head and laughed, a laughter that seemed to ache in her throat. "How could he be anything else? He was begun among the spears!"

Ever since he had first known about the babe, Phaedrus had been taking care not to think too closely about the fact that Murna believed it was Midir's, but now, at her words, suddenly everything in him was crying out to tell her the truth. She had the right to know, and for himself, he felt that something at his heart's core would tear out by the roots if he had to part from her with the thing untold, raising a barrier between them. But he never must tell her; never in all his life or hers, no matter how long or how short that might be.

He put his arms round her, loosely, and carefully at first— strange that he was holding two people in the circle of his arms— then fiercely close. "Listen now: whatever happens, whether I come back to Dun Monaidh to make the victory dance, and we grow old together and watch this son who was begun among the spears become a man, or whether we are not together any more this side of the sunset—*whatever comes*, whatever you hear of me, remember I love you, my Murna."

She put up her hands and took his scarred face between them, and kissed him, and stood for a few moments straining up to rest her forehead against his. "I love you, my gladiator, that shall be helping me to remember."

Phaedrus held her tight against him for a heartbeat longer, then he almost pushed her away. "Go now, go quickly."

And she obeyed without a backward glance.

He stood and watched her going away from him through the

tawny knee-high grass between the furze, striding like a boy in her breeks and tunic, toward where the Companions waited. He saw her fling up her hand to them, and mount into the waiting chariot. ... He went on standing on the ridge, watching until a distant fold of the moors took the chariot and its little escort from his sight.

Then he turned, cursing in his heart with the dark enduring curses of the Gael, so much more potent than those he had learned in the Gladiators' School at Corstopitum, and headed back toward the camp on the skirts of Green Head.

Midway, he met Conory, strolling up through the hazel scrub with Shan's leash swinging in his hand. "You'll not have seen my striped she-devil?" he inquired. "She has slipped her collar."

Phaedrus shook his head. "Never a tail-switch of her." But he had a feeling that it was not really to look for Shan, who was skilled at slipping her collar and was sometimes away on the hunting trail for whole days at a time, that the Captain of his Companions had come that way.

"Ah well, she will come back when she has killed," Conory said, and turning about, fell into step beside Phaedrus.

They walked some way in silence, and then Phaedrus said, "Murna should be safe in Dun Monaidh within three days."

And Conory said, "She will be finding it dull in the women's quarters, after this summer, and she almost alone in there."

"The whole war host will have heard by now," Phaedrus said savagely after a moment.

"Most of them."

"It is an accursed tangle."

"Were you never thinking it was a thing that might happen?"

"Ach, I suppose so."

"And were you never wanting it should happen?"

Phaedrus said, "Murna is *my* woman—mine to me, in the way

that no woman ever was before, and it is warmth in my heart to know that we have begun the making of a child between us."

"But. ..."

"It is my child—but not Midir's."

"The few who know will keep silence."

Phaedrus made an impatient gesture. "That is the kind of thing Sinnoch the Merchant might say. Sa sa, I know it is true. They will keep their side of the bargain as I have kept mine. Besides, they have too much to lose if they let it through their teeth."

"But?" Conory said again.

"Fiends and Furies! She thinks that I am Midir," he groaned. "And I had to let her go, still thinking it."

Conory looked at him thoughtfully, as they walked. "It is in my mind to wonder—just to wonder—if she does— or if for her too, the balance of the blade was wrong, after all."

And Phaedrus stopped dead in his tracks, remembering how she had said "You" and then changed it into "That boy" when she told him the cruel story of that long-ago otter hunt. How she had said, "I love you, my gladiator," not giving him Midir's name. "You think—that?" he said very slowly.

"I don't know. You may know one day; no one else ever will."

"She would never foist a child that she knew was not Midir's onto the Tribe to rule as Horse Lord after me."

"She is a woman, not a man; there's a difference," Conory pointed out kindly. "Women will do strange things for a man, and never feel that they are breaking any faith so long as they do not break it with that one man." And after a silence, "There is this, also, that for the Tribe your son may be better than no Royal Son at all—if it is a son. Remember it will be of the Royal Blood on its mother's side, the same blood as Midir—or as Conory the Captain of your Guard, come to that."

They were moving forward again, threading the steep midge-infested hazel woods that skirted the lower slopes of Green Head, and again they kept silence for a while. Then Phaedrus laughed savagely. "It is a jest for the Gods, isn't it—Liadhan seized the rule and brought back the Old Worship and the Old Ways; and the kings killed each other and came to kingship only by marriage with the Royal Woman; and the daughters were all and the sons nothing. Then Gault and the rest of you rose against Liadhan, to bring back the ways of the Sun People, and you set me up to be Lord of the Dalriadain in her place. And what have I done? I killed the Old King and married the Royal Woman, and my son will draw his right to rule after me from his mother."

"I am not Tuathal the Wise," Conory said after a moment, "but it is in my mind that maybe all the Gods men worship blur into each other a little at the edges. It is in my mind also that there must be Earth Lady as well as Sun Lord, before the barley springs in the furrow."

Phaedrus nodded. He supposed that was the answer. All the answer there was, anyway. Meanwhile they were getting close to the camp, and there was something else he wanted to say to Conory, something that had been in his mind to say to him ever since he knew about the babe. "Conory, if I am killed tomorrow—if I go beyond the sunset before the boy comes to his time for Taking Valor, and you live after me—let you guard him and Murna for me."

"You are very sure that it will be a son."

"Murna says that it will be a son."

"The women have ways of knowing—so they say. See then, if the rule passes to a son, the old pattern is broken after all."

"And you will guard them?"

"I will swear to it, on whatever thing you choose."

"A plain promise will serve."

Conory's sweet, mocking smile was in his voice. "You forget

that I am also of the Royal Blood, and may have sons of my own one day. I will swear."

"Swear then, on the bare blade." They were both half laughing, both in earnest under the laughter. Phaedrus whipped out his dirk, and held it out to Conory as they walked. And Conory, his hand flat along the blade, swore the oldest and most binding oath of the Gaelic People.

"If I break faith with you, may the green earth open and swallow me, may the gray seas roll in and engulf me, may the sky of stars fall and crush me out of life forever."

Something had happened in the camp of the war host while they were away, maybe some news come in. It was in the very air as they came up toward the chariot lines, and glancing aside at his companion, Phaedrus saw that his head was up and his nostrils widened as though to catch an unfamiliar smell. A knot of chari-oteers parted at their approach. Phaedrus called to one of them, young Brys, who had lately returned to him, and the boy came, running lame like a bird trailing a broken wing.

"What is in the wind?" Phaedrus asked.

"My Lord Midir, it is all over the camp that the She-Wolf herself is yonder in Dun Dara!"

Phaedrus and Conory exchanged glances. "So—o," Phaedrus said softly. "The Goddess herself come to be in at the kill."

"That or. ..." Conory checked an instant, his odd eyes narrowed in thought. "Could it be that the Caledones have brought her to put fire into the hearts of their warriors? Could it be that even their strength has an end, and they are throwing in their last weapon against us?"

Phaedrus said, "We have already thrown in ours. Ah well, one way or the other, we shall soon enough be knowing."

16 | *The Last Weapon*

WHEN THE SUN WENT DOWN BEHIND CRUACH MOR TWO evenings later, the Dalriadain were once again masters of Dun Dara; and as the great hills dimmed into the dusk the old stronghold within its turf banks, and the steep slopes that dropped away from it on three sides, were red-flowered with the watch fires of the tattered war host. But away down Glen Croe the great out-thrust shoulder of Black Crag was flowered in the like way, with Caledonian watch fires, so many watch fires, even after these past two day of fighting. And the dead of the Horse People lay mingled with the dead of the Caledones all down the glen.

Sitting before the blind doorway of what had once been the Chieftain's Hall, Phaedrus put the situation into words, more to get it clear in his own mind than anything else, for the men gathered about the Council fire knew it all as well as he did. "This is the way of it, then. We have not the strength left to drive them back to their own side of the Firth; and if we pull back ourselves, leaving them Lords of Black Crag and the lower glen, they'll be over into our herding lands like a stampede of wild horses, and we'll not get them out again until Cruachan falls into Loch Abha. We can keep them penned in the glen just so long as we can hold out here in Dun Dara. But you all know how it is. This has been the driest summer that the oldest of us can remember—see how the furze flares and crackles in the flame—and they have been here before us. They have drunk the old wells dry, and the spring runs so low that it will scarcely serve to water the men, let alone the horses, and the burn is foul with the dead men they heaved into it. We can last out the few days to burn our dead and get our wounded away—no more—while they have all the Firth-head above the burn's outflow to drink dry before they feel the lack of water."

"May it rot their bellies!" growled Oscair, his big freckled hands clenched on his knees.

"If it would, that would be the solving of our problem," Phaedrus said, "but it is in my mind that we will need to be doing something about it ourselves."

Gault, with a bloody clout round his head, looked up from the fire. "And what thing would that be?"

"I do not know yet. Before we can be making any plan, we must come at surer knowledge of the numbers that yet remain to King Bruide and the defenses of his chariot ring. So, my brothers, I am minded for a little night hunting and a closer look at this camp of the Caledones."

There was a quick stir of movement among the Companions, and Diamid said, "We are with you, Midir."

Conory, who had been playing lightly with his dirk as a girl might play with a flower, sheathed it, and made a small soft throat sound to Shan beside his knee, so that she ceased washing herself and with an answering cry sprang to his shoulder. "So, all's ready. We will have a fine hunting, eh, my fanged flower?"

"Three of us should be enough," Phaedrus said quickly. "Na, not you, Finn; you're as brave as a boar, and when you move you make as much noise as one. Nor you, Cathal, with that wound only half healed. Conory, and you, Baruch; you two I take; no more."

"One more." He had already risen heedless of protests, and begun to strip off his necklaces and arm-rings, when he heard the dry tones of Sinnoch the Merchant, who had ridden in that day with his last reserves of horses, and turned to meet the faintly amused gaze under the horse trader's wrinkled lids. "If this were a war trail, I would bide quiet in the shadows, as befits a man of peaceful ways—seeing also that I am but half-born to the Tribe and carry no warrior patterns on my skin. But since it is no more than a hunting trail after all—will you take me for a fourth? I can still move with less noise than a boar, and I know these hills maybe somewhat better than the rest of you."

"The smuggling of mares has its uses," Phaedrus said. "Come then, and show us the way, peaceful merchant man."

And so in a little while, the four hunters stood ready to set out, each with the dirk in his belt for his only weapon, each stripped to the waist, his face and body daubed with fire black over the blurred war paint, and everything that could betray them by fleck of light or jink of sound laid aside. And already, in the light of the Council fire, they seemed to have become shadows; nothing quite distinct about them save for the eyes of the cat on Conory's shoulder that caught the flame light and shone like two green moons.

"We are ready? Then good hunting to us all," Phaedrus said, and the other three caught it up and answered him, "Good hunting to us all."

Sinnoch the Merchant soon proved his value, for it seemed that he did indeed know these hills as other men know the ways of their own steading-yard. They fell in with no Caledonian picket or scouting band and not much more than a Roman hour by Phaedrus's reckoning after setting out, they were crouched among the furze and bilberry-covers above Craeg Dhu, the Black Crag, peering down at the watch fires of the Caledones. Fifty fires at least, Phaedrus reckoned, covering all the great out-thrust shoulder of the hillside; and if one allowed for the usual count of fifty men to a fire. ...

"There's always the chance that they have spread the men more thinly, to make us believe them stronger than they are," Conory murmured.

"It could be. There is no telling from here. I am going in for a closer look."

"I also."

"You also—and Baruch. You are not called the Grass Snake for nothing, Baruch. Get across to the far side yonder, and see what chance an attack might stand by way of the eastern scarp. Sinnoch, let you bide here. It is best that one should stay, lest we need warning of danger, or a diversion making for us. At worst, someone to carry word of what has happened to us back to Gault."

"Have a care, then—remember that they may have dogs. Remember also that there will be watchers posted beyond sling-range of the camp."

"Sa sa, all this we will remember. Do you remember to keep your eyes and ears open for any threat behind us. Give us a vixen's scream for a danger signal, if need be."

And with the words scarcely spoken Phaedrus was creeping forward again, Conory close behind him, and the little striped shadow that was Shan slipping ahead through the bilberry cover. Baruch had already disappeared.

The furze thickened as they dropped lower, so that soon, instead of crouching from clump to clump, they were belly-crawling by narrow winding ways among the furze roots, oozing forward, hand's length by hand's length, every sense on the stretch for danger; but no warning cry came, no sudden leap of spearman or fanged war dog. In the end it seemed as though it was the furze itself that would stop them; an impenetrable wall of furze, black-dark in the light of the moon that had begun to rise. Only, as they cast about for a way through, the smell of dog-fox led them to the mouth of a fox run almost hidden among root-tangle and spiney branches at which Shan arched her back and spat, before flowing forward into it like a liquid shadow. The two men followed her. The run seemed very long, and the stink of it came up into Phaedrus's throat and almost choked him; but just as he began to feel that it must go on forever, it curved sharply downhill, and he caught a glint of firelight at the end of it, and a little later found open ground before him and one of the picket fires scarcely a spear-throw away.

He froze instantly, putting back a foot to warn Conory behind him. He felt the other's touch on his ankle in answer, and a few moments later, Conory was oozing up beside him, with infinite caution parting a spyhole for himself among the furze stems. Shan was crouching between them, and he felt the tense flick of her tail-tip against his neck; but she would make no move on her own account, not when she was hunting with Conory.

Crouching shadow-still in the furze, Phaedrus scanned the men about the picket fire for any sign of sleepiness, but they were awake and watchful, leaning on their spears and staring into the night. Well, he could see enough from here. ...

Not much out of sling-range from where they lay, Bruide's warriors had piled a breastwork of stakes and uprooted thorn bushes across the open hill-shoulder, and drawn up their char-iots just beyond, though clearly their chief defense on that side was the furze itself; while on all other sides they were protected by the steep drop to the glen woods and the river below. The Caledones had taken to themselves a magnificent defensive position, and Phaedrus cursed inwardly as he realized the hopeless-ness of any direct attack. The whole strong-place lay clear in the mingled white and ruddy light of moon and fires—and why not? he thought furiously; the People of Cailleach had no need to hide their strength, and they would be knowing well enough that even from the edge of the furze, if any of the Dalriadain should get so far, they were out of sling-range. Gods! for one Company of the Syrian Archers such as he had seen often enough ride through Corstopitum!

He could see now that the number of fires had been no bluff; the broad hill-shoulder just below him was aswarm with men; men sleeping with their shields for pillows, men wakeful and leaning on their spears. He could hear one man call to another, the whining of a tethered horse from the chariot line, the ding of hammer on field anvil where the smiths labored to repair war gear broken in that day's fighting; the ceaseless, restless stir and lowing of captured cattle. In the midst of all, beside the Great Fire, the Royal Fire, two furze-built bothies stood close together under the grim stag-skull battle standard of Bruide the King. As he strained his eyes toward them, a tall figure rose from beside the fire and crossed to one of the bothies, then turned an instant in the door hole to look up at the dark hill as though aware of eyes watching her out of the furze cover. At that distance, and muffled in the folds of a cloak, there would have been no saying if it were man or woman; not even the gleam of barley-pale hair in the fire-light told who it was, since among the Caledones, as well as the Dalriadain, many of the young warriors bleached their hair. But it was as though hate lent wings to Phaedrus's vision, and he knew Liadhan the She-Wolf as surely as though she stood within hand's reach of him. He had thought that he knew about hate before, but he had never known the kind of hate that gathered somewhere in the dry hollow of his belly as he watched; sharp and piercing hate for Midir's sake, and for Murna's, as well as a broader hate that was for the sake of the Tribe. It seemed to go out from him through the firelit camp to reach her at the heart of it, so that it was small wonder she turned as at a touch, and stood so long staring out and up into the darkness. ... Then she turned again and went into the bothy.

Phaedrus became aware of Shan crouched against his forward-thrust arm, and felt the little wicked currents running through her, and her fur lifting as she caught the hate from him. He felt a touch on his shoulder, a light backward pressure of Conory's hand that meant "Back, now." Well, they had seen what they came to see, and to wait on, so near to one of the pickets, would only be to bide looking for needless trouble. Yet everything in him revolted at the thought of crawling back up that stinking foot-run, and carrying the bitter word to the waiting war host that to attack the Caledones' chariot ring would only be to fling themselves on inevitable disaster; that nothing could come at the enemy up the sheer rocks of Black Crag or through that black tide of furze on a slope that was beyond even the chariot horses.

And then, almost in the same instant, two things happened. Out of the dead stillness that had made the air seem thick to breathe all day, a soft breath of wind came sifting down the Glen, wind that came, for the first time in many weeks, from the West. And quite suddenly, as though of its own accord, his mind said, "Fire could."

For a long moment he made no response to Conory's warning touch, while the long soft breath died away, and another, starting far up the glen, came hushing toward them through the furze. There was a stillness in him like the stillness of revelation. Tuathal the Wise had told him once that it felt like that when the Gods spoke to you. After the summer drought, the furze and parched grass and the thin scrub that wooded the glen floor would burn like touchwood, and with even a light wind behind it, would spread with the speed of stampeding cattle. ...

He yielded at last to the touch on his arm, and slid backward from the mouth of the fox-run. Conory waited an instant to slip the end of the leash coiled about his wrist through Shan's collar, and then came after. It seemed hours before at last they found space to turn round, hours more before they were heading up through the tongues and runnels of the looser furze, toward the place where they had left Sinnoch on watch.

Baruch the Grass Snake had arrived a few moments before them, but none of them spoke any word until all four were well clear and halted in a little hollow of Ben Cornish well on their way back toward Dun Dara. Then Phaedrus broke the silence at last, speaking quickly and at half-breath—even here there was no point in making more sound than need be. "There must be well above two thousand of them still in fighting shape, and from the place where Conory and I lay hid, there was no sign of any possible way of reaching them, even supposing that we could gather up enough men for an attack. How was it from your side, Baruch?"

"The same. What with the hill scarp and that black tide of furze, a few hundred could hold it easily against our number."

"So. Then what now, my children?" Sinnoch's voice was dry and crackling as autumn leaves.

A small silence took them, and in it something made Phaedrus look round at Conory. His face was in black moon shadow, but the angle of his head told Phaedrus that the Captain of his Companions had turned to look at him also. After a few moments, he said softly, "Are you thinking what I am thinking?"

"I am thinking that after this dry summer the whole country-side would burn like a torch if one of those camp fires—or even our own, up on the short grass of Dun Dara—should chance to get out of control."

"Fire!" Baruch whispered.

And the little wind freshened through the long hillside grass.

"Or if a man chanced to drop, say, a burning twig into a grass tussock," Sinnoch said reflectively.

Phaedrus nodded. "Where men cannot go, fire can," and felt the quickening attention of the other three. "A while ago, it was flat calm, but now there's this small wind rising—and from the West! A wind that's a gift from the Gods. If we fire the hillsides say up-valley—about where the westernmost burn comes down from Ben Dornich, it will be on them almost before they know it."

"The captured cattle are corralled on the western side," Baruch said. "They'll stampede, across the camp."

"Surely, and on down the glen, and with our own riders to help the fires along and deal with any breakaways, that should even the odds against us somewhat. At the least, it will clear them from Black Crag."

"Forest fire is like a wild beast on a chain," Sinnoch said, "not to be let loose lightly."

"So long as the wind holds from this quarter, we are safe; and the Firth will serve for a fire break," Conory put in.

"And if the wind changes again?"

"Baruch," Phaedrus said, "will the wind change again before dawn?—No, before tomorrow's noon?"

The little man was silent a moment, while they all watched him, his head cocked, his delicately twitching nose seeming, as it were, to finger the breeze. Then he shook his head. "Before noon it will not have died away, but it will not go round. And I think it will not die before it has had time to do its work."

"Sa. Have you ever known Baruch mistake the wind?" Phaedrus said. "We must pray to Lugh Shining-Spear that he does not begin now."

Baruch, who could be a fiend incarnate in time of fighting, but was oddly gentle before and after, said, "Forest fire moves with the speed of a galloping horse. There'll be wounded among them down there in the chariot ring, some too sore hurt to get away."

"Would the Caledones hold their hands if the thing were the other way on?" Phaedrus said ruthlessly. "If they have wounded, then their sword-brothers must do for them what we have done for our own, before now." For in case of a forced retreat, the Dalriadain had always knifed their own wounded to save them from the mercy of the enemy. Let the Caledones save their own wounded in the same way from the mercy of the fire. He looked round at the other three in the moonlit hollow. "I know what kind of wild beast fire is when one loosens it from the chain. I know it's a wicked weapon we'll be using, and a wicked hazard we'll run in the using of it, but save for making the Caledones a free gift of Earra-Ghyl, is there any other way?"

"No," Conory said after a moment, "there is no other way."

"Sa; and no moment to spare. Baruch, you are the swiftest runner of us all. Back with you to Dun Dara. Tell Gault what we have seen in the Caledones' camp, and the thing we have to do, and bid him turn out every man who can still keep astride a horse and every horse that can still put one foot before another, and send three-fourths of them to meet me in the alder woods where the westernmost burn comes down from Ben Dornich, and himself take the remaining fourth part across the river and down the north bank to the same point. And bid him also to see that five men of his band and ten of mine carry fire-pots under their cloaks."

Baruch was already crouching up with a foot under him. "Any other word, my Lord Midir?"

"Bid him ride as though the Wild Hunt were on his tail. These summer nights are short, and we must set the fire upon them before the chariot ring is astir at dawn, and be ready to throw in our attack the moment they break before the fire."

"I will tell him."

There was the faintest whisper of sound in the long grass, lost almost instantly in the soughing of the little west wind. And only the shadow of a furze bush in the moonlight, where Baruch the Grass Snake had been.

Phaedrus turned back to the other two. "We've a longish wait before us. Might as well be making up toward the meeting place ourselves; at least up there we'll be able to move freely without fear of a Caledonian scouting party on our necks, and we can be filling in some of the time gathering dry grass and branches for torches." He grinned at Conory. "I was wrong when I said we had already thrown in our last weapon; we're throwing it in now."

17 | *The Protection of Rome*

BY NOON, THE WEST WIND HAD DIED INTO THE GRASS, AND the white heat-haze danced again over the glen, over the silence and desolation that had been Glen Croe. The last weapon had done its work. The whole valley was reddened and blackened, the acrid smitch still rising here and there among the charred snags of furze and birch and alder, dead men and horses and cattle, and the jagged wreck of chariots. All across the mouth of the glen and up the Firth shore to its head lay the same trail of dead and broken things, for the coracles beached where the glen ran down to the shore had served to take off only the merest handful of the war host, little more than a bodyguard for the wild and raging woman who had been Liadhan the Queen. And for the rest, there had been the desperate, broken retreat up to the head of the Firth, and the river ford. The dead and broken things lay thickest of all about the ford; some were scattered even on the further side.

Dead of the Dalriadain among the many more dead of the Caledones. Conall and Diamid lay a little way below Black Crag, shoulder touching shoulder as they had fought, and in the mouth of the glen the women, gleaning for wounded among the slain, had found Sinnoch the Merchant: Sinnoch who had never been a warrior, who had been killed, like more than one warrior with Caledonian war paint on his face, not by enemy iron, but by the stampeding cattle. Maybe that was why his dead face had worn a look of wry amusement, as though at a bad jest, when they turned him over.

Where the slain lay thickest by the river ford, the stag-skull standard with saffron tassels torn away, propped drunkenly against an alder tree with its bronze-tipped lines entangled in the branches, marked where King Bruide had turned with his Companions—those that were left to them—to cover the retreat of his tattered war host. Presently, Phaedrus thought, they must raise a grave mound for him and his sword-brothers, when the death fires for their own fallen were burned out. The wolf and the raven could have the rest.

Sitting his borrowed roan beside Conory on a little out-thrust nab of the hillside, he looked down at that scene by the ford and drove one clenched hand into the palm of the other with sudden baffled fury. "That is the second time! Bruide was a king worth the name, and he's food for the ravens, this noon—while *she* ..." his voice strangled in his throat with loathing.

Conory, sitting oddly crooked on his own horse, said, "There will be a third time," and something, a kind of tightness in his voice, made Phaedrus look round. He saw the drawn expression about the other's mouth, but connected it, almost without thought, with the loss of Shan, for the wild cat had gone into battle with her lord as usual, and that was the last that anyone had seen of her—and his own fury claimed him again. "It looks like it, doesn't it? She'll be half across to Baal's Beacon by now, while we sit here waiting for the word of the scouts. I was wrong; we should have pushed straight on. ..."

"You were not wrong. To have hunted tired hounds blindly into those no-man's hunting-runs would have been moon madness. At least the halt will give us a while to rest and bait the horses and put something into our empty bellies that may make us feel less like ghosts ourselves." Conory laughed. "I can smell the fat smell of cooking fires; they do say that captured bullock meat tastes ever the sweetest."

"Then twice captured should be twice as sweet." No good to bide there staring down at the ford and raging. He turned his horse's head back toward their own chariot ring. "Come, then, or we shall miss our share."

Conory wheeled beside him, but as he did so a stone rolled under his horse's off forehoof and the tired beast stumbled. Conory caught his breath in a little choking gasp of pain, and Phaedrus looked round again just in time to fling sideways and catch him as he sagged forward over the horse's neck.

"Steady! What now?"

Conory managed a rather ghastly smile. "I took a spear-thrust in the hip—it must have gone—a bit deeper than I thought."

"You fool!" Phaedrus shouted at him in another kind of fury because he had already lost too many friends for one day. "You *fool!* Why were you not telling me?" Then as the other murmured something quite unintelligible, "Give me the reins. Can you hold on as far as the camp, if I steady you?"

Conory made a great effort against the deadly faintness that was turning him gray-white to the lips, and said quite clearly, through shut teeth, "I've never fallen off a horse yet."

And he did not, though he was riding blind and slumped over the horse's neck as they came up to the picket lines, and Phaedrus, riding knee to knee with him, with a steadying grip on his arm, was almost all that kept him from sliding limply to the ground.

By the nearest of the fires he reined in and called "Hai! Diamid!" before he remembered that it was no use calling Diamid any more. Two or three others came running, young Brys ahead of them, to catch the bridles as he dropped from his borrowed horse to aid Conory down.

"Nor have I ever been lifted off a horse like a screeching captive maiden," said Conory sweetly, opening his eyes which had been half closed; and he set his hands on the horse's withers to swing his sound leg over, and crumpled quietly into Phaedrus's arms in a dead faint.

Phaedrus gathered him up, shaking his head impatiently at the hands that came out to help. "Na, leave be. I have him—where are the Healer Priests?"

Aluin Bear's Paw pointed, with a hand whose back was furred with thick dark hair. "Up yonder by that hazel-tump in the loop of the burn."

Conory was extraordinarily light to carry, even unconscious. Phaedrus thought suddenly that Murna would not be so very much lighter. But the weight of his own weariness was added to the weight of the slight figure in his arms, so that he was gasping when he reached the hazel trees where several Sun Priests with their strangely crested heads were moving among the men who sat or lay there stretched out in the shade.

For one horrible moment, as he laid his friend down, Phaedrus thought that he was dead, but when he put a hand over his heart he felt it beating faintly under his fingers; and the Healer Priest who come up behind him said, "Na na, his spirit is out of his body, but it will come back."

"You are sure?" Phaedrus demanded.

A gray smile touched the Priest's face. He also was a tired man. "There is always a risk that the spirit may lose its way. I shall know better when I have seen the wound." He sent one of the women for water from the low-running stream and, kneeling down, began to cut away the plaid cloth of Conory's breeks to come at the spear-thrust in his hip, and clicked his tongue over it like an old woman, and called to a young priest for his instruments.

Phaedrus said nothing, but stood by while the wound was cleansed and salved, glad that for this while at least Conory was out of his body and need not feel the surgeon's probe that fetched out splintered bone. When the thing was finished and the wound lashed tight, he said, "Will it mend?"

The Priest looked up with a start, having quite forgotten his presence. "He'll go lame on that leg to the end of his days; but if he does not take the wound fever, he'll be astride a horse again by winter." His tired face gentled. "There's no good that you can do here, my Lord Midir. Go you and eat and get what rest you can."

Back among the cooking fires, the lumps of half-raw bullock meat were being given out to men who ate like starving wolves, or were too weary to eat at all; and one of the scouts had just come in with word of having picked up the trail of Liadhan and the small band with her and followed until it was sure that they were making for the Black Glen and the Waters of Baal's Beacon.

Phaedrus listened, gnawing his way through a great wedge of meat that was black on the outside and still dripped red within. Then he spoke urgently with Gault the Strong. "Scrape me together two or three score men; there must be so many among the war host who can keep on horseback a few hours longer."

"The war host is something smaller than it used to be," Gault said savagely.

"That I had noticed. Nonetheless, I must have at least two score to push on with me now. For the others, let you rest the men and horses but gather every single one you can and hold them ready to bring on after me when I send back word."

"That I will do," Gault said, "but as to the two score—do your own dirty work, my Lord of the Horse Herd. They're asleep on their feet; but if you can wake them, they'll answer to your call better than they will to mine." He smiled, that harsh, bitten-off smile of his. "Did I not promise you that you should be as much the King as you showed yourself strong for?"

"You did, and behold, I am the Horse Lord, and men come at my call."

And for an instant, eye looking into eye, both of them remembered that quiet-surfaced struggle for the soul of a little Dark Hunter, that had been also a trial of strength for the leadership of the Tribe.

There were only seven of the Companions left now, and of those Baruch the Grass Snake was away with the scouting band. Brys brought the number up to seven again; and surprisingly, Vron, Sinnoch's old fore rider, came forward to make the eighth, with his disreputable sheepskin hat still on the back of his head. Dergdian joined them, leaving the leadership of his own men to a kinsman, and Tyrnon and Nial Mac Cairbre. ... They came forward in ones and twos, men with red-rimmed eyes and scorched and blackened faces, several with a bloody rag knotted somewhere about them, until in a little while Phaedrus had more than the three score that he had first called for.

It took longer to find the horses than it had done to find the men, for the poor beasts were utterly spent, and while that was being done, each man was making ready as best he could, bundling five days' supply of bannock and meat in his rolled-up cloak. Brys, still proudly careful of his duties as the King's armor-bearer, though now he was one of the Companions, had brought Phaedrus's cloak with the great war-brooch still in it down from Dun Dara in the before-dawn darkness, that the Horse Lord should not ride into battle without it, and dealt with making up his lord's bundle as well as his own, and seeing to both their weapons.

For while the ready-making was going on, Phaedrus had gone upstream to the hazel tump where the Healer Priests were still busy with the wounded.

Conory had come back into his body again, and lay with his head and shoulders propped against the leaning stem of a hazel, looking down at something that crouched against his flank. He looked round at Phaedrus's step, and moved his hand quickly in a tiny gesture that was at once warning to Phaedrus and restraint and reassurance to the thing that crouched there so tensely still, and Phaedrus, checking beside him and looking down, saw that it was Shan.

Her collar was gone and she was a pitiable sight, her striped fur almost all singed off; but somehow she had come out of the fighting and found her lord again, and her fighting spirit was quite unquenched, judging by the way she tensed and spat at his approach, before she quietened under Conory's hand; and her narrowed eyes looking up at him were as bright and wicked as ever he had seen them.

It was stupid, he thought, at a time like this, to feel this rush of relief and gladness because one small wicked-tempered wild cat had come alive through the fighting and the fire. And yet—it would have been even harder to leave Conory here and go on without him, if she had not. ...

"So—she is back from her hunting yet again," he said. It was the easy and obvious thing to say, when the things that needed saying were too difficult and stuck in one's throat. "They do say that every cat is born into the world with nine lives."

Conory was fondling the poor singed ears, and Shan, her fierceness now quite laid aside, was butting her head into the hollow of his hand and crooning to him. "Then counting the day I found her, that should be leaving her six yet to run," he said, speaking as lightly as Phaedrus had done.

Phaedrus squatted down beside him and looked questioningly into his face. "How is it with you, now?"

"None so ill. What news is in the camp? It seems so long that I have been lying up here."

"The first scout has come back with word of Liadhan's trail toward the Black Glen. I'm away after her now with three score or so of our warriors. That counts what are left of the Companions."

"How many *are* left of us? Of the Companions?" Conory asked after a moment.

"Seven fit to ride, and you here."

"I am sore at heart to be missing this hunting."

"We have hunted well together these past months," Phaedrus said.

And looking down into the pale bright eyes that were so like Murna's despite the odd set of them, he thought suddenly of how they had first met his across the heads of other men in the Cave of the Hunter, less than a year ago. Gods! Less than a year! And yet he seemed to have lived a whole lifetime since the night in that private room in the Rose of Paestum, almost as long since that first meeting with Conory—and the Roman world had gone away from him, small and remote and unreal as a scene reflected in a polished helmet. He remembered with sudden piercing clearness how he had seen Conory then—a wasp-waisted creature with paint on its eyelids and strung glass beads on its wrists. And he had always thought himself a good judge of men! Fool that he had been not to see the tempered blade inside the fantastic silken sheath.

"If you should be back in Dun Monaidh ahead of me, tell Murna—tell Murna to be looking out for me. Remember, if the need be, I give them into your charge."

Pain was pulling at the corners of Conory's mouth, but a trace of his old lazy smile was there too. "Surely, I will tell her, but I do not think that she will need the telling. Be easy in your heart for Murna and the babe."

Phaedrus put a hand on his shoulder and gripped it an instant, wordlessly—Shan watching the while with laid-back ears in case he meant some harm after all—then he scrambled to his feet and went back downstream to where the horses stood ready, too weary to stamp and fidget in their usual way, though not much more weary than the men who were to ride them.

They had trouble with the horses at the ford, for the smell of blood was strong there, and a raven flapping up under the very nose of Finn's mount sent the poor beast half wild with terror. But they got across at last, and turning aside from the trail of the main retreat, that was marked here and there by dead horses in the trampled grass, here and there by dead men, headed Southwest to pick up the trail of the She-Wolf. It was old Vron, riding ahead as he had been used to do with the pack train, who found it first, and sat waiting for them to come up, then pointed out the hours-old horse droppings. "They had horses waiting on the other side," he informed them with gloomy triumph.

The shadows were lengthening and they had come three or four Roman miles, pushing themselves and the weary horses to the very limit of endurance, when a darker shadow uncoiled itself from a tump of hill juniper, and came to meet them.

"Sa sa—Baruch the Grass Snake." Phaedrus looked down at the little man standing at his horse's shoulder. "What word?"

"I followed the She-Wolf and their pack till they were over the ridge yonder into the Black Glen." He turned and pointed toward a lift of the high moors maybe a mile away. "There was a camp of the Caledones, and the Queen was waiting for her Lord. I lay hid under cover—there is good bracken cover—and watched while she and Liadhan spoke together awhile. Then the first fringe of their beaten war host came over the hill and down to the camp, and then I heard the Queen scream. It must have been when they told her her Lord was slain. She screamed and pulled out handfuls of her own hair. There began to be a great crowd, and I could not see what happened, nor hear anything that passed between her and Liadhan, but Liadhan came out from the throng in the Queen's own chariot and with her few priests riding about her, and with no one else at all—aiee! But the horses had terror on them! And when the Caledones harnessed up and turned northward again for the Druim Alban passes, they took the old chariot way that leads South along the loch shore to the Red Crests' fort on the Cluta."

With the muttered exclamation of the war band in his ears, Phaedrus said, "A Roman fort! She could not be making for that!"

"There is no other place, I am thinking, that she could be making for, down *that* trail," put in old Vron, who had shared his master's special knowledge of the border hills.

"But—Light of the Sun! Liadhan to throw herself on the Red Crests' mercy!"

"And what can have parted her from the Caledones?"

Aluin asked the question, and gray-muzzled Dergdian answered it. "Bruide who was her kinsman is dead. It is in my mind that, left without a strong king, the Queen, maybe even her people, may well feel that there is no room for another Goddess-on-Earth in the Cailleach's hunting-runs. I'd not put it past belief that Liadhan smells danger in that, too."

"As I smell danger in her going to the Red Crests," Phaedrus said harshly. "Wherever she goes, she carries with her deadly danger to the Dalriadain; and among the Red Crests, who do not know her, she will be fire in stubble. Little Grass Snake, get back again to Gault the Strong and tell him all that you have just told me." Then to the horsemen behind him, "Come—it seems we have a clear trail to follow, anyway, but we must ride quickly on it."

Toward evening, three days later, the little war band rode out from the thick breathless shadows of Coit Caledon, the Wood of the Caledones, and checked among the tangled thickets of hazel and elder that made up the forest verge, looking out across the emptiness of cleared land that shone tawny pale in the hazed sunlight and up the steep tumble of thin grass and black outcrop to where the old fortress of Theodosia crouched on the crest of its great out-thrust rock above the waters of the Cluta. It might have been a further outcrop itself, it seemed so deeply rooted in its rock, with the white wing-flicker of the gulls rising and falling all about it. Even at that distance it had a half-deserted look, but Roman standards hung limp and straight in the still air above the Praetorian Gate, vivid as streaks of colored flame against the somber masses of storm cloud piling up behind. And as Phaedrus sat his tired horse under the broad eyes of the forest verge, and looked up toward it with eyes narrowed against the glare, the brooding stillness was torn across by the sound of Roman trumpets that he had not heard for a year.

All their efforts to ride the She-Wolf down before she could reach the shelter of the old Naval Station had been hopeless from the start, for she had fresh horses, while their own poor beasts had been far spent before ever they began that ride. They had to rest them again and again, and more than once they had had to lie close to avoid an Auxiliary patrol, which had not made for speed. And so—Liadhan was safe behind Roman walls. And what now?

"What now?" Dergdian asked, like an echo of his own thoughts.

"We will try first what the mere asking will do," Phaedrus said, his gaze still on the distant gatehouse. "That may at least tell us whether she is still within the fort."

And so, when they urged the weary horses on again, each man carried his spear reversed, for a token that he came in peace; and Phaedrus, riding a little in advance, had broken a green branch from a wayfaring tree and carried it in his hand.

Trumpets sounded again, high above them, as they passed through the huddle of the small native town at the foot of the rock and headed up the zigzag track beyond. And when Phaedrus let the red mare stumble to a halt—poor beast, he had no need to rein her in—before the high timber gate, the ramparts were manned on either side, and an Auxiliary Centurion looking down from the Guardhouse roof demanded, "Strangers, what is your business here?"

"To speak with your Commander."

"And who would you think you are, to demand to speak with the Commander?"

"I am Midir, Lord of the Dalriadain. I come in peace." Phaedrus raised the green branch in his hand. "But it would be well that the Commander come out to speak with me, none the less."

"Midir of the Dalriadain, d'ye say?"

Knowing that with Liadhan behind those walls the name must have an effect one way or the other, he had gambled on it working in the way they needed. He could only hope that it was doing so, when the Centurion stared a moment, muttered something half under his breath, and disappeared. There was a quick barking of orders from within the gates, and then nothing more for a while.

He sat the red mare in the sultry sunlight, on the ditch causeway, reining her head up with a ruthless hand and ignoring the sallies that the sentries on the ramparts did not suppose he understood, about one-valley kings riding broken-winded nags and mistaking themselves for Caesar.

At last the sentries grew abruptly silent, and stood back, and a new head and shoulders appeared over the timber breastwork above him. A bronze helmet shimmered in the veiled sunlight and a red horsehair crest cut its own shape out of the heat-pearled sky; and under the forehead band was a thin dark face with a nose too big for it, that he had seen before.

"Greeting to you, Midir of the Dalriadain. You wish to speak with me across the green branch?"

Phaedrus spoke, for the benefit of the sentries, in Latin very much purer than their own. "Greeting to you, Commander. Did the mare make a good hunting pony?"

The dark eyes suddenly alerted in the soldier's face, and he leaned forward across the breastwork. "I have seen you before?"

"More than a year ago. I have somewhat changed, maybe." Phaedrus, meeting the questioning stare that had no recognition in it, was sharply aware of that change, the fine bronze-hilted dirk at his side, the tattooed device that was almost like a four petaled flower on his forehead, half hidden by the blurred traces of war paint, the great knotted scar that made havoc of one side of his face. "I was a pack driver of Sinnoch the Merchant's, and you were Captain of a troop of Frontier Wolves. Quick promotion, Commander."

"So-o, I remember. And now you are King of the Dalriadain? Quick promotion, my Lord Midir; but by the look of you it did not come without fighting."

"It did not come without fighting. When we last met, I was on my road North to win back the kingship that Liadhan, my father's half-sister, robbed me of when he died. I have fought for it; and many others fought with me, to free Earra-Ghyl from the

She-Wolf. And we had the victory. But *she* escaped to the Cale-dones, and brought war between them and us, and now that her welcome among them grows thin she escapes again, to refuge under the shadow of the Eagles."

"It is a good story, but what has it to do with me?"

"It has this to do with you, that you hold the She-Wolf even now within your gates, and I come to demand her return."

The dark gaze flickered over the little band of tattered and gray-weary riders. "You should bring a greater war host with you when you come demanding to the gates of a Roman fort."

"There will be more of us in a while and a while," Phaedrus said with cool effrontery.

"Then demand again, when you have enough men behind you to back your demand."

"You refuse, then?"

"I refuse to hand over, merely because some usurping adven-turer bids me, a queen who has thrown herself upon the protec-tion of Rome."

Rage rose scalding as vomit into Phaedrus's throat, and he swallowed it, knowing that an angry swordsman was too often one with the edge of his skill blunted. "I am no usurper!" (He had quite forgotten that that was exactly what he was.) "I am my father's only son. This woman seized the rule, even as I told you, when he died. She would have had me slain, but that I—escaped—and for seven years she has ruled my people unlawfully and according to ways that were hateful to them. Therefore they rose against her at last, and I—came back to lead them. Does that make me the usurper?"

"It was not so, that the Queen told it," said Titus Hilarion.

"Would she be likely to come to you for shelter with the truth—*that* truth—on her tongue?"

"Maybe not." The Fort Commander settled his elbows on the parapet and leaned forward conversationally. "But even supposing that every word of this tale of yours is true, why trouble to hound her further? You have your kingship back. She does not stand between you and the Sun. And myself, I'd say vengeance was inclined to be a waste of time."

"While she lives, she is the shadow of Death over the Dalriadain." (No use to say "You do not know her as you did not know Cartimandua, a hundred years ago. You do not know that if you keep her, you will listen to her, and as sure as there is thunder coming, you will find yourselves marching North one day to set her back in the Royal Seat, and believing that the peace of the Frontier depends on it." You could only say "She is the shadow of Death over the Dalriadain," and leave it at that.)

The Commander straightened from the breastwork and stood looking down at the horsemen below him, his mouth turning straight and hard. "All that is nothing to Rome. Let the tribes beyond the Pale fight out their own feuds. The Queen has appealed to the protection of Rome, and until the Legate bids me give her up to you, I shall not do so. Is it understood?"

There was a long silence, and in the distance a low mutter of thunder quivered along the skyline.

Then Phaedrus said, "It is understood," and dashed the wayfaring branch to the ground. He brought the mare round in a plunging turn, snorting from the savage jab of his heel and the bit tearing at her mouth. "Away!"

There was no more talking to be done.

18 | *The Whistler in the Dark Woods*

GUIDED BY OLD VRON, THEY HOLED UP FOR THE NIGHT IN A shallow valley, where a burn that had barely enough water to cover its stones wound out through the low-lying forest to join Baal's Ruin on its way past Theodosia to the Firth of Cluta. And at dusk, Phaedrus and the old fore rider cut southward through the woods and marshes to the coast, and worked their way in for a closer look at the seaward side of the place. Theodosia had been a great Naval Station once, in the time of Agricola when the patrol galleys had come and gone as regularly as shuttles in a loom, up and down the Firth of Cluta; and the size of the old fort crouched on its crag above the empty docks and weed-grown slipways told its own tale of past power. Now, clearly, it was no more than an outpost fort for the Northern Wall, but strong still. Phaedrus doubted bitterly whether there would be much that they could do against it, even when Gault brought up what was left of the war host. And as he watched the towering rock mass turn black and menacing against the coppery sunset far across the pale waters of the Firth, where the low shoreline of Valentia lay like a bank of mist, a beacon fire sprang up from the Roman Signal Station. Theodosia might be far from the nearest fortress on the Wall, but it was in close touch across the water.

Back in the glen where the hobbled ponies had lain themselves down, too tired even to graze, the war band had made a fire. The Red Crests would know well enough that they had not simply ridden out of the district, so it seemed best to make no pretenses at secrecy. They ate the last of the meat, which by now was stinking. Tomorrow and the next day they could keep going on the strips of smoked deer meat and the last of the stirabout. After that, if the thing still dragged on, they would have to turn hunter—in a countryside that looked to have been long since hunted all but bare by the Red Crests.

Now Phaedrus sprawled on one elbow by the fire, his thoughts ranging loosely, as the thoughts of a man will when he is too tired to keep them on any one thing. Faces came and went through his mind: Murna's, and Conory's, and Sinnoch's dead face with that look of wry amusement as though at a bad jest; the dark face under the horsehair crest looking down at him from the ramparts of Theodosia. ... Sinnoch had said that he would command a fort before he was thirty, unless he was dead in a bog or broken for going too much his own way. But it was odd to see him again like this—as though the strange past year were coming full circle back to its starting place again. Some pattern being completed, each loose end carefully secured as it was finished with, as the women fastened off each color as it was done at the end of a pattern on the loom. And then he thought of Murna's face again, and the way her hair smelled when it was wet. ...

Midway between sleeping and waking, he heard something— a little plaintive whistling among the trees below the camp that might almost be the call of some night bird; almost, but not quite. Still half asleep, he cocked a listening ear. And as he listened, the whistling came again. It was the five-note call that he and Midir had used as a signal to each other in that shared month in the Onnum Cock loft!

Now he was wide awake and listening with every nerve in his body. The call came again, softly insistent, and the faces of the others in the firelight told him that they heard it too. Finn's hand was stealing to his dirk, and he was up on one knee; others were making the same move. "Spy!" somebody whispered.

Phaedrus sprang to his feet. "Fools! Would a spy come whistling so near our fire. That is a call—and for me."

"Whose call?" Dergdian demanded tersely.

"A friend's—or a friend's ghost."

"Leave it alone, Lord." Brys's face was sharp with sudden fear for his Lord. "It is not healthy to answer such calls!"

And old Vron grunted in agreement. "The boy is in the right of it—I remember when I was a young man. ..."

But Phaedrus was away, heading down the slippery grass slope that dropped away into the trees. Ahead of him, the call sounded again, farther off, as though whoever—whatever—it was that called had heard him coming and moved back. It was a dark night, seeming all the darker for the brief flicker of lightning from time to time far off among the hills, the old moon not yet risen, and a thin thunder-wrack covering the stars; and once among the trees, Phaedrus could scarcely see his hand before his face. These were no thin birch and hazel woods such as those of Earra-Ghyl, but the dense black fleece of forest that covered all the low country from the great hills of Valentia northward into the unknown; damp-oak forest, thicketed with yew and holly, and on the north skirts of the hills the tall whispering pines. An ancient forest that seemed to Phaedrus to be watching with hostile eyes that could see in the dark like Shan's. Low-hanging branches whipped his face, and time and again he blundered into a tree trunk or stumbled into a hole left by the uptorn roots of some long-fallen giant; and always, whenever he checked to listen, the call came again, as far ahead as ever. It was leading him farther and farther from the camp. But he had no doubts, whether it was by some strange and almost unbelievable chance Midir ahead of him, or Midir's ghost, this following through the dark woods was some part of the pattern that was being worked out.

The slope of the land had leveled out beneath his feet, and he could hear the small drought voice of the burn very close in the darkness; and at last he came out onto the bank just where it spread into a chain of pools and the tail of the last pool ran out into Baal's River.

It was at that moment that he suddenly knew that the whistler was no longer far ahead, but close beside him. It was no sound or movement, just the sense of somebody there in the darkness, within arm's reach of him. He whipped round, and in doing so caught his foot in an arched root and almost pitched headlong down the bank. He recovered himself, cursing under his breath, and something that was only a denser darkness moved close by, and he heard the merest breath of a laugh.

"A blind man has the advantage in the dark."

"*Midir!* Is it you indeed?—or your ghost?"

"Did you think it might be my ghost, then?"

"I—was not sure."

"Yet you came."

"I came."

Hands came out of the darkness and fastened on his shoulders in the old familiar way; and they were warm and strong with life, as Phaedrus put his own up to cover them. "Feel. No ghost," Midir said.

After the first few moments, their meeting again had slipped into place so that Phaedrus felt it to be something not at all surprising that had simply been waiting for them in the future, until the time came for it to happen. He still did not know whether he liked Midir, and he still knew that that did not matter, that far down at the root of things they belonged together, as though perhaps they had been meant to come into the world as one person and had somehow got split up and come into it as two.

He said, "But I do not understand. How do you come to be here?"

"You were easy enough to follow from the Fort—I heard the way you went, and that gave me the start of the trail. Tired horses smell strong, and I had the smoke of your fire to guide me the last part of my way."

"Sa, that I see, but I was meaning, how do you come to be North of the Wall?"

"My old master died, and still needing to eat now and then, I set out to find work for myself. Also, I'd a mind to gain tidings if I could of how this matter of the Horse Lord went, after we had taken so great pains with it. I came to Theodosia. There is always a welcome for a good leather worker, wherever the Red Crests are. They were glad to see me in these parts." Midir's tone changed. "And you? You are the Horse Lord sure enough—ach, I know: news travels on the wind in these parts. Beside, if the thing had gone against you, you would have been unpleasantly dead long before this, instead of standing here under my hands. But it seems that you have not yet taken my vengeance for me, as you promised."

"I will take it yet," Phaedrus said.

"Maybe. Or maybe I will take it for myself, after all." There was a cold, lingering softness in his voice that made something crawl in Phaedrus's belly. But when he spoke again, his voice sounded as usual. "But I am wasting time, when there is little enough to spare. Listen, Phaedrus. The Fort Commander has sent word to the Signal Station across the Firth—the boat went at dusk. He has asked for a swift rowing galley and an escort from the Walls-end Fort. And on tomorrow's night tide, they will send her across into Valentia."

"How do you know?"

"Now you sound like a Red Crest. The British town that huddles under generally knows more than the Fort Commander supposes."

Phaedrus was silent a moment, then he burst out, "Fiends and Furies! I had hoped that they would at least have held her until some word came from the Legate or the Governor!"

"It is in my mind that the Commander Titus Hilarion seeks to get her away quickly lest the Frontier goes up in flames with her still in his hands."

Phaedrus was watching the pale swirl of the water. "The thing that is clear beyond all else," he said at last, "is that Liadhan must never set foot on board that galley."

"How many spears are there with you?"

"Three score, more or less."

"Not enough. Where is the rest of the war host?"

"Not at home eating honey cakes!" Phaedrus was up in arms on the instant to defend his own. "Dead, a good few of them. All summer we have been fighting; did *that* word not reach you? Three days since, we fought—aiee! quite a battle, and after, I could scarcely find three score fit to bestride a horse, to ride this trail with me. Gault is bringing on all that he can raise, so soon as they and the horses can tell night from day, but flesh and blood is flesh and blood, for all the heart that's in it. I doubt that they can be here for two days yet!"

Midir said softly, "Yes! I was right, I was right! Assuredly you are the Horse Lord, Phaedrus, my brother."

"At all events I sometimes catch myself believing that I am." For an instant memory flickered up in Phaedrus of the Little Dark Chieftain and his magic. "Do you not believe I am the Horse Lord?" he had said; and the little man had said "I do not know. But when you see that feather again, you will be." But it was gone at once, leaving no more trace than the golden plover's feather in the narrow dark hand.

For a long moment there was no sound between them save the liquid running of the burn and the small nighttime stirrings of the forest.

Then Phaedrus said abruptly, "For the thing that must be done, I am thinking that one man might stand a better chance than a whole war host."

"Two men, anyway," Midir said, and from his tone, Phaedrus knew that he had been thinking along the same lines.

"Two?"

Another silence. Then Midir broke it, speaking in short quick bursts with long pauses between, as though he were thinking the thing out as he went along. "Listen now; this could be the way of it. The galleys will not put in until well after dark; and if they will wait for dark to put in, that can only mean that they intend sailing again before dawn. At dusk, you must send in. ..." he checked. "Have you a good dirk thrower with you?"

Phaedrus's mind had caught the direction, now. "One or two," he said, and then, "One, at least."

"Sa, at dusk, then, send him in. In the general run of things, they do not keep guards down there; there's not much to guard in empty galley sheds and broken-down jetties, and they'd find it none so easy if they tried, with the town spreading into the dockyard all along the northern edge of the harbor and the fisherfolk storing their nets in the ruins, and no man to say where one begins and the other ends. But it is in my mind they'll have a guard posted tomorrow night!"

"And how does our dirk thrower get through?"

"Ach—I leave that to you—to him. Choose a man who is used to stalking game, and he'll find a way through."

"So. And then?"

"There's only one way down the rock on the seaward side—very steep—so steep at the bottom that it ends in a wooden stair. They must bring her that way; even the Red Crests would not be fool enough to take her out by the Praetorian Gate and half-circle round through the town. There are the remains of store-sheds and the like close up to the stair foot on the north side—good enough cover, well within knife range. Let your man lie up there, and when she comes to the foot of the stair—they are bound to have a torch or two to light her down—that will be the time for him to throw—and to pray that he throws straight!"

There was a little silence; and in the midst of the silence, somewhere away in the trees, the small sharp sound of a snapping twig.

The two froze as they stood, hearts suddenly racing. "What was that?" Phaedrus whispered, and the other's hand tightened on his shoulder.

"Listen."

For what seemed an hour they stood listening, every nerve on the stretch. But there was nothing more to hear but the little night-time rustlings and sighings of the woods behind them. At last Midir let his breath go with a little sigh. "Nothing."

"I will be going to make sure."

"How?" Midir said.

No, there was no way of making sure—and no need; he had heard such little sharp unexplained sounds often enough before now. "The dry summer has made the forest noisy with dead twigs."

They listened a moment longer, all the same, then returned urgently to the point where they had broken off.

"I'd not say it was a good plan," Phaedrus said, "but it's possible, and I can't think of a better. It has one sore spot in it, though—it will be death to the man with the dirk."

"Surely, if he were alone. That is where the second man comes in—to draw off the hunt."

"I was forgetting about the second man," Phaedrus said. "Well? Do I send him in with the other?"

"Na, *you* do not send him in at all. I shall wander in to talk with the fishermen when they bring in the catch at evening—it won't be the first time—and find means to go to ground until the time comes."

"You?" Phaedrus said.

"Why not? They will not see my face when I run from them. I know that ground well; with luck I shall lead them a fair way before I fall over anything—maybe farther than they will go themselves; torches are unsure light for a chase. They will not know me, until they capture me, for the blind leather worker from the town."

"And when they do capture you?"

"I shall have a fine excuse. See now: I went down to talk with the fishermen and bargain for a fish for my supper. I was tired, and the air thunder-heavy; and I crawled into a corner and fell asleep. The sudden uproar woke me, and I was frightened. A sudden uproar is a frightening thing to a blind man, my Phaedrus—and I ran."

"It holds together," Phaedrus said slowly.

"Surely, it holds together."

"But it would be madness for you to try it, Midir— don't you see. ..."

Midir cut in. "No, I don't see—I don't *see*; that's what you mean, isn't it? You are not believing that I can do the thing, because I am blind! I know what I can do, better than you can! If any man of yours does it, he will die; there is no escape round the south side of the rock. But I can do it and like enough live to tell the tale—not that that greatly interests me just now. ... Also, it is my right. My *right* to have a small share in my own vengeance, and maybe a small share in saving the Tribe also." He broke off, and added in a tone of deliberate lightness, "It is strange that I should trouble about that. Long ago I ceased to feel that I belong to them. But I still do not want to see the Dalriadain trampled into the mud."

"Just as I have come to feel that I belong to them, and they to me. I also would not see the Dalriadain go down." He broke off, and was silent a moment. "Come then, and take your rightful share." And checked again. "I am not liking it, this slaying-in-the-dark, but it must be done; it is her life or the Tribe's—*it must be done!*"

"It must be done," Midir said.

A low, long-drawn mutter of thunder trembled into the silence. The woods seemed to have grown very still, and in the stillness the voice of the burn sounded unnaturally loud. "The storm is coming," Midir said. "Phuh! There is no air to breathe."

"It is as though the woods knew it—and were waiting."

They stood together, a short while longer, quickly going over the few remaining details, then parted without any leave-taking, Midir turning back toward the bothy-town that huddled at the foot of Theodosia Rock, Phaedrus heading up the glen once more.

Another thread of the finishing pattern had been woven into place.

It was not until he caught the first flicker of the watch fire through the trees, that he realized that Midir had asked no word of anyone, not even of Conory. He was puzzled for the moment, and then he understood that here, so near his own people who were so completely lost to him, his only hope lay in not asking, not wanting to know. "Long ago I ceased to feel that I belong to them," he had said; and that was his armor.

He whistled to warn the Companions of his coming, and men were afoot and faces turned to him as he came into the firelight. Finn began a question, and then stopped; no one else spoke, but the question was in all their faces, and Phaedras answered it. "No, no ghost. An old friend of mine who I did not know was North of the Wall—a leather worker in the town, who slipped out with news for me."

"Why did he not come up to the camp?" Dergdian asked.

"Maybe he had no wish to risk getting caught up with the war host of the Dalriadain; it was only me that he had his news for." Phaedrus squatted down on his haunches well back from the fire, but near enough for the smoke to keep the midges away; and sitting with his arms folded across his knees, told them of what had passed between himself and Midir—or at least as much of it as they needed to know.

When he came to the end, Dergdian, the oldest and most cautious among them, said, "It is in my mind to wonder what price the Red Crest may demand for the slaying of a Goddess under their protection."

Phaedrus had thought of that, too. "Liadhan means little to the Red Crests, and her slaying will mean little, save that by it, we shall have set their authority at nought, and that they will *not* like. ... If the luck runs our way, they may never even be able to prove that the dirk came from the Dalriadain. If they do, they will maybe march North to teach us more respect for our betters. Then we shall drive off the cattle and horse herds—giving thanks to Lugh Shining-Spear that we are not a corn-growing people rooted to our fields—and take to the hills and islands, and play wolf pack on their flanks until winter turns them South again. They may burn down a hall here and there, but thatch and turf and timber are none so hard to replace; at the worst, they may burn off what they can of the pasture. But there's rain coming soon. When the storm breaks, the weather will break with it. If Liadhan lives and has her way with them, if they march North to thrust her back into the Royal Place and hold her there with their swords, as they did in the earlier days for that other She-Wolf Cartimandua, that will be another—a darker story."

All round the fire, men's voices answered him quick and fierce, eyes red-sparked with an old anger above the rims of their shields.

"Sa, it is well thought out," Dergdian said. "Then it seems there is only one question left to settle: who is the best dirk thrower amongst us?"

The Companions glanced at each other. Niall began "I—"

But Phaedrus said, "I am." He looked round at them in the fire-light. "The throwing-knife is not really our weapon, here in the North, but one learns strange skills in the Gladiators' School."

"No!" Niall said quickly. "My Lord Midir, I did not learn it in the Gladiators' School, but I've a fair aim with a dirk, nonetheless. Let me go."

"No," Phaedrus said. He looked at face after protesting face. "I am the best dirk thrower round this fire tonight; it is as simple as that. Also—this is a matter between Liadhan and me."

"It is between Liadhan and all of us," Finn said.

"But since we cannot all settle it with her, it is right that the King should settle it for the rest."

"It is not fitting work for the King."

"It is not fitting work for any man. But one man must do it, and only the King can do it for the whole Tribe."

19 | *The Dirk Thrower*

WHEN DAWN CAME THE THREATENING STORM HAD STILL NOT broken. A little wind had got up, brushing fitfully through the treetops, but there was no freshness in it. And the sense of coming storm made Phaedrus feel increasingly, as the day dragged by, that if anyone touched him he would give off sparks like a cat.

Thunder was grumbling again in the distance, when the time came for him to make ready, but they had heard it more than once that day, and each time it had gone away again. This time it would probably do the same. He hoped so, much as he longed for the relief of its coming, for a thunderstorm in the next few hours might complicate and confuse things hopelessly. He put on his war-tattered cloak, partly because he could pull the loose hood forward over his head if he needed to hide his face; partly with a certain feeling for the fitness of things, in a way a play actor's feeling for the shape of the pattern that he was making. It was the King's cloak. Brys had brought it down for him from Dun Dara on the night they fired Glen Croe, that he might not go into battle without it. Now he was going out against Liadhan for what, he knew, one way or the other would be the last time. And he flung on the cloak as though for battle, settled the folds at the shoulder to give free play to his right arm, and thrust in the great bronze war brooch with its splendor of blue and green enamel.

Brys, who had been standing by, came forward with his dirk freshly burnished and whetted to a razor keenness. Phaedrus took it and felt the edge with his thumb, then nodded. "Sa sa!

With this, one could draw blood from the wind!" and slipped it silkenly into the deerskin sheath at his belt.

"Take me with you!" Brys said, suddenly and desperately. "My Lord Midir—let me come with you!"

Phaedrus touched the boy's shoulder kindly enough. "I'll not be needing my armor-bearer on this trail."

He turned to the rest of the war band; they were all there, save for the two who were watching the river fords against the time when Gault came seeking them. He had already given them their orders, that they were to bide here, no man coming with him save old Vron as far as the forest verge, that there might be no target of moving men large enough to catch the eye of any Red Crest scouts; and whatever happened, there was to be no attack on the Fort, even when Gault came with the war host. In their present weakened state, once they lifted a spear against the Fort, they were done. He could only hope that he had got that through to them, knowing as he did the hotness of their heads and the little skill they had in counting the cost. Dergdian understood, at all events. He could trust Dergdian to hold this lot, anyway, in leash.

They sacrificed to Lugh Shining-Spear together, the small quick sacrifice of barley meal moistened with a few drops of blood from each warrior's thumb, which the Sun Lord accepted when there was no living sacrifice to be had—for at a time like this, no God worth praying to could even wish for one of the horses.

And when that was done, there was nothing more to hold Phaedrus from his setting out.

They watched him go in silence, no one raising a protesting voice. All that had been finished with last night. If the Sun Lord willed it, he would come back; if not, and the Mark was on his forehead, then the Mark was on his forehead. Either way, it was the King's trail and no one else's; between him and Liadhan, between him and the High Gods, and they had accepted that it was so.

It was already dusk when he came with old Vron to the edge of the woods, close to the place where the ancient chariot road forded Baal's River. An unnaturally early dusk under a piled tumult of blue-black clouds, their underbellies stained here and there with dull copper light from the unseen westering sun. The storm had held off so far, but it was churning round them in closing circles; not long now, Phaedrus thought, before it broke.

He whispered to the shadow in the battered sheepskin hat beside him, "Wait here and watch till I am well into the bothies; then back with you, and tell them that all goes well so far."

The old fore rider grunted by way of reply, a grunt which might mean anything. Phaedrus waited for no more, but slipped out from the gloom of the woodshore and down through the low-growing scrub to the chariot road.

There was no walled or hedged cantonment at Theodosia; the steep rise of the rock left no space for more than the fort itself on the crest, and the more level ground below it was too far outside the walls for bath house and married quarters and granaries. Only a huddle of native bothies had sprung up along the foot of the rock on its landward side, with a wine shop thrown in for good measure. And being in a kind of no-man's land—for within a day's trail of the Northern Wall the old tribal territories had not much meaning save in time of war—it was a place through which the rags of many tribes came and went. And so there was no encircling dike with its gateway stopped at twilight by the night-time thorn bush, and Phaedrus loped in by the track that turned from the chariot road like a man at the end of a journey, without let or hindrance of any kind. Neither men nor hounds took any especial notice of him, as they would have done of a stranger in a tribal dun, as he made his way between the crowding bothies, keeping always well clear of the firelight that shone here and there through hut doorways or from little courtyards. If any man spoke to him or even looked at him hard, he was going to ask for the wine shop, which he knew from Midir lay in the right direction; but no one did. It was all very easy—almost too easy. ...

He passed quite close to the wine shop and saw the smoking light of oil lamps spilling from the doorway, and heard a sudden burst of singing that brought back with a vivid flash of memory the dark streets and crowded wine shops of Corstopitum.

> "Six poor soldiers, marching home from Gaul,
> Five Centurions, bully-big and tall.
> Four brave Legates, who never saw a fight;
> Three grave Senators, to set the world to right.
> Two wise Consuls, going out to dine,
> But one shall be our Emperor, and pay for the wine."

They had sung the same counting-out song to slightly different words in the Gladiators' School, and with the same clamoring of someone's name at the end—the name of whoever was to be Emperor and stand treat for the rest.

Phaedrus left the lighted doorway behind him, and walked on. There was beginning to be a different smell in the air, the smell of salt water mingling with the stink of the little dirty town. And he became suddenly aware of the crying of gulls made restless by the coming storm. The bothies began to thin out, and gleams of fire or lamplight became fewer and farther between, and he knew that the time had come for going still more cautiously.

A short way farther—and he dropped to his belly in the black gloom between a store-shed wall and a ragged pile of driftwood, and lay flat looking out across a patch of open ground, hearing the tramp-tramp-tramp of a sentry's feet, coming closer—closer—and dying away again. He could see the man, a dark bulk in the deepening dusk, moving steadily across the open space, and before his footsteps had died away into the lap of water and the crying of the gulls, the footsteps of another sentry took up the beat, and a second dark figure crossed the open space, turned, and paced back; and a few moments later the first man had reappeared. Midir had been quite right; the fringes of the old dockyard were being patrolled.

Phaedrus lay still for what seemed a long time, watching and listening, while the lightning flickered closer, showing him the pacing figures with acid clarity every now and then, trying to decide what point in that steady passing and re-passing would give him his best chance. And gradually he found that though both sentries were within sound all the while, there was one moment in each turn when one sentry had his back to him and the other's sight was blanked by the corner of what looked like a derelict sail loft. Still he waited, getting the timing by heart, and found that it never varied; every time there was that one blind moment, just long enough, he reckoned, to get him across, but with certainly nothing to spare.

The next time it came, he got to his feet and slipped forward to the very last nail's-breadth of his shelter, then froze, crouching like a runner before a race, while the second sentry came up and passed, turned and passed again, and the first returned. This time, the instant the man's back was toward him, he loosed forward like an arrow from a bow. His soft rawhide brogues made no more sound than bare feet on the sunbaked earth. The open space seemed all at once appallingly wide, the dusk still appallingly thin, and he could hear the footsteps of the second sentry—in another heartbeat he would round the corner of the derelict sail loft.

He just made it, and, as the man came into view, dropped beside a dark pile of nets against the sail-loft wall and lay still, praying that no lightning flash would betray him, praying that the sentry would not look that way and notice that the pile of nets was bigger than it had been before. The footsteps came on, closer, closer—passed without checking. A few moments later Phaedrus was oozing forward again, into a narrow alleyway between the sail loft and the gutted shell of another building. Sand and shingle had drifted deep in the narrow space, and dry dagger-sharp dune thistles had seeded themselves thickly along the wall. The dry rustling of them sounded so loud in his ears each time he moved that it seemed it must bring the Red Crests down upon him every instant; but at the end of the building the sand drift ceased, and he knew with an almost sick relief that he was clear through the patrol line. But he had no means of knowing whether there were more guards about, and his heart was still drubbing against his breastbone as he worked his way forward with agonizing caution through the wilderness of derelict buildings and rotting weed-grown jetties. At last he found himself crouching in the doorway of a half-roofless store-shed of some kind, close in to the great upthrust of rock that towered over him like some vast menacing beast about to strike; and saw in the faint lightning-flicker the wooden steps at the foot of the zigzag track from the fort above. Looking far up, as the lightning flicked again, beyond the rock ledges cushioned with the dry brown ghosts of sea-pinks, he saw the head of the track where it swerved up the last steep stretch, and the harsh outline of the fort against the sky; and at the southern end, where the rocks dropped almost sheer into the sea, he saw the out-thrust catapult platform from which in the old days the great stone-hurler batteries must have covered the entrance to the anchorage and dockyard.

There had been no sign of the galley alongside the one serviceable jetty, or even of a stern brazier out to sea; but it was not quite full dark yet. He had a long wait ahead of him. He put his hand to his dirk, and felt that it was loose and easy in the sheath. Now that he was so near to the thing he felt curiously empty, as though everything had been drained out of him except the knowledge of what he had to do. He did not even feel anything about that; he only knew, very clearly inside the cold echoing emptiness of his own head, that he had come to kill Liadhan, and how, and why. Presently, he would feel again, but not now.

He whistled softly, not the old five-note call, which was too obviously man-made, but the high thin "pee-wheeet" of a plover, twice repeated, which was the agreed signal. No answer came. Only the fretful gulls still wheeled crying about the face of the rock, only the lap of water and the low mutter of thunder like the first distant waking of the wolfskin war drums.

Was Midir not there yet? Had something gone wrong? He whistled once again and, even as he did so, heard a stir of movement behind him. His hand was on his dirk, but before he could whip round he felt a numbing blow on the back of his neck, and pitched forward into a darkness that buzzed and roared and was full of shooting stars.

It seemed to him that he never quite lost consciousness, but was aware of a vast army of hands dragging and wrenching at him, and hollow booming voices at a great distance all the while. But he was trapped in a kind of half consciousness like a swimmer trapped by weed below the surface of the water. He fought against it, heart hammering and blood roaring in his ears, and broke surface at last, to find that his hands were bound behind him and he was already being manhandled up the wooden stair. He began to struggle, and somebody struck him across the mouth with a hand that had a heavy ring on it, saying with a curse, "That's enough of that!" And he gave up struggling for the present. It was useless anyhow.

So—he was in the hands of men from the fort. He had walked into a trap—fool and double fool that he was! But who had set the trap and who had sprung it? Confusedly, through the swimming and throbbing of his head, he remembered the stick that had snapped in the summer-dry forest!

But who?—who?—that did not matter now; there was something else—someone. ... The sudden remembrance shot through him bringing him back to full consciousness with a crash. If he had been betrayed, then so had Midir! Midir! What had become of Midir?

As the little knot of Frontier Wolves, with Phaedrus stumbling in their midst, started up the steep track that ended at the Water Gate of Theodosia Fort, Midir was breaking out of the small strong lock-up behind the main guard house.

20 | *The Hostage*

THE DECURION ON GUARD HAD ORDERED A SMALL LAMP TO be left burning in a niche high on the lock-up wall, so that they could keep an eye on their prisoner through the grill in the door, for he seemed so crazily violent that he might be up to any lunacy. The Decurion had known such a man bite through his own wrists before now, and bleed to death under the noses of the guard, and he wasn't taking any chances. The Commander had ordered the man to be kept close till morning and brought up for questioning again, and kept close and brought up for questioning he was going to be.

Midir, exploring his prison by smell and delicate sense of touch, had found the lamp within a hundred heartbeats of there being no more heavy breathing behind the bars of the door-squint. When he knew exactly where it was, so that he could reach it in an instant from any part of the cell, he began hammering on the door and yelling. Presently someone came and cursed him, and he quietened for a short while, and then returned to his hammering and shouting. As time went by, the shouts became a hoarse raging, rose above the nearing storm on a growing note of hysteria, a howling that sounded more like a rabid wolf than a man—and then fell suddenly and ominously silent.

That silence fetched the Decurion at a hurried march, with one of the guards tramping behind him. When he looked through the grill, he saw the prisoner with the lamp in his hands, seemingly in the act of setting fire to his bedding straw. The Decurion shouted at him not to be a fool, cursed the Auxiliary for not having brought a torch, as he fumbled an instant with the padlock, and slammed up the door bar.

At sound of the voice and the rattle of the key in the padlock, Midir turned a wild face toward the doorway, and seemed to hesitate. Then as the door crashed open and hobnailed feet pounded toward him, he pinched out the little flame and tossed the lamp aside and, springing up, side-stepped from the line of the suddenly stumbling rush.

There was a startled shout, a curse, and then more feet. Two to one, but, as he had said to Phaedrus, a blind man has the advantage in the dark. There were a few moments of chaos. Somebody pitched over his out-thrust leg and, crashing head foremost into the opposite wall, crumpled down it with a grunt. Midir's hands found a man's throat and closed on it, and his thumbs jabbed upward at the pulse under the angle of the jaw.

Next instant he was outside, the door slammed behind him. He felt for and found the bar and dropped it into place. There was a groan and the sound of somebody retching his heart up, as he turned away in search of a hiding place—a search in which a blind man did *not* have the advantage. However, he reckoned it would be a little while before there was any serious outcry from the lock-up to lead to the discovery of his escape.

It would be too late to warn Phaedrus, but if he could escape recapture, there might be something he could do—he didn't know what, but something—when they brought their second prisoner in. And even as he set off up what seemed to be an alleyway between high-sounding buildings, a smother of voices and the clear-cut orders of an officer sounded across the fort from the direction of the gate that gave onto the old water stair. And all was swallowed up in a whiplash crack of thunder and a long hollow booming as the storm that had circled them so long burst full overhead.

He heard hurrying feet, men brushed past him, going all one way, tossing a word or a question from one to another, and he went with them—partly because he did not have much choice, partly because he guessed the meaning of the sudden stir—keeping his head well down, for somewhere not far off he smelled the resin smoke of a pine-knot torch.

To Phaedrus, sagging between his captors in the open space inside the sea-gate, that clap of thunder seemed part of the dizzy roaring inside his own head. Vaguely, he was aware of torches, and the jink of torchlight on bronze, and faces pressing in, all eyes and mouths, and he was confronting the Duty Centurion. "So our friend in the fox-face hat *was* telling the truth!" the Centurion was saying. "Bring him up to the Praetorium, the Commander wants a word with him." Then, rounding on the crowding Auxiliaries, "All right, you lot get back to your barrack rows; there's nothing more to see here."

A flash of lightning cut like a knife between earth and heaven, picking out every detail of the scene with a blue-white glare, and the thunder broke with a coughing roar, like the war song of the wolfskin drums, as the onlookers began to melt away.

But the Centurion was wrong, for as the white whip-crack of lightning came again, suddenly the challenge of the sentry sounded from the ramparts! "Who comes?"

And a woman's clear scornful voice answered, "The Queen of the Dalriadain."

And Phaedrus, wrenching round in the hands of his captors, saw in the white nicker, that was now almost incessant, the tall triumphant figure of Liadhan standing at the head of the rampart stair, looking down at him. Strange to think that this was only the third time he had ever seen her. She had been so much part of his life, this past year. ... She seemed something that belonged to the storm; the lightning made a silver wildfire of her hair, and the lightning was in her eyes. "I came to see this—this *thing* that would have called itself Horse Lord and King of the Dalriadain in my stead; this *thing* that tonight would have slain me who am the Goddess-on-Earth!" and she laughed until her laughter was swallowed up in the echoing crash of the thunder.

There was a moment of utter blackness, for after the lightning the flare of the torches was not so much light as a red flowering of the dark. And in the dark, Phaedrus sensed rather than saw something move in toward the foot of the rampart, and cast about oddly, like a hound seeking for a lost scent, until it came to the steps.

It was halfway up when the Decurion of the Gate Guard saw it, and started forward, shouting "Here! You. ..."

The figure flung itself forward and up, and seemed to reach the rampart walk at a bound. And in that instant the lightning flared again, and Phaedrus saw that it was Midir.

Liadhan saw, too. Her eyes stared in her head, and her mouth opened to a cry. *"Midir!"* But the name was blurred in her throat, and in the tumult and confusion of the storm no one save Midir himself, and Phaedrus standing rigid in the grip of his captors, knew what name she cried.

Midir spoke softly, bitterly mocking; and in the instant of prickling silence before the next thunder-peal, every word came clear to those below: "Goddess-on-Earth, it was not wise to cry out," and sprang toward her. She flinched back and turned to run, with death close at her heels.

The instant's stillness exploded into action. Men were running from all directions. The Commander's voice cut through the tumult. "Spear! Bring him down!" A flung spear missed the blind man by a thumb's breadth and thudded into the rampart timbers—but it was scarcely possible to believe in those moments that he was blind. Men were closing in on him, racing along the ramparts, up the rampart steps; another spear actually grazed his shoulder, and falling, tripped the man behind him and brought him sprawling down, causing an instant's confusion; and in that instant, Midir's outstretched hand found a fold of Liadhan's mantle, and then his arms were fast round her. In the gloom it was as though the two figures far along the rampart fused into one. Liadhan screamed again and again, like a trapped hare.

Then a searing flash split the night in two. For a long moment the whole sky was one flickering blast of greenish light that seemed to blind and dazzle and beat down at the very soul. And for that one last moment, Midir appeared poised on the very edge of the raised catapult platform, with Liadhan struggling in his arms, the lightning flare playing all around them both.

Then, the woman still locked against him, he sprang outward into blazing space. In the same instant, the darkness cracked back again, and the pursuers blundered together in the place where he had been. The dreadful hare-like screaming broke off as though cut with a knife.

Phaedrus thought of the black jagged rocks and the tide running far below.

Then the thunder came, peel on clanging, crashing peel that seemed to shake the very roots of the great rock, and boomed hollow under the vault of the heavens, and rolled and reverberated away into the hills. For Phaedrus, the night had turned unreal, and the torchlight and the quick tramp of feet and the shouted orders seemed all a part of the chaos within his own throbbing head. The only thing he knew with any clearness, as his guards marched him away up one nightmare alleyway and down another, was that the first of the longed-for rain was falling in great spattering drops, and the smell of rain on parched earth was rising all about him.

They came to a square courtyard surrounded by buildings, and then there was the soft glow of lamplight on the lime-washed walls of a small, barely furnished room, with the rain hushing down outside, and the lightning stabbing beyond the small high window, and the thunder booming fainter and fainter among the hills.

Someone gave him a drink of the sour watered vinegar that was the Legions' marching-wine, and that and the steady light and enclosed quietness of the room cleared his head. He looked about him and saw a big writing table with papyrus rolls on it, a couple of chests and camp chairs, a gay native rug hanging half over an open doorway that gave a glimpse of a sleeping cubicle beyond. The Commander's quarters. ... Somebody, sometime, had said something about orders that he was to be taken to the Commander's private quarters in the Praetorium, and held under guard until the Commander came. There must have been orders about giving him a drink, too.

He leaned against the wall, dragged down by a great weight of weariness, and stared at the little flame-tongue of the lamp, while the thunder boomed fainter and fainter into the distance and only the rain teemed down; not thinking very clearly of anything save that Midir had taken his own revenge, and for him the pattern was complete—and that Liadhan would never again carry the threat of destruction to the Dalriadain. ...

A quick, heavy step came along the colonnade, and the men on guard over him straightened to attention as the door was flung open and the Commander came striding in, pulling his sodden cloak from his shoulders and shaking himself like a wet dog. His quick glance took in Phaedrus straightening from the wall. "Ah, good—thanks, Optio, I shall not be needing you for the moment, but keep your men within call."

When the three had saluted and gone, he spoke to Phaedrus, not as captor to captive, but with formal courtesy, as one leader of men to another.

"I regret that you have been held waiting for me so long."

"You have had urgent matters to attend to," Phaedrus said grimly.

"I have had—urgent matters to attend to, yes."

The Commander crossed to his writing table, but remained standing beside it, and Phaedrus understood perfectly, with a certain amused respect, that Titus Hilarion, for all his courtesy of speech, would not bid a prisoner to sit in his presence—the presence of Roman authority—but that he would not sit down himself while keeping the other standing.

"What do you know of the man who did the thing?" The question shot out and took Phaedrus unawares, for he had been expecting his own part in that night's events to be the first matter for questions or accusation.

"Know of him?" he said, to gain time. "What should I know of him?"

"Something, I imagine, since he went seeking you with word that we intended sending Liadhan across by galley into Valentia tonight, though how he came by that information, Mithras alone knows—and to plot out with you this plan for killing her, which would quite possibly have succeeded if you had not been over-heard."

Phaedrus remembered the stick that had cracked in the dark woods. "Who was it?" he demanded.

"One of the three priests she has—she had with her. He noticed a certain likeness between you two, and when the man—he was a leather worker in the native village, blind, poor devil—slipped away and headed for the woods last night, it seemed to the priest that there might be something to be gained by following him. An unpleasant little beast in a foxskin headdress, and stinks like the Black Pit of Ahriman, but it seems his instinct was sound and his report was a true one."

"Well?"

"It is hard to see why a blind leather worker should take so much interest in the death of a queen. This one took a very great interest. Now why?"

"Likely for the same reason as he killed her in the end."

"A grudge of some sort? Some real or fancied wrong to be avenged? Do you know what it was?"

"The wrong was real enough—it was his wrong, and he avenged it. It has nothing to do with me."

"So you do know something of him?"

"In the days when I was a gladiator, he mended my sandal straps a few times."

"No kin to you, then? He flew the same-colored hair, and it seemed to me also, when I questioned him earlier this evening, that he shared a certain likeness with the Lord of the Dalriadain."

"None that I know of," Phaedrus said. "There's a good deal of red hair among the Tribes, and it's hard to judge the likeness between two men when one lacks eyes and the other has half a cheek torn away."

The level eyes of the soldier looked at him for a long considering moment, with a little frown. Then he shrugged and changed the subject, as one who is not at all sure that he has got at the truth, but knows that if he has not, he will get no nearer to it.

"But it was not to ask you these things that I bade them hold you here against my coming."

"Na, I would be thinking not." The old faintly dangerous smile was on Phaedrus's lips. "Say whatever it is that you have to say to your prisoner."

"I had rather think of you as—a possible hostage," the Commander said, and checked. "Not even quite that—as a bargaining counter."

"I—do not understand," Phaedrus said slowly.

"Yet the thing is simple enough; I propose to hand you back to your own people in exchange for one thousand of your young men, to serve with the Auxiliaries."

There was a long, harsh silence, filled by the drenching of the rain. Phaedrus felt for a moment as though he had taken a blow between the eyes. He was remembering the desolation of Valentia, the deserted raths, the pasture lands gone back to heath and bramble because of the young men gone to fill the ranks of the Auxiliaries along the German Lines. And for Earra-Ghyl there would be a greater evil, for with a thousand of their remaining warriors gone they would be left with none save the women to take up the swords when the Caledones seized their chance and came swarming in. No more children born, either; as it was, there were too many women, now, who would never go to a husband's hearth.

"That was the thing you had to say to me."

"The thousand would have to be paid first, of course," the Commander said.

Phaedrus was still thinking with an odd detachment, as though he stood outside himself, looking on. Strange that now it was he and not Liadhan who was the danger to the Dalriadain. "And if they refuse to pay the price, or if I refuse to be ransomed by the lives of my best warriors?" he said at last.

"Then I shall most probably send you South to be safe held as—a guest of the Empire. In that case you might certainly be called a hostage. Of course there is an alternative. It might well be a simpler way in the end to crucify you for an example to your kind."

"An example? What am I supposed to have done?"

"Nothing. You were merely taken in the attempt. That is the injustice of life."

"You are not afraid of bringing down the wrath of the North against your Wall?"

"It is only when the Caledones and the Dalriadain link shields that there is danger to the Wall." The Roman's voice and eyes were inflexible, but Phaedrus knew that the only feeling between them was liking; which made it all rather stupid and sad. Hilarion was a good soldier, doing his duty by the peace of the Frontier, and not enjoying it.

"I—must have time to think," he said, slowly.

"You have until sunrise."

"And whatever I decide, after my thinking, I must have speech with my own people, that they may hear it from my mouth."

"You shall have that also, as I had speech with you, from the rampart at the Praetorian Gate."

They looked at each other, a long, straight, steady look. Then Phaedrus said, "It is Liadhan, not Midir, who was the usurper, you know."

"I think I believe you. That is your justification before your own Gods. But Rome reckons little of justification beside the fact of danger to the Frontier. When a spark falls on a grass tuft, here on the borders, we stamp it out before it can become a forest fire."

He crossed to the door, his eyes never leaving Phaedrus's face, and opening it, called, "Optio."

There was a tramp of feet, and the Optio entered with his two men behind him. "Sir?"

"Take him away and keep him well under guard until I send for him again—under guard! He is not to be left unwatched one instant. We have had one escape already tonight."

21 | *The Mark of the Horse Lord*

Squatting under the lamp, the two Auxiliaries were playing a game of chance to pass the time. At first the rattle of the falling dice had maddened Phaedrus, sitting on the bench on the far end of the narrow stone-walled chamber. But now it had ceased to matter, indeed he heard it scarcely more than he heard the drip-drip-drip of rain under the eaves. He was listening for only one thing, for any sound of fighting in the world outside that would mean an attack by his own people, praying to all the Gods that ever he had heard of that it would not come; that they would obey his orders; that at least they would have enough sense to wait till morning. It did not come. Once, as the night wore on, he heard faint sounds of activity that could only mean the arrival of the galley—it must have been delayed by the storm—and he wondered how Hilarion would be meeting the Escort Commander. For the rest, elbows on knees and cloak huddled about him, for it had turned chilly after the storm and he was bone-cold with weariness, he sat withdrawn from his surroundings deep into his own thoughts, as he had been used to do in the old days, before the Arena trumpets sounded.

He had overmuch thinking to do, and not overmuch time, for the trumpets had sounded for midnight watch-setting a good while since. He tried to think about the time to come, and the likely way that things would go for the Tribe. But his mind went ranging back over the past year, remembering the surprised look on Vortimax's dead face, and the strange light feel of the Wooden

Foil in his hand, and the moment of stepping forward alone into freedom that was as strange and lonely to him as death. ... Remembering again the cock loft at Onnum, and the small tormenting pain of the tattooing needle on his forehead; and the feel of wrestling with Midir. He thought of Murna who had fought beside him all that summer, and the babe that had been begun among the spears. He wished that he could have seen the babe, even once. Well, Conory would keep his promise to guard them; he would trust Conory with his life—he smiled in his mind at the thought—he would trust him with Murna's life and the child's, which was more to the point.

But despite what he had said to the Commander, he had no need to think what choice he was going to make. It was as though the choice had been made long ago, and was as familiar as the folds of an old cloak. It was he who had led the Tribe into this new danger, and only he could pull them out from it again. Rome had power over the Dalriadain by right of holding him hostage. No hostage—no power; it was as simple as that, on the surface. But suddenly he was remembering that giant horned figure on the back wall of the Cave of the Hunter, and Midir's voice saying of his father, "He went out to meet his boar. There had been much fighting and the Red Crests had burned off all the pasture that they could reach, and then a wet autumn and the cattle died. It was famine time, you see ..." He hadn't understood, then. He did not really understand now—his head only knew that when it had to be one or the other, there was not much else you could do but pay away your own life for the Tribe's. But something deep within him understood that it was not only among those who had followed the dark, ancient ways of Earth Mother that the King died for the People; only among the Sun People the King himself chose when the time was come.

"He went out to meet his boar. ... It was famine time, you see. ..."

The odd thing was that he never once thought to himself that he was not, after all, the King; that the true Horse Lord had leaped to his death a few hours ago, taking the woman Liadhan with him. It was as though, growing into the kingship through this past year, Red Phaedrus the Gladiator had grown into this other thing, too, because without it, the kingship would not be complete.

Outside, the rain water still dripped from the eaves, but the rain had stopped. The lamp was guttering into the first gray light of dawn, and the trumpets were sounding cockcrow, and presently a tramp of feet sounded outside and the two Auxiliaries pouched their dice and got up. Phaedrus got up too, even before the door rattled open and the Centurion's voice said, "The Commander has sent for his prisoner."

He was stiff and sore as a rheumaticky old man—he grinned to himself at the thought. That was something he would never have to put up with, anyway. He took his time with studied insolence, knowing well enough that the Commander would have given orders that he was not to be treated like a common captive, raked his hair as best he could with his fingers, settled the folds of his warworn cloak across his shoulders—lightly touching the great brooch that fastened it. They had taken his dirk, of course— odd that no one ever thought of a brooch with a pin as thick as a corn stalk and longer than a man's forefinger as a weapon, even in a camp of the Eagles where they learned, just as one did in the Gladiators' School, that two inches in the right place were enough.

"Quite ready, Centurion," he said, when the last detail, even to the dazzlingly insolent play actor's smile, was perfectly to his satisfaction.

"I rejoice to hear it," said the Centurion with feeling, and gestured him to go out first. Outside in the gray dawn light a small guard of the Frontier Wolves were waiting. Phaedrus laughed at the sight of them.

"You're taking no chances! Do you think I am Cuchulain, to make the hero's salmon-leap over these ramparts and away?"

"Get on!" the Centurion said, his patience fraying badly. "Guard, march!"

In the room where Phaedrus had stood before the fort Commander last night, the lamp burned low and guttering, and Titus Hilarion, in the same drenched clothes, now somewhat dried on him, red-eyed and gray-faced so that suddenly he looked like an old man instead of a young one, rose from behind the littered table and the report he had clearly been writing.

"Well?" he said, when Phaedrus came to a halt before him.

"Well?" Phaedrus said, a little mocking.

"Have you made up your mind?"

Phaedrus gave an exaggerated shrug. "I've little enough choice, come to think of it, have I? A tribe doesn't thrive without its leader—and they say it's none so bad a life in the Auxiliaries. Yes, for myself, I accept your terms."

He thought he saw a flicker of disappointment in the Roman's eyes. But he only said, "So. A wise decision."

"There were conditions, remember. I am to have speech with my people and tell them of these terms, myself. The final word must be for them to speak."

"Surely." The Commander reached for his sword, which lay on the bench beside him, and slipped the belt over his head. "The sentries report a band of them waiting before the Praetorian Gate now; your reserves, it seems, came in last night, and their leader—a dark man, broad-shouldered and short in the leg. ..."

"Gault the Strong."

"So? He is well named, I should judge—Gault the Strong came in with a band of them, demanding word of you. I spoke with him in the Gate and swore to him that you should be safe until dawn, so long as he and his men attempted no attack on the fort, and that at sunrise you would speak to them yourself as to the terms for your release."

Phaedrus settled the folds of his cloak again on his shoulder, and said pleasantly, "I think I heard sounds of the galley a good while after midnight. She was delayed by the storm?"

"Yes."

"How inconvenient for you that she was not delayed a while longer. Ah, but I am sure you will find means to carry out your plan despite any counter orders."

Hilarion's brows flickered up. "Fortunately the Escort Commander has not the power to give me counter orders. All he can do is to take back my report to the Commander of the Wall."

"Sa. That should give you time."

"Time to handle the thing my own way, and maybe avoid a clash along the Frontier."

"Yes, you want the quiet of the Frontier. You told me. That is why you will exchange me for all that is left of Earra-Ghyl's fighting power." Phaedrus looked at him straightly. "Has a mere Fort Commander the right to do that?"

"No," the other said crisply.

"And how if the Governor Sylvanus prefers the kudos of a captured king to the more serviceable but less dramatic gain of a heavy draft for the Auxiliaries, which after all, will go to strengthen the Eagles for another Governor in another province of the Empire? Will he be pleased with the Fort Commander who made that choice?"

"No," the other said again, "but it so happens that I am more interested in the peace of the Frontier than in Sylvanus Varus's chance of catching the Emperor's eye." A small bitter smile flicked at the corners of his mouth for an instant. "Rome will not risk losing face before the Barbarians by repudiating my action, though undoubtedly she will repudiate *me*."

"Sa. I was thinking that. You will be broken for what happened last night in any case, Commander." Phaedrus glanced at the half-written report on the table and felt a stirring of sympathy for this man who would have to go on living and face, in all likelihood, unjust disgrace and the ruin of his career. "Best keep me to sweeten the Governor, and leave the peace of the Frontier to the man who takes your place. That way at least they may give you another Cohort in another part of the Empire, after they have kicked you enough."

"Is that the faith they taught you in the Arena?"

Phaedrus laughed. "The world is a hungry place for a broken soldier, just as it is for a gladiator who has won his Wooden Foil. If you grow hungry enough you may come to the Arena yet, as you would have had me come to the Frontier Wolves."

"Maybe."

"Offer a pigeon in my name, for old time's sake, the first time you sacrifice at the Altar of Vengeance."

"I'll remember."

Phaedrus half turned toward the doorway, beyond which the courtyard was coming back to form and color, and the sky over the roof ridges was already full of light. "Shall we be going? A pity, it would be, if the sun were before us."

"Surely." The Commander crossed to the door beside him and spoke to the Centurion of the Guard. "Escort to the Praetorian Gate, Centurion."

The escort formed up, and with the tramp of nailed sandals all round him and the Commander at his side, Phaedrus fell into the long-paced swaggering parade march, as they went through the camp, where men were beginning to stir and horses shifting and stamping in the stable lines, toward the Praetorian Gate.

He outpaced his escort in the last few yards, and turned to face them on the lowest step of the rampart stair. "I go to speak with my own people, and I go alone. From this place you can hear every word that I speak; there is no need that any man of the Red Crests come further with me." His eyes met Hilarion's, and their gaze locked and held for a long moment. Then the Fort Commander put up his hand in a gesture that might very nearly have been a friendly salute. "Very well."

So Phaedrus climbed the rampart stair alone. Out of the tail of his eye he was aware of a knot of soldiers standing some way along the rampart walk on either side, but they were a good distance off and it would take almost as long for them to reach him as it would for the men behind him to come springing up the rampart stair.

The sun was just rising, and it was going to be a glorious day after the night's storm. The morning seemed clear-washed and new as the first morning of the world, and above the hoarse never-ceasing surge of the tide below the headland rose the thin sweet crying of the plover and the harsh laughter of gulls. Far off northwestward, clear in the cool after-storm light, Cruachan caught the first rays of the sun. Phaedrus suddenly knew again the feeling of being light on his feet and lucky, the feeling that most of the Arena-trained knew well, that it was your lucky day, the day when the God's face was toward you. ...

He looked down. Yes, he had been right about the drop. Clearly the Red Crests thought that it was enough to hold him from escaping that way, or they would not have allowed him up here without the guards close at his sides, and they were probably right. But here on the landward side, it was not far enough to be sure of the other thing, even if one dived head foremost, especially for a man trained how to fall. Well, he had his means of making sure.

Lastly, he looked at the knot of horsemen who had been waiting a little way off, and now at sight of him were urging their horses in closer. He saw the squat dark figure of the leader, a bloody clout round the head, and was glad that it was Gault, good, level-headed, old Gault, who had had the sense not to bring the war host out in force and so betray its strength—or rather its pitiful weakness—to the Red Crests.

They were quite close under the Gate now; the hand of the Centurion away to the right flashed up, "Near enough!"

And they checked their horses.

They were looking up at him, tossing up their spears to bring them crashing down across shield rims in the Royal Salute, and now they sat their horses, silent, waiting for him to speak. Gault and Dergdian, Niall and hairy Aluin and Finn, young Brys with a white, sullen-set face. ... He wondered if they were thinking in their hearts that he had betrayed them now. It was Brys that he minded about most.

He leaned forward, his hands braced on the split-timber coping of the breastwork. They were quite close; he need scarcely raise his voice to reach them across the dry ditch.

"The Light of the Sun on you, Gault the Strong; you are well come."

"And on you, Midir of the Dalriadain."

He knew that they must have some idea of what had happened, even if they did not know the whole story. Better, though, that they should hear it from his own mouth also. "Liadhan the She-Wolf is dead, though not by my dirk."

Silence greeted his words. Gault broke it at last. "I have men with me—enough, maybe; you have but to say the word. ..."

Was that in some way for the benefit of the listening Red Crests? Or simply that the squat dark warrior with the bitten mouth was so much a fighting man through and through that his heart turned to battle even when he knew that battle, any attempt at rescue, had no possible place in what was happening at all; or was it a direct question from the only man among that little band who knew the truth about him: "You are willing? You who are not the King?"

Either way, the answer was the same. "There shall be no fighting, my brothers. No attack on this fort." He had spoken in the common British tongue that would be understood both by the knot of horsemen across the ditch and the Red Crests in the Fort behind him; but now he changed quickly to the highly inflected speech of Earra-Ghyl, which would be scarcely, if at all, intelligible to the Red Crests. "No fighting now—or afterward. To attack this place with the war bands we have left to us would only be to fling them on disaster. It would mean the death of the Dalriadain as surely as though Liadhan stood beside you to urge you on. I keep my faith with you, now; and after, you shall keep yours with me." Out of the tail of his eye he saw the men on either side begin to move in closer, distrusting the almost foreign tongue, and changed back to the common British speech. "Sinnoch would have said that was a fair bargain."

"We will keep faith with you," Gault said simply.

And Phaedrus saw in all their upturned faces, even on Gault's, that they knew and accepted what he was going to do, because he was the King, the Horse Lord, and had the King's Right.

How loudly the plover were calling, disturbed by the horses. For a moment their pied wing-flicker seemed all about him as a whole cloud of them swirled across the fort, and among the thinner calling of the rest, he thought he caught the sweeter woodwind whistle of golden plover, who sometimes flocked with the lesser of their kind. They swept on and sank again like a falling cloud of storm-spray. And out of the sky where they had passed, a single feather came drifting down, twisting and circling on the quiet air. It drifted past Phaedrus's face and settled on the parapet almost touching his hand—a dark feather, spangled with the clearest and most singing gold—clung there an instant, and then lifted off again, and went circling and side-clipping on down toward the ditch.

Phaedrus said, "It was told to me that you have had speech already with the Chief of the Red Crests here in this Fort, and that he gave you his word that I should speak with you at sunrise, and see, he has kept his word."

The men below were silent, waiting.

"The Chief of the Red Crests offers these terms for my release; that he will sell me back to you at his own price, and his price is one thousand of the best of our young warriors, to serve as Auxiliary troops with the Eagles."

There was a faint stir among the little band of horsemen, and a pony threw up its head in protest against a sudden jab of the bit. But nobody spoke. They were waiting. They were his people.

"But it is in my mind that I do not like to be bought and sold, I who have been a slave; and so I have thought of a better way. ... It is this!"

He had been playing idly with the great enameled brooch at his shoulder as he spoke, working it free. He had it in the hollow of his hand now. His fingers closed over it so that only the tip of the deadly pin that was almost as long as a small dagger projected between them. He had plenty of time to find the place, the two-inch place just to the left of the breastbone, that meant a quick death. A good exit. The old instinct for good exits and entrances that the Arena had trained into him was still with him now.

The freed folds of his cloak fell away from him as he got a knee across the rampart coping and next instant had sprung erect. There was a shouting and a running of feet behind him and on either side, and a strange deep cry from his own men below, but it all came to his ears like the roaring of a circus crowd. The sun, still rising far North with summer, had sprung clear of the hills and shone full into his eyes as he turned a little to face it, in a golden dazzle that touched as though in greeting the Mark of the Horse Lord on his forehead. He opened his fingers, freeing the whole deadly length of the great pin, and drove it home.

The taste of blood rushed into his mouth. He plunged forward into the sun dazzle and felt himself falling. He never felt the jagged stones in the ditch.

Rosemary Sutcliff (England, 1920–1992) wrote over fifty books for young people. Her first two were published in 1950 and her last were published posthumously. She received the following awards: the Carnegie Award for *The Lantern Bearers*, The Boston Globe–Horn Book Award for *Tristan and Iseult*, a Hans Christian Andersen Highly Commended Author Award in 1974 for her body of work, an Order of the British Empire in 1975, the Phoenix Award for *The Mark of the Horse Lord*, and a Commander of the British Empire in the year of her death. Her books have been translated into several languages and have been published throughout the world.